Black Bird, Black Bird

By

Shane Bates

Table of Contents

Acknowledgments

I want to thank my wife, Michelle, my parents, Jerry and Paulette Bates, and my sister, Tanya Bates for all their support and advice.

I've enjoyed writing this book. I hope everyone enjoys it as much as I have enjoyed writing it.

"Blackbird, Blackbird"

Part One

It was a normal day just like any other day except on this day, there he lay, Robert Ashton.

Robert's grandson, Tommy came over to check on his grandfather and found his sixty-seven-year-old grandfather on the floor unresponsive. Let me go back to when I first met Mr. Robert Ashston.

It was spring April 2012. I applied online for a job with the Tennessee Power Association. I was eating breakfast with my wife Michelle when my phone rang. I looked at the screen and it said unidentified number. I didn't answer.

She asked, "You not going to get that?"

I said, "No, unidentified number." I laughed and said, "If it's important, they will call back. Nothing, see it was our car's extended warranty." We laughed again even harder when the phone rang again vibrating on the table. Rosie jumped twice barking eagerly letting us know she knew something was happening. I threw her a piece of bacon.

"Oh must be important," Michelle said.

In my Thurston Howell, the third voice I answered, "Hello, yes, this is he." My wife giggled pointing at me.

And on the other end, I heard, "Yes, this is Ben Adams with the Tennessee Power Association. I'm calling about an online application you filled out in October of last year."

I cleared my throat answering yes, in my serious normal voice while giving my wife the throat slash a couple of times to knock it off. She went into the kitchen and returned with the coffee pot filling my cup as I spoke with Mr. Adams.

"We are looking to hire a new facilities worker."

"Oh wow yes, it had been awhile and I almost forgot after not hearing anything."

"Well, we move slowly round here. I'm the shop foreman, Ben Adams. Can't remember if I mentioned that or not. We wanted to call you in to meet and interview, face to face. You seem to be more than qualified, and the lead horse for the position so far. Want to get someone hired before the upcoming mowing season. You do know how to mow, don't you?"

"Are you serious?" I said half-heartedly laughing.

"You'd be surprised how many knuckleheads we get that don't have a clue."

Well, I asked when.

"How about Tuesday at 7:00 a.m. sharp? Gimme some time to get some coffee in me."

"Yes, sir, I will be there at 7:00 a.m. sharp. Should I bring my resume?"

"Naw really don't need anything. I have your online application printed right here in front of me. Mr. Avery Wayne Jackson, 34, oh you are a Christmas baby. Veteran I see, served in the National Guard for three years. Yep, you would fit in right nice here. See you Tuesday, Mr. Jackson. I texted you the address and call if you have any problems."

"Yes sir I'll be there, thank you."

Michelle heard me hang up and asked, "Who was that?"

I said, "Remember when I filled out those applications back in October when I got laid off from the plant? Well, I just received a call from the Tennessee Power Association saying they have looked over my application and I was more than qualified for an opening they have available soon."

She was so happy leaping into the air, doing her happy dance. Rosie barked running in circles and jumping around. We hugged and I said, "Hey it's just an Interview."

"Tennessee Power Association, wow!" She exclaimed, "That would be nice!"

Michelle and I met at community college and she is the love of my life. I knew the moment I saw her I had to have her. She's always struck me as a very strong, independent thinker, adventurous, loving, caring, and big-hearted, but not one to be pushed around or run over. She studied accounting hoping to land a job with a Fortune 500 company and move to the big city. But as we grew closer dating a year and a half later, her plans changed to our plans. After graduating, three months later, we were married. I got a job down at the plant where my father worked and retired from Tella Co. I often wondered if people knew my name or if it was, you're Jerry's son. Either way, I answered. It was a great little job and, a pretty good income to keep our bills paid. We were buying our first home, which we shared with our little Jack Russell named Rosie. She was seven and a half pounds of pure energy. Yes, she was the queen of the house. Kind enough to let us live there too.

Michelle got a job at a lawyer's office across town full-time. The Ted Winston Law Firm. Mister Winston was an older gentleman in his seventies but still sharp as a tack and semi-retired but still had his Law firm to keep him busy being a widower. He always calls Michelle "Granddaughter." Michelle is very fond of "Teddy" as she calls him and just about everyone else in town is too. She is always telling me stories about the children's charities he donates to. Mr. Winston is super nice to her and the other secretary, Mary Catherine Taylor. Mary Catherine is a divorced mother of two mischievous teenage boys, big boys. Michelle says that Mary Catherine is like a freight train smoking so much. Lighting one off the other. But, she is nice and laid back. I told Michelle I thought those boys' father must have been Andra the giant. Those boys are huge, I mean a couple of hosses. When tax season rolls around Teddy allows Mary Catherine and Michelle to prepare people's taxes for a small fee there at the office on certain days of the week.

Everything was good in our world until the plant announced in 2011 that there would be some layoffs due to cutbacks. A few of our companies' plants were moving to Mexico, and being one of the youngest, I got the axe.

I drew my unemployment and worked under the table with a lawn care service my buddy owned, so we weren't starving. And being young, we were so happy together. Michelle worked just as hard putting in all the hours she could at the office. She also would go in on Sundays to clean up. I would always tell her it's us against the world. She would say we are the three musketeers. My response was you think we should get a dog now. But I always wanted so much more for her.

...

I pulled up early Tuesday morning to the Tennessee Power Association's maintenance building. The sun was just starting to rise it was a cool morning. There were six vehicles already there in the parking lot. The first thing I noticed when I walked through the gate was a nice fenced-in paved parking lot with two more vehicles parked inside, a grey extended cab Chevy 4x4 truck and an old brown Ford four-door Escort. There was a fleet of new light blue matching Dodge trucks and trailers, two new Kubota mini excavators, a John Deere bulldozer, and a John Deere backhoe. A John Deere skid steer, two new Kubota M7040 4×4 cab tractors, one still had plastic on the seat. Two Kubota 4×4 side by side utility vehicles with spray herbicide spray rigs in the back, four Kubota 60-inch cut zero-turn lawnmowers. Two John Deere 997 60-inch cut zero turn mowers tucked under a six-bay shed. Like a team of Clydesdales pawing the ground ready to work. That place was equipped with the best of the best. I would have guessed easily three-quarters of a million dollars' worth of equipment sitting there. I walked into the Maintenance building ten minutes before my scheduled interview time. A few steps in on my left was a door that led to two offices with desk, chairs, computers, two more steps on my right was a conference room with two tables and chairs around it. A 65-inch big-screen TV was on the wall with a group of nine men watching the morning news talking and drinking coffee. In an open area straight ahead, I could see a full kitchen, and a little further, a bathroom sign above the door. I could see through the window in the door that led to the shop area. There were four bays with electric garage doors. Several tool boxes, a work table, an air compressor, a drill press, floor jacks, an overhead Crain, two welders, one was a MIG welder, a band saw, and yes, I got a warm tingly feeling looking at all those tools. Tennessee Power Association is no joke I was very, very impressed to say the least.

"Can I help you?" One of the men spoke up.

I responded, "Yes, I'm Avery Jackson I have an Interview at 7:00 this morning."

"Fresh meat," the men said and laughed. His comment got a few laughs from around the table.

The man I was talking to said, "Crews!" in a stern voice.

"Well, he is. Well, might be."

"Ignore him, Terry heehaws with everybody like that. I'm Ben Adams, the shop foreman. I spoke with you on the phone the other day. I will be one of the people conducting your interview and the guy with the funny hat, that is Carlton Rogers, and he will also be conducting your interview. Beside him is Josh Stanford, that feller there is Timmy Mason, that man is Paul Killion, and beside him is Robert Landry, if they look alike it's cause they're cousins.

Josh muttered, "Probably inbred."

"Military man," Terry Crews said pointing at me.

Ben said, "How you know Crews?

"I can just tell by the build, hair, and that he was ten minutes early for his interview."

Crews squinted and said, "National Guard."

I said, "Yes sir, three years."

"Don't call me sir! I was an NCO. I had to work for a living, I'm a prior military man myself. Army supply sergeant eighteen years."

"What was your MOS?"

"19 Delta Cavalry Scout."

"Well, how'd you know he was in the guard?" Ben asked.

"I saw his application on your desk."

Everyone except Ben thought that was funny.

"Crews, I've told you, keep your ass out of my office." As the laughter died down. Ben continued, "And that there fella is Steven Benson and that old guy in the overalls is Rocky Thomas, and that's Chris Williams there." Ben then looked at me and said, "Well, Mr. Jackson, you bout ready to get started?

"Yes sir, I believe I am, if y'all are." I looked at everyone and said, "It was nice to meet you all, hope I can get in here and work with y'all."

I no more got the words out of my mouth and Rocky Thomas said, "We not gettin it done settin' here a-talkin' about it. Let's go get er done boys."

They all got up and went into the shop then out the door to those four trucks and began loading the gooseneck trailers with mowers and equipment. Then began cranking up and driving out to different locations around the area.

It was just us three in the office, Ben and Carlton shared an office. They each had a copy of my application reading and occasionally asked me questions about my answers to the application.

"Avery Wayne Jackson 34. So you have experience working in maintenance over at Tella Co?"

"Yes, a little bit of everything you could say."

"You said in community college you took diesel mechanics, welding stick, or MIG. So you can use a torch? You have shot grade with laser and GPS Tremble. You have experience with various types of equipment. Can you back a trailer?" Carlton asked.

"Yes, I can," I replied. I have driven tractors all my life pulling and backing trailers on the farm. Tractor with a box blade, front loader, bush hog, I do own a zero-turn mower myself."

Ben asked, "You run a chainsaw?"

"Yes sir, I've cut lots of firewood.

Ben said, "Well, TPA has a Veterans Preference and you are the only veteran applying, and that goes in your favor. Your application looks very good Mr. Jackson. We will look at your…"

And about that time the door burst open and like a breeze that just blew through, a little short man walking fast, walked right past me not saying a word to anyone. He went into the other office and shut the door which had a name plate that read Irishman. He had a little straw fedora and a stubby cigar in the side of his mouth.

Ben gathered his thoughts and said, "We'll take a look at everything and discuss everything and give you a"

The door opened again. We heard a voice say, "Benny, get in here."

Ben got up, looked back at me, and said, "We'll give you a call." And went into the office and shut the door.

Carlton laughed and said, "And that's our Regional Supervisor, Robert Ashton. Robert Ashton was in his mid-fifties, single, with one daughter and grandson. His first wife Evelyn died giving birth to their daughter Rebecca. He had been married another time for a short time. He had made the statement Evelyn was the only woman for him. Flat-top haircut, his signature, Ray Ban sunglasses, and is about 5'5" spunky I'd say. He had been with the Tennessee Power Association for thirty years and pretty much assembled the maintenance division. Before he came along TPA depended on subcontractors for the majority of all work being done. His pitch was, 'Why be at the mercy of subcontractors when we can do the work ourselves? Invest in ourselves building our infrastructure.' And that is where the TPA facility was born. Now they are state-wide and four border states. TPA is buying up power plants, substations, and switchyards, selling power, and pushing it across the power grid of the United States like many other companies. Duke Energy Carolinas, Georgia Power, Consumers Energy, Dominion Energy, Consolidated Edison, and many more. NextEra Energy based on market value headquartered in Florida is the largest in the world with an estimated value of 158.6 Billion U.S. dollars. With the talk of electric vehicles in the future, electricity is and will be a really big business."

I asked Carlton if he had time to show me around before I left. He said, "Sure."

We walked out into the shop and looked around looking at all the tools and equipment. I looked up and noticed it had an upstairs which had boxes of toilet paper, paper towels, Lysol spray, Pine-Sol, Insect repellent, Lava soap, Dial antibacterial hand soap, and more. "You sure got a lot of supplies up there."

We go around to all the substations, and switchyards making sure they are stocked with everything they might need. "How long you worked here?"

"Eleven years now. I like it here a lot. Everybody is like family here. Shoot before I came here I was working as a Walmart door greeter. I also owned my own business, well half of it, me and my half-brother, Arty." He said grinning with pride. "I was working on computers. I was passing out a few of my business cards one day, and Mr. Ashton came in and I gave him a card and he said, 'You pretty good with computers?' I said, 'Yes sir I am. Fix em, program em, files, I can do it all.' He asked me if I would like to come to work for him. He said I'd make some good money and he was right. He has sure took care of me, covered my butt a few times. And he's got a smokin' hot daughter." Carlton smiled big, "I'd sure like to call him my daddy-in-law. She fixin' to be a veterinarian makin' that big money. She already got a kid I think, a boy. Her name is Rebecca Ashton. Dr. Rebecca Rogers sounds good to me."

We laughed and walked on looking at everything there. Carlton seemed to be a likable guy, a cut-up for sure. "Well," I said, "I don't wanna hold you any longer, I guess I'll be on my way. Thanks for showing me around, Carlton."

"You bet, buddy."

It was tax season and Michelle was working late nights and long hours preparing people's taxes, the 15th was fast approaching and you always have those who wait until the last minute. She would come in and I would have her bathwater run for a good soak in the tub with some bubble bath and wine to relax and wind down after a long day. I would light a candle and sit on the floor; it was a great time for us to talk. She laughed and said, "Boy, our Friday nights look different as we get older."

I frowned and said, "It will get better, I promise." She asked me if I was getting worried. "It's the waiting, not knowing. Heck, it's been almost a week now," I said impatiently. What if they weren't impressed or went with another guy? Seems they would've let me know something."

"Well, baby, be positive and no news is good news. And yes I'm sure they would have let you know one way or the other."

The next day was very busy with people coming in and out getting their taxes done. Mary Catherine was with a husband and wife doing their taxes when her two o'clock appointment came in and Michelle asked if they wanted to wait or, she would be glad to take them. They nodded and sat down at her desk. "Hello, I'm Michelle how are y'all doing today?"

"We doing pretty good, I'm Rocky Thomas and this is my wife, Joan. We need you to just look over this here tax form. My daughter said mine was pretty easy and she could do it but I would rather someone who knows for sure what they doin' take a look at it."

Rocky handed her the paperwork and Michelle went over it and agreed, "Yes, your daughter did a very good job, we may have to hire her here." It was all filled out correctly. Deductions, allowances, sign here, and date. Do you want me to mail it with the rest of these, or do you want to take it to the post office and mail it?"

Rocky said, "You can. How much do I owe you?"

"Well, your daughter did all the work, twenty dollars too much?"

He reached down into his overalls and pulled out a wad of crisp twenty-dollar bills. He peeled one off and said, "Thank you, Mrs. Jackson." She had a puzzled look and Rocky said, "You Avery's wife."

She said, "Yes, how did you know?

He said, "I seen them pictures and recognized him from when he came in for his interview."

Michelle said, "Oh yes, I see now, he mentioned you. I've just seen a million faces and names; I didn't put it together. Have they filled the position?" she asked him in a low voice. "Avery is really sweating it."

He winked and smiled. "Don't tell I told you but he will be getting a call Monday to go take his drug test and report to work Tuesday, if everything goes right."

"Oh, he's going to be so thrilled! Thank you, thank you, Mr., and Mrs. Thomas." They got up and waved at Mary Catherine as they were leaving. Michelle, very excited, yelled, "Thanks again!" smiling from ear to ear. "Y'all come back" waving goodbye. Late that night as she was soaking in her warm bubble bath, she said, "I know a secret that you don't know."

I had no idea what she could be talking about and said, “Well, ain’t you something! In my big bad wolf growl, I said, “What you know girly girl?”

“I can’t tell ya. If I told ya I’d have to kill ya.”

“I think that wine is kickin’ in.

“If I killed ya, TPA would have to find someone to replace ya. Cause you couldn’t answer the phone when they call Monday morning to tell you, you got the job!!!”

“What??”

“Yes, they are going to call you Monday morning to tell you to go take your drug test and report to work Tuesday!!!’

“How do you know that?”

“Mr. and Mrs. Thomas came in today to have someone look at their tax form. I was the lucky one who helped them. He saw you in the pictures on my desk. I mentioned the interview, and said you were sweating it not hearing anything, and Mr. Thomas said you would hear something Monday. So this is our little secret. Can’t tell anyone.”

“I won’t tell a soul.” As I put my hands on each side of her wet head and gently pulled her face to mine, our lips met and embraced a deep passionate kiss, her lips had a hint of strawberry from the sweet sangria. She stood up, her body wet, glistening from the glow of the candle. I stood up and wrapped her in a towel drying her off, teasing parts of her body kissing and licking her damp body. I picked her up in my arms carrying her into the bedroom and we fell onto our bed kissing enjoying a night of making love, pleasuring each other. She lay motionless drifting off far, far away. I felt a sense of happiness and I exhaled with a sigh of relief, excitement, knowing our lives were going to change for the better with this new job.

I woke up earlier than normal on Monday. I actually woke up before my alarm clock went off. So I reached over and cut it off and lay there looking at the ceiling. Rosie didn't appreciate me waking her up and got up leaving the room with an attitude headed for the couch. I could hear Michelle already up blow drying her hair. The aroma of coffee filled the house. So I got up and headed into the kitchen to fix me a cup. I went to the bathroom door and pushed it open some to see Michelle bent over blow drying her long blonde hair. She raised up and yelled, "Shit! You scared me!"

I laughed and said, "I didn't mean to. Let me in, I gotta piss."

She laughed and said, "You better save it, they will be calling here in a little while."

"No way I can hold it, I'll just have to make more." I went back to the kitchen sat down drinking on my second cup of coffee with some French vanilla tasting so good. Michelle came in and got her purse off the table gave me a big kiss and said, "Bye, I love you, gotta go. Keep me posted, love you, bye."

I knew she had to be at work by 8:00. I picked up my phone and began scrolling looking at news and weather. Then clearing out some old messages and voice mails when my phone rang. I looked at the clock and it was 7:33. Unidentified and thought, it's them or a call about my car's extended warranty.

"Hello."

"Hey Avery, this is Ben with TPA. I wanted to give you the good news that you have been chosen to fill the opening we have, if you are still interested."

"Yes, sir I am!"

"Well, that's great to hear! Today go to Dickson General hospital to the waiting room there in the back and tell them you are there for your drug screen for TPA, it's already set up. Just whenever you get ready. They will fax me the results and If you don't hear anything from me, be here in the morning at seven. Make sure you have on work boots safety toe, that's mandatory and also bring a void bank check for your direct deposit. Also driver's license and social security card or birth certificate. Then we can finish up your hire in package and you should be ready to go. I'm sure I'm forgetting something."

"Yes sir, that sounds good. Thank you and see you in the morning."

The next morning I woke up with a feeling of so much excitement. Michelle hugged me telling me how proud she was of me wishing me good luck on my first day. She gave me a big kiss telling me bye as she headed out the door for work herself. Rosie looked up at me like what the hell is going on. I slipped on my boots, pitched her a treat, and was off to my first day of work at my new job at the Tennessee Power Association. I went in to a very warm welcome from everyone there at work.

Everyone was in the conference room talking, drinking coffee, watching the News Channel 3 out of Nashville.

Ben said, “sit down Avery, join the party.”

Steven and Carlton were talking politics and Crews spoke up and said, “he’s a sorry sum bitch.”

I gathered he sure was not a fan of the president. Steven said, “Now that’s your opinion, settle down, some of us believe he’s doing a good job.”

I looked at Rocky, he smiled and gave me a nod. Timmy Mason and Paul Killion were talking about Monday night Football. Robert Landry was reading a TPA safety memo shaking his head.

Josh Stanford said, “Snakes are out and movin.’ Saw a copper head fishing yesterday. He was a nice one.”

Chris Williams sat quietly half asleep; his ball cap pulled low over his eyes. Ben spoke up saying, “Guys, I believe everyone has met Avery our newest member to the team. Let’s be our brother’s keeper and help him get adjusted to our system around here. That being said, Avery safety is big around TPA and we here at this base are proud of our safety program and accident free status now for two years.”

Crews spoke up calling Carlton’s name some laughing around the table.

Carlton yelled, “Hey, that tractor jumped outta gear.”

Crews said, "Uh, you don't park on a hill and not scotch it, everybody know that." He continued saying he took out power to half the county when it hit that pole and transformer.

Ben said, "Ok guys, let's stay focused. Has anybody got anything that needs to be discussed about safety?"

"This ain't really safety but I got it on my mind," Rocky said. "That keypad at West Hickman is still broken, not workin'."

Ben said, "Ok, I have reported it. I'll check back with Tony Kyle about a new electrical box or keypad whatever we need to get er fixed. Anyone else got anything?"

Carlton spoke up, "They called from Vanleer and said they need toilet paper and soap."

Crews said, "We have left some both times when we was there. Somebody carryin' that shit home. Ok, y'all be safe out there it's not necessarily y'all it's the other idiots on the road. I'll see y'all this afternoon."

Ben looked at me and Carlton and said, "Avery, you ready to finish your hire in?"

"Yes sir."

Everyone else got up exiting out the shop door then I heard trucks cranking up and leaving the parking lot. We sat in the office filling out paperwork. Ben asked if I had my OSHA 10 which I handed him to make a copy of, along with my driver's license, and social security card. "I also have my fork lift certification."

Carlton said, "That was a plus for getting this job, all your certifications were in your favor. What about that void check for your direct deposit? Your rate of pay is $28.92 an hour. Then after ninety days, it moves to $35.00 then you top out at $40.00 plus bonuses, paid vacation time, insurance, and 401k."

I exhaled and said, "Wow!"

Carlton laughed and said, "Welcome aboard, Avery."

We heard a vehicle pull up outside and Ben said, "That should be Robert."

The shop door opened and Mr. Ashton came in the office door. "Hey guys how y'all doing this morning?"

We were just finishing up Mr. Jackson's paperwork. "Hello, I'm Robert Ashton."

As he extended his hand, I stood up shaking his hand. "Hello, I'm Avery Jackson, nice to meet you."

"I'm the regional supervisor here at TPA and we are glad to have you. I looked over your application and thank you for your service. I wish this country had more fine young men like you, Avery."

"Thank you, sir."

Ben said, "Avery that's about got it, if I think of anything else, I'll let you know. You can go out into the shop area and clean up, familiarize yourself with everything."

I left the office, went out into the shop, and the first thing I noticed was a Kubota ZD 331 60-inch cut zero-turn mower and a John Deere 997 60-inch cut zero-turn mower. I had seen both of these new mowers in the Tennessee Agricultural magazine. They still had plastic on the seats.

I heard the door behind me and, Ben walked up and said, “Whatcha think of these machines? We just got them in.”

I replied, “Pretty.”

Ben said, “Hell, they should be. They sure think a lot of them. He pushed the green button on the wall and the bay door began to rise. He said, “Pick you one, pull that plastic off the seat, let’s try 'em out.”

I said, “Really?”

“Oh yeah, we gonna have to sooner or later.” I put on my new hard hat and safety glasses and fired it up. He pointed to his ear which was my clue to put my earplugs in. You know what they say, nothing runs like a Deere, and they are right! It was nice, a lot nicer than mine at home. Oh, I’d say eighteen thousand dollars more nice. Handled and road like a Cadillac. I made a few rounds in the upper parking lot and returned to the shop. As I drove up and killed the engine I could hear Mr. Ashton yelling at Carlton very loudly and a loud crash.

“Dang Carlton, you know better. You have been doing this long enough to know better!”

“I just forgot Robert.”

“We have to stay two steps ahead so there’s nothing that leads back to us.” I heard the office door open. I hurried to the back bay of the shop when I heard a truck crank and speed off. I turned and walked toward the office; I could still see smoke hanging in the air in this nonsmoking building. I pushed the office door open slowly seeing Carlton squatted down picking up the phone and some files off the floor.

“You ok?”

“Oh yeah, the little Irishman can get fired up sometimes. He doesn’t mean anything by it just gets excited.” I heard the other mower coming through the gate and I looked at Carlton and then back outside. He said, “Go on, it’s all good, thanks, Avery.”

Later that night I told Michelle how strange it was seeing the aggression Mr. Ashton showed toward Carlton. “Maybe it was something I wasn’t supposed to see or something I misunderstood. But, other than that incident, my day went great.” I told her about the new equipment that came in and being the first to test them out. The warm welcome everyone gave me when I came in that morning. To say I was looking forward to it would be an understatement. The next morning was a new day and when I walked into the building, I felt great. Everyone was so nice; the atmosphere was very lax. Ben came in and said I was riding with Chris that day. We loaded up and headed out. We hit the Interstate heading to Chesterfield where there is a substation. We unloaded, got it mowed in three hours then he used his keys to open the door and we went inside. Big cabinets buzzing with monitors, gages, and instrument panels.

“Chris, how long have you been here?”

He said, "Three years."

"How do you like it?"

"It's different but I like it, we come to work, do our job then go home."

Chris was younger than me, I'd guess his early thirties. His class ring was in 2002. He was a very well-mannered young man. We left Chesterfield and headed back to base. We pulled in that afternoon a few trucks were back already. I noticed the dozer and track hoe were gone. Then the next day the backhoe and skid steer were gone. As we were getting from work one day, two of our trucks were coming in late. It was Rocky and Crews. The next day was a different location, substation, and switchyard. But same routine. Working a four ten schedule the weeks went fast. I learned all the locations, got my own set of keys and fuel card. After a few months, I received my ninety day raise, then next thing I knew six months had come and gone.

We were gathered around the table in the conference room having our morning pow wow as Paul Killion likes to call it. Then the news reporter calls my name and there's my face on the big screen being interviewed for what the reporter called heroic, lifesaving actions. Everyone in the room cheered and congratulated me. I said it's not that big of a deal. I had gone to Oakdale 500 to spray herbicide that particular day and was on my way back, rolling down the Interstate when I see a woman waving her arms screaming help. I pulled off ran back to her. She screamed, "My husband! My husband!"

As I told her to call 911, I leaned in the window and saw him holding his chest. I went running to the truck, grabbed the

AED (Automated External Defibrillator), and ran back jumping into action trying to save his life. I didn't really think about, I just did it. Wasn't long Dickson General's ambulance service arrived. As we loaded Mr. Jenkins into the ambulance, Mrs. Jenkins hugged me.

"God Bless you Avery!!"

They took off, sirens wailing headed east on forty to Dickson General. When I finally returned to base that afternoon everyone wanted to hear my story.

Ben said. "Avery tell us all about it and don't leave out one single detail."

TPA took some credit sharing the free positive publicity claiming it was their idea to put AED's in all of their trucks and the classes on the proper way to use them. I received a safety award at the regional safety dinner presented by the Tennessee Power Association division director, Tom Shepherd and division supervisor, Bryan Funt, and our regional supervisor, Robert Ashton. They thanked me for representing the company and doing a good deed. Mr. and Mrs. Jenkins were there also thanking me.

Albert said, "If it wasn't for you, Avery, I wouldn't be here today," as tears rolled down Alice's face. I was just glad I could help. Lots of pictures were taken.

Tom Shepherd said there would big a big write up in the TPA monthly newsletter telling my heroic story. After the ceremony, Tom and Bryan told me if I ever needed anything give them a call. It was a great time and dinner.

After the safety meeting was over, Tom and Bryan loaded up in the TPA helicopter and headed back to Nashville. Michelle took off from work that day to see me receive my award and meet all my coworkers. It was a great day. It was getting close to the annual Christmas party they always have and Carlton was asking us all trying to get an idea of how many might attend. I was very excited about it since I'd never been to one.

Steven asked, "What if we don't wanna come?"

Chris spoke up saying, "Yeah what if we don't wanna come.

Carlton said, "If you don't come, you don't get paid. You can bring your girlfriend, Shawn, and Chris you can bring your boyfriend." Everyone laughed.

Chris said, "Well, who you bringing we all know that answer.

"You should know, Chris, I'm bringing your mom and I hope she wears those tight jeans I like." Everyone laughed hysterically!! Chris punched Carlton in the arm.

Ben came in saying, "What are you idiots up to?"

Carlton responded saying, "They asked what if they don't wanna come."

Mr. Ashton came through the door and said, "We all gonna be there. We have rented a nice place. The Lodge At Montgomery Bell State Park ballroom. Very nice and the food is excellent."

Crews said, "We gonna eat good."

Mr. Ashton continued saying, "You can bring another person, anybody you want. This is for adults! Alcohol will be served."

Timmy laughed and told Robert and Paul, "No strippers."

Robert said, "I don't think our wives would like that at all."

Paul said laughing, "Mine might!"

Crews asked Rocky if he was going to bring the apple pie. Rocky bout spits his coffee out.

Josh said, "They should have deserts on the buffet."

Crews said, "You Idiot, not that kind of apple pie. You kids today."

I knew Michelle would enjoy it. Later that day I called Montgomery Bell Motel and made reservations for us to stay the weekend of December 14th. I thought after the dinner party was over we would take our party upstairs and have some more fun. Jackson party of two!!

We all headed out in different directions. I had been riding with Steven for the past couple of weeks and he was great to work with. A laid-back guy. I liked him. We were about the same age and he loved showing me pictures of his twin girls, Lisa, and Leslie. But, I had heard he had a gambling problem. He would ask me who I thought was going to win certain games. Just conversation but sometimes I felt he wanted my advice.

One day after we had finished work and going back to base, I said, “Who is using the dozer, track hoe and skid steer, and backhoe?”

He said, “They are using it on a job. Rocky, Crews, Timmy, Josh.”

“Oh, I didn’t know, I just knew I would see them coming in late when we were heading home in the afternoons.”

“Yeah, workin’ on a job.”

I asked him, “You going to the Christmas party Friday night?”

“Yeah, I reckon, watch Crews, Josh, and Timmy act crazy.”

“This place we’re going is nice. You bringing anybody?” I asked him.

“Yeah, same ole gal I been seeing.”

“What about you?”

“Yes, my wife. I think she will enjoy cutting’ loose a little that weekend.”

The Lodge at Montgomery Bell was indeed a beautiful place. The park was very well-manicured. There were cabins, camping areas, hiking trails, horseshoe pits. Basketball and tennis courts, an eighteen hole golf course. A lake for fishing and a pool. That place was nice!!

Michelle and I got there early and checked into our room relaxing before the party. We opened the curtains in our room, being on the fourth floor you could see the wildlife in the woods frolicking around, deer and squirrels everywhere. People enjoying the nature walks in the wood before it got too dark to see. As the sun was sinking in the sky you could see headlights snaking their way through the woods.

We finished getting ready and Michelle had her makeup on, and put her diamond stud earrings in asking me, “How do I look?”

“You look beautiful as always, baby.”

‘You think this dress is too tight?”

‘No, it will definitely turn heads.”

We left our room, go on the elevator and was heading down to the first floor when the elevator stopped on the second floor and the door opened and an attractive young lady and Robert Ashton stepped in.

“Hello, Michelle, Avery, how you doing today?”

“Fine sir, and you?”

“This is my beautiful daughter, Rebecca.”

“Nice to meet you,” Michelle and I said.

“You look stunning,” Michelle said to Rebecca.

“Thank you, and you as well.”

The elevator stopped, we all stepped out, and walked toward the ballroom. Michelle and I stopped at the gift shop and bought us two small keychains to remember the event.

She said, “A little keepsake.”

I said, “Let’s go get this party started.”

She laughed and said, “You party animal you.”

We walked into the ballroom and several people were there, some we knew, and some we didn’t. Everyone was pretty casual, boots, jeans, dress pants, slacks, dresses. Very comfortable I have to say.

Joan Thomas yelled at Michelle. “Hey girl, how you doin'?”

Michelle smiled and said, “Doing good.”

“Is this your man I have been hearing so much about?”

“Yes, my better half, Avery.”

“Hello, nice to meet you.”

Rocky had a nice hair and beard trim with new dark blue overalls on. He said, "Hey feller, pretty lady, how you doin'?"

Michelle hugged him and said, "Doing good, ready to have a good time."

Everyone was mixing and mingling, drinks were being served, and appetizers were on the tables. Lots of talking. Crews had his friend Caroline with him. Paul and Julie Killion, Robert Landry, his wife Christin, and Timmy were there alone. His wife was working. Josh had a young lady with him, Michelle thought someone should have carded her. Carlton and his sister showed up late, Ben and his wife, Angela. Steven had a very attractive woman with him. Some of us thought she was a call girl; her name was Ylonda. Crews said she was way too hot for Steven. And Chris brought his fiancé, Mitzy. Bryan Funt showed up an hour after everyone else. I don't know if anyone knew he was going to be there. Michelle was working the room talking to people while I was talking to Ben. They wheeled in the buffet and it was steak, shrimp, catfish, chicken, white beans, turnip greens, cornbread, baked potatoes, corn on the cob, asparagus, and rolls. Then in came the dessert bar.

I heard Josh tell Crews, "See, told you they'd have apple pie." That got a good laugh. Michelle and I fixed our plates sat down and began eating. I enjoyed my medium rare steak. It was a juicy perfectly seasoned steak. Michelle loved her catfish and said it was seasoned and cooked exactly the way she liked it. Good food with some cold beer hit the spot. Everyone was having a good time.

After they cleared the tables, Bryan Funt took to the podium first and congratulated us all on a great year and an outstanding safety program, mentioning my life-saving event, and thanking us again. He thanked Mr. Robert Ashton and congratulated him as well on running a tight ship. Mr. Ashton then thanked Ben who also got up to the podium and thanked us all and told us we are the definition of excellence, working as a team to get it done. Not long after that Bryan Funt left the Lodge said he was going back to Nashville, and had tickets to a hockey game the next day. Robert Ashton and Ben thanked him for coming and told him to be careful on his way home. Soon after the crowd was getting a little louder, and after all the talking and praises, the drinks were flowing. The DJ started playing some great country music and classic rock. People were conversing, mixing, mingling, dancing, and having a great time. I saw Timmy and Josh taking sips from a mason jar and thought yep there it is. Rocky had broken out that apple pie moonshine. The laughter and party went on for another three hours. They opened the ballroom doors and other Lodge guests came in hearing the great music. Carlton was doing some kind of walk like an Egyptian dance and splitting his pants. Timmy and Josh were yelling come on in join the party. As we slow danced and the evening was winding down, Michelle and I agreed it was time to call it a night down here and take our party upstairs. We didn't make it to the room, she attacked me in the elevator kissing me forcefully, and she bit my lip. I wrapped my arms around her waist putting my hands on her ass cheeks pulling her closer. I heard the ding of the second floor, then another ding, of the third floor. She took in a deep breath, then exhaled, breathing faster unbuttoning my top two buttons of my shirt and kissing the top of my chest. I bent down picking her up into my arms, she wrapped her legs around me tightly then another ding, and the doors opened. I stepped into the hallway to my left and three doors down was our room. I got the key card from my back pocket holding her with one arm the door opened and Inside we went. Pulling each other's clothes off as fast as we could. It was intense lovemaking, enjoying each other's bodies and achieving the satisfaction we hadn't had in a while.

It was so quiet, candle flickering, laying there in bed still wrapped in each other's arms talking I apologized for not giving her the attention she deserved. We talked about what fun the evening had been. I promised her we would slow down, enjoy life more, and travel if she wanted. We continued talking in whispers.

She said, "I found something very interesting on the ballroom floor earlier tonight. An envelope I picked up under a chair. It was open and there was money in the envelope. A whole lot of money. I saw five 1,000 dollar bands in there."

I said, Wow, that was a lot of money! Who's envelope was it?"

"Carlton's, It had his name on the outside. I looked around, saw him, and waved, he came over, and I asked him if he was missing anything. He checked his jacket pockets and then said, 'Did you find something?' I handed it back to him and he thanked me several times. He leaned in close and said this can be our little secret. Sliding backward doing a little dance move laughing getting himself another beer from a waiter who was walking by winking at me taking a big drink from the beer then pulling me out onto the dance floor. He wasn't a bad dancer either," she said laughing.

I told her I saw him take a few sips from the mason jar earlier.

"Well, he wasn't the only one," she said giggling. "I had a couple of little sips myself."

I could tell she was still a little tipsy for sure. We talked more about the night but I was very intrigued tryin' to figure out why Carlton would have an envelope with 5,000 dollars at a party.

Before drifting off to sleep she muttered in a low whisper, "Crews had one too."

I said, "What?"

"Yes, I'm sure of it. I saw it in the garbage by the door at the women's bathroom ripped open, crumpled up, empty."

I lay there thinking. Not able to sleep, thinking about what Michelle said she saw. I looked over at the clock it was 4:15 and thought, it's Sunday morning if they hadn't cleaned up the ballroom that trash might still be there before the dayshift came in but I had to go now.

I got up easy not to wake Michelle, slipped on my shorts, t-shirt, and flip-flops, grabbed my wallet, and key card, and eased out the door. I got into the elevator, went down to the lobby, and found the ballroom door closed. I opened the door and went in, it was dark. I turned my phone light on dimly and found the garbage can close to our table, and started looking through it and I saw an envelope with red writing. I grabbed it, and it said Timmy. Confused I then remembered her saying by the restrooms. I went over, started looking through it and there it was. Another envelope with red writing but when I shined my light on it, it said Rock. I could hear voices outside the door. I knew I had to hurry. Then I looked in the can again deeper and saw another envelope with red writing and this one said Crews. I picked it up something was still inside a small card that said, It's been a good year here's to many more. About that time the door opened I turned my light off standing in the dark slipping the card Into my pocket.

The lights came on and a security guard yelled, "Hey you, what the hell are you doing in here?" I started to walk toward him he pulled his gun. "Put your hands up asshole! Yeah, come in Alex. Alex go ahead. I'm gonna need your help in #2 ballroom."

"10-4 on my way."

"I'm sorry, officer."

"Shut up, I'll do the talkin.' What are you doing in here?"

"I am a guest here and I lost my wallet which had my room key in it."

"So you saying you're a guest here?"

"Yes sir."

"What's your name, mister?"

"Avery Jackson, room 421, here's my ID."

"Yeah, how bout cha Tanya?"

"Yeah go ahead, Glen. Tanya can you look at your registry and see who we got in room 421?"

"Sure can. Glen, we got Mr. Avery Jackson signed in that room 'til Sunday afternoon."

"10-4, thanks, Tanya. Mr. Jackson, you can put your hands down now, sir. Sorry for being so rough with you. We have people come in through side doors that don't shut completely, come in here getting food and alcohol left out after parties."

"What's going on, Glen?" Alex arrived walking very fast eyeing me as he entered the room. Alex was a big black guy who looked to be about 6"6" and 285 pounds.

"Everything is alright, Alex. We can't be too careful, you know."

"I completely understand, officer, sorry for the inconvenience. I left the ballroom and got on the elevator going up to the fourth floor. The elevator stopped on the second floor, and the doors opened, to my surprise, it was Rebecca Ashton.

"Hello, Avery."

"Good morning, Miss Ashton."

"You can call me, Becca, my close friends do. Would you like to be my friend Avery? Do you want to get to know me, Avery?" She giggled with a mischievous intent. Very flirtatious, she touched my cheek. My back was against the back of the elevator I couldn't go anywhere. She giggled and said, "Oh my,

I've got him cornered now." She put her hand above my knee sliding it up my inner thigh toward my crotch. She smelled of cigarettes and whiskey. I heard the ding, the doors opened, and there stood her father. He looked very stern at us.

"Good morning, sir." She never turned around not caring at all. I put my hand on her shoulders moving her aside.

"Rebecca, where have you been? I jumped out, hung a left, said, "Nice seeing you both and was on my way three doors away to my room, opening the door and inside I went. I was looking out the peephole, then listening. Hearing them get louder they were arguing about something then silence. The sun was soon to rise, I slid back into bed, the room pitch black, the sheets were cold, and Michelle's body warm as we snuggled. Seems I fell asleep as soon as my head hit the pillow. Later that day and into the night we enjoyed room service, movies, wine, candles, and the big jacuzzi tub. But, I couldn't help but think, wonder I guess, why or what so much money would be doin' changing hands like that. I mean if there was five thousand in each envelope heck that alone is twenty thousand in cash. My next thought was how many envelopes were there, and for what? Trying to process what was goin' on. Maybe I was just letting my mind run. Probably a very simple explanation. Michelle could tell I was thinking hard and after I told her what else I had seen. We discussed several scenarios but nothing made sense. I had several questions, and I knew exactly who to talk to about these questions.

Monday morning at the pow wow the room was a buzz with talk and laughter. Everyone had a great time I gathered. I know my wife and I enjoyed our three-day "mini vaca."

Ben cleared his throat saying, "Alright the weekend's over, let's focus on today, the task at hand. Any safety concerns we need to discuss?" Hearing no one. Ben said, "Let's get to it, folks."

We loaded up and were on the road again. Going to Cordova substation to paint a bathroom and put up new LED lights.

I had thought of how I might bring it up to Steven to see if he knew anything. "So, good time the other night?" '

"Yeah, it was. You and ole girl seeing each other long?"

"Well, you know, when it's convenient."

"Hey, I noticed something the other night at the party."

"What's that?"

"Carlton lost an envelope with a lot of money in it. Michelle found it and gave it back to him. Wonder what that was about?"

"You can never tell, man. They say Carlton is smart as a whip. I've heard his IQ is like Einstein's high."

"Really?"

"Yeah, and computers, If you looked up computer whiz his picture is beside the definition."

"Really?"

“Oh yeah, they say that’s why Ashton hired him.”

“You have been here a pretty good while, you seen any strange stuff?”

“Yeah, every day working with you.”

“No serious.”

“Well, I mean, it’s all family. What, you don’t know.”

“No, fill me in man.”

“Well, Ben is Timmy and Josh’s uncle.”

“What?”

“Yeah, no interviews, Ben just hired them.”

“Wow, yeah crazy. Hell, I had to jump through hoops.”

“And I’ve heard Paul and Robert are family too. Crews and Rocky do whatever Ashton wants; they work at his house a lot.”

“They do?”

“Oh, yeah, they have been over there clearing his bottom, building a huge lake.”

“Is that where the equipment has been these past few weeks? Is that why they are working late?”

"Dude, Ben takes equipment home and Timmy used TPA equipment to clear land he's building that big new house for his wife trying to make her happy. I know what's been making her happy. I saw her in the parking garage with some dude at Dickson General and they were getting' down."

Steven said I don't care too much for Timmy so he can find out the hard way for all I care. He started laughing, "She's pretty hot too, wearing them tight-ass scrubs." We laughed as we were driving on to Cordova.

On our way back, Steven said, "Avery, listen the best thing you could do is forget anything we have talked about and Dang sure forget about seeing that envelope. It was probably nothing. I'm telling you, Avery, these people are like the redneck mafia. They are profiting off each other and they won't like someone coming in messing up the money flow. I'm telling you this because I like you and Michelle. I keep my mouth shut. I need this job and insurance for my girls."

I hadn't thought of it that way. It's not just me involved in this, whatever this is. Christmas this year was our best I would say. I felt better about having more room to breathe as far as our finances with the new job and the work. We had both worked so hard to get ahead. It was relaxing with family and friends; our stress levels were low to none. I was able to finally get things I had heard Michelle wishing for in years past, not that she ever thought of herself first. But, sometimes she would drop a hint. A new flat iron straightener with ceramic plates, a beautiful diamond ring I couldn't afford when we first got married, and earrings to match. That salesman had me going. A new electric skillet. And a stocking full of treats. And Rosie always loves Christmas, especially opening her stocking filled with treats. We spent our New Year with friends at a New Year's eve party at a local bar and grill. It was a great band there that night, 24 Seven out of West Tennessee, and they rocked it!! It was a wonderful time ringing in the New Year.

The first day back Into the new year was full of surprises to say the least. Ben, informed us we would be traveling south down Mississippi to take care of several switchyards and substations. I thought wow that's a lot of windshield time. I asked if we should pack, and Ben said no we would drive down there the other side of Tupelo, work that day, then drive all the way home, which I thought was crazy.

Crews said, "Yeah, boys, gonna be some good overtime."

The next day, it seemed like we loaded up everything. Mowers, spray rigs, chainsaws skid steer. We were rolling down 45, five trucks in a convoy with a million in equipment, manpower, and fuel. I seemed to be the only one who thought it was strange we were so far away from home. I asked Steven if they had ever traveled this far before, and he said yes, they had several different times since he had been there. I asked why, he said these subcontractors didn't do a good job or sometimes not at all. He said they had gone to several locations. One not far from the Louisiana state line. I couldn't help but think it was odd but enjoyed the ride and work. Sixteen-hour days for a week made for a great check. And place after place was grown up needing attention. After we had everything spiffed up, Ben would take pictures. Then, we were loaded up heading to the next place or home.

The next week Rocky and Crews would leave out going south with equipment to tidy up a few more places. It was more maintenance plumbing, painting, building offices, and remodeling. We were very busy those days, weeks went fast. It was a Tuesday I was at the base helping take inventory and I was checking and matching serial numbers.

Carlton said, "Just initial, sign, and date it after you match them, check the box." I was checking everything there and couldn't find five pieces of the equipment on the checklist. A tractor, a John Deere riding lawn mower, a John Deere zero turn mower, a Ditch witch trenching machine, and a Hustler zero turn mower. I asked Carlton about it and he said they were probably transferred to another base being used there. He said he would call them for verification. Carlton was ordering chemicals for the season and sent me to the chemical building and it was pretty much empty. Except for a few things. I came back and told him there were fourteen cases of an aquatic spay for the watershed lakes and that was it. He asked if I would go get the mail.

I said, "Yes, sure." I went up to the upper parking lot to our mailbox and got the mail. You can sure tell spring is upon us, sale papers with those spring deals. Lowes promotion deals, Tractor Supply credit card information. I noticed one envelope was marked R.E.R. Construction. Another was from Ferrell Brothers Investors addressed to Mr. Robert Ashton. Co-op, Evens Petroleum, Dodge, Red Door Tires, Airgas, Rowell Sand and Gravel Company, Bad Boy sales event paper, Harbor Freight promotion paper. The first day of spring wasn't too far off. I took the mail into the office. Carlton was on the phone I sat down at Ben's desk and looked down in his drawer which was open just enough to see an envelope with red writing that said Ben. I wanted to see what was in it if anything at all. I turned the chair around and eased the drawer, picked it up to see it was empty then slowly put it back closing the drawer. It just made my curiosity run wild once again. If some here are getting paid, for what was it they were getting paid? I had noticed things for sure. Things disappear around here like those chemicals from last year that weren't used, gone. I talked with Michelle about the suspicious things I saw but, maybe I shouldn't have seen but I do suspect. I mean we could be talking forty thousand or more. And who is involved? How deep does this go? I will not bring it up, I will sit back until it affects me personally.

March came and went the days starting to warm. It had been almost a year since I was first hired on. Our lives seemed to be more relaxed with the extra money my new job had brought in. Tax season was in full swing Michelle was so busy at work filing tax returns. But she had mentioned slowing down some. But, she said she enjoyed helping people and the excitement. Things at work were going great, until April fourth, 2013.

...

We were at the base having our morning pow-wow when the phone rang. Carlton answered and said, "Yes, yes, I understand. Ben, phone call."

He got up and went into the other room for a while. Rocky told everyone, "Let's get to it we need to go spray herbicide at three substations."

We were getting up and Ben came in and said, "We could have some guests come by asking questions about a tractor that is missing from the fleet. It was at Centerville being used to bush hog and now it's gone."

"Gone, what you mean gone?"

Ben looked agitated, "Well, hell Crews, it's stolen, might as well say."

As we went out into the shop to get equipment to get loaded up and head out I heard Ben telling Timmy and Josh hold back, they were going on a secret mission. We were cruising along I asked Steven if he knew or heard anything about the stolen tractor.

"Well, no but think about it. Who had the keys? What did they haul it with? What did they haul it on? To me, it sure sounds fishy."

I said, "Yeah, that is a good point." The next morning as we were leaving out to go mow at Vanleer I saw Robert Ashton pulling into the base with a trailer and riding John Deere mower.

I heard Steven say, "There it is. The little John Deere that was bought East Hickman 151, Ashton has had it."

I exclaimed, "What? He just took it?"

"Yep, who's gonna say anything? You say something, they will find a way to get rid of you."

That afternoon Chris was in the shop working on the mower. I walked in, "Nice mower."

"Yes, new blades, belts, seat, and oil change."

"Nice!"

The next day it disappeared. I never saw it again. Michelle and I had been talking about the things I noticed at work and I started thinking, on that list was a John Deere riding lawn mower. Now it had me wondering if that was the mower on the list. We never heard anything else about the stolen tractor anymore. I thought, whoever took it had the means and the know-how. I asked Steven one day about the money flow in our department.

He said, "Our department gets so much money to budget every year. So, at the end of the year you have to get rid of it or the next year you don't get as much. It's like you have to break even and that's it, break even or have a loss. I've heard of equipment being buried to get rid of it. Then they say it was old and scrapped to buy new equipment. Just between you and me, Avery, there's lots of money involved here. You've heard the old saying, you don't let the left hand know what the right hand is doing. Well, there you go."

I asked him if he had ever gotten an envelope.

He laughed and said, "What?"

I told him again about the envelope but, this time I told him the rest of what I knew. He sat there in disbelief. We talked about the amount of money that could be involved here.

He said, "Well now I'm pissed cause I haven't gotten any money."

I told him we would have to be quiet about this until we knew more information.

"I told you they were like the mob. It's that mob mentality, certain ones are getting big pay offs."

Now I had to ask myself, is he in on it? And did you just tip your hand? We shall see. Michelle and I would sit and discuss the possibilities. But, we both agreed the picture is getting clearer. Once again, I thought, as long as I'm not involved, why should I care as long as I'm not breaking the law.

The next day was great, Steven and I went to Oakdale 500, mowed, and checked supplies.

That night Michelle told me she had seen Rebecca Ashton that day at the office. She was getting taxes done. She is so nice and pretty too. She was asking about you and how long we had been together. She said I had myself quite a catch. Laughing Michelle said, "I might otta watch her around you."

I said, "Oh now you're exaggerating, I'm sure." Never mentioning the elevator incident, her trying to seduce me. The next morning at base we were gathered in the conference room discussing the day's work scope when the phone rang.

Ben answered and said, "Yes, sure will, I understand. Carlton, phone call." He left the room then later returned telling Ben he had to go toward Milledgeville. We continued with our safety meeting. Then work assignments and Steven and I were on the road again. We no longer got out of the parking lot and I asked, "What's in Milledgeville?"

He said, "Well I do know Ashton lives there."

"Oh, I just heard Carlton say he was going there. Yeah, probably to work at Ashton's house."

"Really?"

"Yeah, they go there all the time. I mean Crews and Rocky laid carpet and tile. That big ass lake was dug with TPA equipment, fuel, and manpower. That's where Timmy, Josh, Crews, and Rocky were going for weeks. You gotta peep game, Avery!! Watch everything and everybody. We are probably the only ones not getting those envelopes. We are not in the loop but that's ok with me. My dad told me to watch them all. I'm sure they all know but my father is the Dickson County District Attorney."

"Oh wow, Steven, cool but I didn't know. You are new so they have eyes on you. Trying to get a read on you to see if you can be trusted. They keep it all from me but I see things, too buddy. A few days I came in only to be greeted by Ben at the door."

"Congratulations, Avery you have won the door prize!"

"What?"

"Yes, you go on up to Dickson General to take a random drug test."

"Oh heck, you had me going there, Ben," everyone laughing along. Steven had just come in behind me.

Ben said, "Yep, you too, Benson. Yall, go make us proud guys!"

So, we went on up there, walked in, and told them we were there for drug test TPA.

The receptionist asked, “Are you Josh Stanford and Timmy Mason?”

With a surprised look on my face, I said, “No, I’m Avery Jackson.”

Steven spoke up and said, “I’m Steven Benson.”

We both received a clipboard and took a seat.

“You see,” Steven said, “Ben covered for his boys knowing they couldn’t pass the drug test.”

“Well,” I said, “I wasn’t going to take it.”

“That is automatic termination, Avery. Just play along and act as if we know nothing about the switch. Don’t make any waves, no red flags. Right, no problem, you’re good, right?”

“Oh, yes,” I said.

So that’s exactly what we did and returned to base. They were none the wiser we knew the game they were playing. Did it bother me? I mean, a little, knowing we are all not held to the same standards, rules, and regulations. Steven and I both agreed we would keep this secret. I told Michelle about what had happened that day and she too thought it was shady. I told her and she also agreed. So what if they couldn’t pass the drug test. I knew I could anytime, and now they will too.

It was graduation day for Rebecca Ashton now, after many years of study, she will be a veterinarian. Robert Ashton was so proud of his daughter. He gifted her with a new car for a graduation present. A new 2014 Black Corvette Stingray. A very beautiful car and expensive for sure. A few months after her graduation Rebecca bought a nice new home in the upper part of town. Chris pulled the house up on the Realtors page. Like 400,000 dollars' worth of house. Wow!!

Crews said, "Her mom left her a lot of money from her side of the family, that's why Robert married her."

I used my GI Bill for college classes. But, still school for eight years is a lot of money. That evening I was telling Michelle about Rebecca's new home.

She was like, "Dang girl." Then she said, "You are gonna leave me for the hot young veterinarian with the big house and fast car." She laughed and said, "Hell, I might be lesbian for all that." Flicking her tongue at me.

I said to her, "You could look at her tax papers you filled out, right?"

"Well, I didn't actually fill them out. Mary Catherine did them, so I don't know if we still have them."

"That sure would answer a lot of our questions, right? You feel like a little trip?"

"Are you serious?"

"It's not but 8:45."

"Ok, let's go."

We got to the office and went inside to her inbox. We looked and looked, and found nothing. We looked at the registry and there it was Rebecca Ashton. Why couldn't we find it then? We went to Mary Catherine's desk looking for something, anything. I looked in the trash can looking for something. There it was, a post-it note with R.E.R. *Rebecca Ashton* Mary Catherine made some little stars around her name. R.E.R. I had seen this somewhere. But where? What does this have to do with Rebecca Ashton? This makes no sense to me or us.

We locked the office and were back home by 10:00 very confused. So we googled R.E.R. and found several company listings. That next day I asked Steven if he had ever heard of R.E.R. construction. He had not heard of them either.

Michelle said she would talk to Mary Catherine about R.E.R. and Rebecca Ashton.

"Girl, you know I can't remember what she looked like. I've seen a million faces and I rock them all." They laughed out saying cause I'm wanted dead or alive.

Teddy said, "You girls alright?"

They continued to laugh. "We're fine Teddy, just going crazy from all these people and taxes."

Teddy said, "I bet it'll be a short trip."

They all laughed, Mary Catherine spitting her coffee, "Awe, Teddy made a funny."

Michelle continued searching R.E.R. but wasn't finding much.

At work that day I also asked Carlton if he had any idea what R.E.R. was. He said he hadn't heard of them.

We came in on May 7th, 2013, Ben told us we had a hot job at Cedar Ridge Lake. Some of the lake inspectors noticed there was a sinkhole in the spillway that needed to be fixed immediately.

He handed his TPA credit card to Timmy and said, "Go get y'all some new rubber boots at Tractor Supply."

We got in there and I noticed some of the guys getting expensive camouflage insulated hunting boots.

They said, "Get what you want."

But I got the plain Jane rubber work boots.

They laughed and said, "No one knows what we're getting, no one checks the receipts. Ashton signs everything. It all goes through him and nothing will be said."

And they were right, nothing was ever mentioned. I mean what eight hundred dollars' worth of boots to a company that makes billions? I still laugh every time I hear, due to high fuel costs, TPA will have to raise your rates. Yep, that one still gets me after seeing all the waste. After thinking about the boots and what they said, 'Everything goes through Ashton.' Maybe that is something to think about. It's like the old saying I guess, follow the money. If Ashton signs, approves, and pays all the bills, he is the money. But, does he know about any of the shady deals going on in this department?

I asked Michelle and Mary Catherine to continue searching R.E.R. and call me if they found anything interesting. When Mary Catherine said, “I’ve got a friend over at the bank, we could take a look at her finances. I mean, buying that big new house.”

“What bank?”

“Well, her tax return is to be deposited into her checking account at Farmers Bank Of Dickson. Hell, for that matter I’ve got her social security number here on file. You just need her last four to check her bank account. Like Teddy always says, follow the money.”

So Mary Catherine gives Michelle, Rebecca’s last four of her social security number 7221. Mary Catherine told Michelle to make sure you dial *67 so our number doesn’t show up.

“Good thinking, girl.”

“Good afternoon, Farmers First Bank Of Dickson, Abigail speaking.”

Michelle said, “Yes, I’d like to check my checking account please.”

“What’s your last four/”

“7221 this is Rebecca Ashton.”

“What’s the full name on the account?”

Mary Catherine pointing to the top of the folder.

“Rebecca Lynn Ashton.”

“Um, did you say checking?”

“Yes.”

“I’m not finding anything. Here it is, savings.”

“Yes, that’s what I thought I said.”

$422,047.63”

Michelle almost dropped the phone saying, “Ok, thank you.” Abigail hung up quickly.

Mary Catherine wrote it down and said, “Holy shit!”

Michelle said, “Dang! I’ve got to tell Avery. This is very interesting.” Michelle took pictures of the file to compare any information.

That night Michelle and I were trying to put the piece together. Make it make sense. We had a dry eraser board writing it all down. So, we have Robert and Rebecca. We know Rebecca has a lot of money. Eight years of school, new house. Crews said her mother’s family had money. They left her pretty well off with a lot of money if that is even correct. I knew I needed to find out more about her mother. I guess a name would be a great start. Surely there has to be a marriage license. I remembered Carlton had to go to Savanah and that is in Hardin County Tennessee. So that's where I'll start. I told Steven my idea he said he would help.

So we called the courthouse. "Hardin County courthouse, how may I help you?"

Steven said, "Hello, I'm Trent Vance with Patriot Insurance trying to verify a marriage license for Mr. Robert Ashston and Mrs. Ashton but her name is smeared, an ink smudge on my copy. Can you tell me the name on the certificate?"

"Let me go to our records, some of our records are on the computer we are transitioning over from old files to the computer. Ah yes, here it is, Evelyn Lynn Renfro, married James Robert Ashton 1969."

"Ok, thank you very much." As soon as he hung up, I congratulated him on such a fine performance.

I said, "Pretty good right off the top of your head like that."

So that night we added Evelyn to the board. Robert, Evelyn, Rebecca Ashton. And lots of money. We still couldn't put everything together. The wine was definitely hindering our thought process. What if Rebecca's money is old family money? She's been in school. "What did it say on her tax return?"

"I didn't think to look but I did take a few pictures of the file. Get my phone let's look at the pictures and see if it tells us anything."

It had an occupation, secretary at R.E.R. construction. I looked at the Board candlelight flickering off the board.

Michelle said, "My goodness, there it is right in front of us."

I said, "What, what do you see?"

"R.E.R., right there!! Robert, Evelyn, Rebecca."

So, now we believe we know who R.E.R. construction really is. Now we have to find out how it's involved with TPA. Not only that but the other players in this web of lies and deceit. Michelle said she would keep digging into this.

The next morning I went in and went to the restrooms where our lockers were and unlocked my locker, and I saw something that scared the hell out of me. An envelope with my name in red ink. I looked around but I knew I was the only one in there. I opened the envelope and saw five 1,000-dollar bands inside. I didn't know what to do. I felt sick to my stomach. I picked my lock up looking to see if I could tell how they got in. I left the envelope, locked the door, and went to the conference room acting as if nothing was out of the ordinary.

"Morning," Crews said.

I responded, "Good morning."

Steven looked at me with a funny look as if he could tell something wasn't right. Ben came in and started the safety meeting as usual.

Timmy smirked and said, "Everything OK Avery?"

"Fine," I said trying to keep a straight face. But, that was becoming hard to do feeling my face getting red and blood pressure rising.

The pow-wow was over I stepped outside as fast as I could trying to act normal.

Steven and I got in the truck and he said, "You ok, buddy? I didn't know what to say. "We are too far into this to keep secrets, Avery."

"You're right, I should tell you for sure. This morning I opened my locker and found an envelope with five grand inside it."

"What the hell?"

"Yeah, I'm a little torn up right now."

"What did you do with it?"

"I left it, put the lock back on my locker, and got the hell out of there. It was like all the others I had seen." We were silent driving an hour west toward Martinsville Tennessee to a substation, not saying a word.

When Steven said, "What are we going to do?"

"I don't know yet. I didn't move the money, who's to say I even knew it was there? Maybe I didn't open my locker."

That evening I told Michelle about the surprise waiting in my locker this morning and what my next move should be. "I left five thousand dollars in my locker today. I've got to be very careful about this."

Michelle said, "I believe your envelope is a test. They are watching to see what you do. You have to take the cash. Put on rubber gloves put them in a zip lock bag bring them home we can put them in the lockbox. When you opened it, was it sealed or just closed?"

"Sealed! So someone might have licked it. Which could give us DNA and fingerprints."

"Right!! Boy, watching all those reruns of CSI has really paid off. I still have that other envelope from Montgomery Bell Lodge in my sock drawer too."

"Great, we will put those together as possible evidence and in our lockbox."

The next day Steven and I went down to Boliver Tennessee to a substation way out in the boondocks. We talked all the way discussing everything going on. Trying to figure out all the players involved. Before we left, we both heard Ben tell Timmy and Josh to get the saws sharpened and ready to go. Steven said they were going out to one of the lakes to cut timber. They cut the timber to clear around the lakes then sell the timber to a logging company which just happens to be Ben's brother, and Timmy and Josh's father. Then they charge TPA and get a nice kickback from the timber. Their hands are clean and clear except for all the cash they get put in them.

He laughed and said, "These good old boys have been slick leggin' TPA for years. And no one looks twice."

"Wow!" I said, "This is crazy!!!"

Steven said, "Hell Avery, we probably don't know the half of it."

Friday morning I got up and decided to take a ride southwest to Savanah. I knew Robert Ashton lived on 22 South out of Milledgeville. So that was my goal for the day Do some private investigating. I sure looked the part. Hat, shades, binoculars, and borrowed Mary Catherine's camera and my wife's car. I just needed the fake mustache. The trip was about an hour and fifty minutes to Milledgeville. I drove south just a few miles and there it was. A long paved driveway with a huge lake on both sides of the drive. A massive log home with a pool. Surrounded by Bradford pear trees, a few magnolias, and dogwoods. Further out, a barn house with stables, a riding arena, and fenced-in pastures. This place looked like the Yellowstone ranch, just in the south. I mean huge!! Then down by the barn, I noticed something. You couldn't miss the bright orange Kubota M7040 4x4 tractor and bulldozer sitting there. I thought, must be nice having friends use equipment and fuel at your disposal whenever you needed it. I drove on down the road not to be noticed then turned around. I came back driving slowly. Out in the country hardly none to no traffic. I saw the bulldozer moving.

Looking through my binoculars I saw Timmy Mason running the dozer. He was going towards the new lake levy. I took the camera and zoomed in and could see the TPA stickers on the side of the dozer snapping several pictures. I raised the camera some and said, "Smile, Timmy, you're on candid camera," again snapping several photos. I thought to myself wonder if this is TPA overtime.

After my surveillance work, I headed back to Milledgeville. I had worked up an appetite and stopped at a little place I saw on the way down. I pulled into the parking lot of Paulette's Country Cookin went inside and sat down in a booth by the window to grab a bite to eat.

A pretty red-haired girl came to my table and said, "Hello, I'm Sadie, your waitress," handing me a menu. "What would you like to drink?"

"I'll have sweet tea."

She brought my tea and asked if I'd like lemon?

I said, "No thank you," and she was gone again. The place was pretty full with people. Some men sitting drinking coffee talking. People eating laughing, a radio playing some Patsy Cline in the back ground. A small bell on the door would ring when people would come and go. The atmosphere was very relaxing, calming, homely.

She returned asking, "Do you know yet what you might like?"

I said, "What's good?"

She laughed saying, "Everything is good, my grandma cooks everything fresh."

I looked around seeing a little chalkboard that read special. Pot roast, chicken pot pie, turnip greens black-eyed peas, biscuits, or cornbread, pecan pie, chess pie, ice cream. I handed her the menu back and said, "I'd like that special."

“Oh, good choice,” she said, “I forgot to mention the special.”

“I’ll have that pot roast over two biscuits.”

She went to the kitchen and came back with a plate loaded down with roast, potatoes, carrots over two biscuits my mouth was watering ready to get in it. I heard the bell ring but paid no attention, my focus was on my plate in front of me. I came up with the fork full meat to my mouth and felt a hand on my shoulder.

“Avery is that you?”

I knew that voice, looking up our eyes met.

“Well what a surprise this is, you are a long way from home. What brings you down to this neck of the woods, my neck of the woods.”

I was still in disbelief. I felt my pulse rate jump. “I have family down this way.”

“Oh, really, where abouts?”

“Ah, Selmer.” Seeing that on a road sign 28 miles south of here.

“Mind if I sit down, it’s pretty crowded in here.” Family In Selmer what their name I might know them.

“Bill and Linda Jackson.”

"No, don't know them," he said.

"Mr. Ashton," Sadie said, "How are you today?"

"Fine, sugar. You doin good?"

"Yes sir. What you having today?"

He said, "Coffee and chess pie."

She looked at me asking if I needed anything.

I replied, "I'm good, thank you."

He said, "Everyone has said what a great coworker you are to work with Avery. You are very dependable, with great work ethics. We need all of that there. Everyone is one big happy family."

I said, "Absolutely, Mr. Ashton," as she brought his coffee and pie, and we continued to eat, looking out the window. The silence between us grew awkward. I was finishing up fast as I could trying not to be obvious.

He spoke up and said, "See those two old dogs, Avery?"

I looked out seeing two dogs, one on a chain at the house next to the restaurant parking lot while Sadie brought my bill, laying it on the table.

I said, "Yes, I see them."

He said, "See that one on the chain with his hair raised?"

I said, “Yes. That old dog is giving him a warning.”

He laughed and said, “He don’t like that other dog comin’ in his yard sniffin’ round.

I stood up and said, “I think you’re right.”

He grabbed my bill and said, “Oh, I know I am, Avery. I got this.” Looking into my eyes, he said it again. “I got this, Avery.”

“Thank you, sir.” I threw down a ten thanking him again, and walking out the door, then to my car pretty quick. After getting into my car, I could see him staring at me through the window. It was a cold icy stare. On my way home I thought, what the hell just happened. When I got home I told Michelle I got busted. I told her the story that I had told him but didn’t think he bought it. I also believe he was making a point for Dang sure.

I had thought about that envelope all night. I wasn’t going to be part of their dirty game. I wasn’t going to do it. I had a plan. I got up, went out to the garage, got a piece of cardboard I’d say 10×10 and painted it black to match the lockers. The next morning I went in and went straight to my locker. I put on a rubber glove to not touch the envelope putting it into a zip lock bag. I then took and taped the bag to the top of my locker. I took the cardboard out from under my shirt and taped it over the bag and envelope giving the appearance of the top of the locker. I mean nobody ever looks up in the top of a locker. I then put the lock back on and locking it. Then, I stuck the key inside and broke it off inside the lock. There Is really nothing in there I need anyways. Now I will know if someone has been in there unless they cut the lock off. Then, I know for sure. Steven didn't come in that morning.

I texted him and he said, "all good, my girls were sick last night."

I was alone today and as I pulled through the gate leaving the parking lot, I noticed the mail truck was just pulling up. I stopped by the mailbox and told her I would help her out and take the mail.

She smiled and said, "Sure, thank you."

I smiled back, "You're welcome."

Looking at the mail I saw exactly what I hoped to see, an envelope addressed to R.E.R Construction and Robert Ashton from Ferrell Brothers Investors. I took those two envelopes and put them in the trunk of my car. I put everything else in the box. I mean there's no cameras, who's to say I took it. And yes, I will put it back tomorrow. That's what I told myself all the way home that evening. Later that night Michelle and I sat down on the bed with our board between us.

"Avery, I can't believe you took this mail."

"I didn't!! It's here in my hand. I just borrowed it. I will put it back in the morning."

We opened it, looked at it, took a few pictures, and sealed it back, and it goes back into the mailbox at work first thing in the morning.

"So, which one first? Ferrell Brothers Investors, or R.E.R?"

"Ok," she said, "Ferrell Brothers it is." I have a box cutter blade here to delicately open it. She handed me the blade. I slid the box cutter blade under the flap of the envelope and worked it up and down slowly. Ever so easily lifting the flap up opening the envelope to see its contents. It was a check receipt for a deposit of $644,000 that had been deposited into an offshore bank account.

"Holy Smoke!!! It seems R.E.R. is a shell company. Which means we don't actually know who owns this company. But, we do know, and we are sure of it. This also means stock." I asked her how a company that isn't a real company has stock.

It's all just ghost companies. It could be to avoid taxes or to hide their identity from the government, or the people they are swindling the money from. Let's open the other it could help answer the questions we have. Rosie jumped up starring at the window growling, then barking her hair on her neck raised. We looked at each knowing she had never done that. She didn't move starring at the window. We opened the second envelope and she read quietly. She looked up and nodded to me. She leaned over and whispered R.E.R. is buying up lots of TPA stock. Rosie laid down still starring at the window. I leaned over and whispered in her ear are we just being paranoid I mean whispering in our own house. But, here we were still whispering. But, I have an idea.

We laid down for bed she said, "Be careful Avery, this is way bigger than we thought."

The next day I took the envelopes back to work and put them back in the mailbox. We saw what we needed to see, took a few pictures, no one knew anything. I told Michelle to have Mary Catherine call me. She called and I told her my plan. That night a car pulled up down the street. Mary Catherine's two boys Trevor and Troy Bailey were in that car. Both were 6' 3" ish, 260 plus pounds. Highly recruited by several colleges. Both on the wrestling team and captains on the football team. About 8:30 we went into our room turned on our light and the radio.

Not long after we went into our room we heard a loud ruckus outside our window. Rosie was on our bed going crazy. Her hair raised barking and growling. I ran outside and across the neighbor's yard.

"He got away," the boys said laughing pretty hard.

I said, "What happened?"

"You were right Avery!! We beat the hell out of some dude trying to look in your window. I mean beat the brakes off his ass."

I gave them each a twenty, they both thanked me. Told me I didn't have to pay them. Said their mom would have their hides for taking this money.

I told them it would be our little secret.

"Yell at us if you need us to whoop some more ass, Avery this was fun."

I went in and told Michelle what had happened. I said, "Somebody got a big surprise, two big surprises."

The next morning I went into work and into the conference room taking a seat. Looking around, I noticed Josh with a black eye and swollen lip. We got up to go to work and I could tell he would be sore for a long time. Steven laughed so hard when I told him about the ass whipping Josh got. We were rolling down Interstate laughing our asses off. We were headed to Oakdale 500.

That night I told Michelle what I had seen at work.

She said, "He deserved what he got. Avery, do you think we should contact the authorities and report this to TPA?"

"Not yet honey, not just yet."

The next day I went in to work. Like every morning everyone was gathered in the conference room watching the morning News Channel 3. The same reporter who had interviewed me was doing a story about the illegal sale of cannabis oils, vapes, and gummies, to minors. There he was cameras in the owner's face.

"Sir, do you have anything you would like to say about these allegations?"

"No comment," the owner said.

"And there you have it. I'm Ken Katel with an exclusive that you will only see here on News Channel 3."

Crews said, “That old boy gets up in their faces, he don’t care.”

I spoke up and said, “Yeah, great guy, super nice. If I ever have a story, I’d want him reporting it. He digs and digs ‘til he gets to the bottom, or top, I guess,” laughing out loud.

I could tell some in there were squirming. I definitely caught some stares. After the safety meeting, Ben asked to speak with me.

I went into his office and he said warmly, “Sit down, Avery, sit down,” smiling.

Carlton was also in there smiling like a mule eatin’ briers. “Everything alright, Avery?”

“Yes sir, everything is fine.”

“You been here almost a year and a half now, what you think about it?”

“I love it here!! Great atmosphere, people are nice, the job is challenging, something different every day.”

Carlton spoke up and said, “Yeah, never a dull moment.”

Ben said, “Well, just checking on you.”

I thanked them both, got up, opened the door, and walked out. Down the hall I saw Josh. His eye, a deeper shade of purple, almost black. As he walked through the shop door and I followed him into the shop.

"Dang man, you alright Josh? What in the world happened to your eye and lip?"

He looked at me gritting his teeth and said, "I fell."

I thought, yeah, fell into a fist. "Bless you're heart man, you be careful, buddy." Doing my best to be antagonizing.

He said, "Oh, I will Avery, you do the same."

I got to the truck, Steven had all the equipment fueled up and ready to go. I got in and he said, "What was that about?"

"I felt like it was intimidation. But, I don't know if they are just trying to get a read on me or what."

That next morning in the safety meeting the phone rang. Ben answered and said, "Yes, he is here. I sure will, yes." Ben said, "Avery, phone call, it's Ken Katel with News Channel 3. I took the phone and went out into the hallway.

"Hello, yes Mr. Katel, oh fine. Ah yes, No it's not right now. Can I call you back in a couple of hours I'm in a meeting here at work? Yes, be glad to meet and talk. Oh yes very interesting. Thank you Mr. Katel."

I walked back into the conference room and everyone had crazy looks on their faces. I said, "they wanted to do a follow-up from last year's story." I don't know if they bought it but I think so. What they didn't know was that it was actually Troy Bailey over at Teddy's office on his mother's phone. I knew that would raise some eyebrows. And yes, I was poking the bear. Michelle was getting off work that night and her and Mary

Catherine walked to their cars, said goodbye to one another and Michelle's phone rang as she got into her car. She said hello and no one said anything. She said hello again, nothing but silence. Michelle cranked up turning on her lights, buckling her seat belt as Mary Catherine drove by beeping her horn. Michelle put her car in drive pulling out onto main street. As she pulled out, she noticed a truck behind her pulling out too with its lights on bright. She had turned right and it did too, right on her bumper it seemed.

She said out loud, "OK you wanna play games, we're gonna see how good your insurance is?"

She slammed on her brakes, and saw headlights coming straight for her from behind; she braced for impact. Hearing tires squall, sliding at the last second, swerving and just bumping the right side of her bumper, and then hung a right onto Long Street. She opened her eyes almost crying.

Mary Catherine pulled up jumping out with her hazard lights on. "Girl, you alright? I was right there at the gas station, heard tires screeching, seen a truck about to hit you. It was on purpose; I know it was."

I got there as soon as I could she was so upset and scared. The cops came and made a report. Mary Catherine described the truck. Extended cab gold looking Chevy I a Dodge. They thanked her for her help she hugged Michelle and we parked her car in the Gas station parking lot and I drove us home.

After a warm bath, a grilled cheese sandwich, and a glass of wine, she was fast asleep. This was getting out of hand, now they put my wife's life in danger. I went in the next morning and as I walked by Ben's truck, I saw a smudge of white paint. I know it was him but didn't say anything. I couldn't prove anything. I thought all day about this whole thing and still didn't have all the pieces. I talked with Steven picking his brain trying to figure it out.

"I told you, Avery, they are like the mob. It's all about the money. We have to find the money." He said, "Carlton deals with the books around here. He's got shit on those computers. We don't know his password, and I wouldn't know how to find it. There has to be receipts, paper, files something. We have to find where R.E.R. is getting all that money. That afternoon Steven and I returned to base and a white Tahoe was in the parking lot. We went inside to the conference room and Ben was in there with two people I didn't know, a man and women.

Ben turned to see me in the doorway and said, "Ah yes, here he is."

The two stood up and the man said, "Avery Jackson, hello I'm Detective Jack Allen and this is my partner, Lieutenant Jo Ann Forrester."

"Hello," I said extending my hand.

Ben got up and said, "I will give y'all some privacy."

They said, "Thank you. We are here investigating some equipment missing from Tennessee Power Association."

"Yes, I heard something about that."

"You did, that's strange," Lieutenant Forrester said, "It's strange because you signed off on the equipment check list as accounted for and present. Matching the serial numbers, checking the box means accounted for and here."

"Is it here, Mr. Jackson? I don't believe so. The detective pulled a copy of the checklist showing me the paper. Is this not signed and dated by you, Mr. Jackson? Is this not your signature?"

I said, "All these boxes were not checked, and I told Carlton these five were unaccounted for."

The lieutenant's voice raised. "These boxes are checked!!"

"I can see they are but, I didn't check them."

"Well, then who did?"

"I can't answer that. Carlton can clear this up. I told them I'm not saying anything else unless I have an attorney."

They laughed and said, "You are not under arrest. Do you need an attorney?" Detective Allen asked.

"Do I? Or are we just talking?"

"Maybe it is just misplaced, a misunderstanding and will turn up soon." They stood up and said, "We will be in touch, Mr. Jackson, "then turned and handed me a card and walked out.

Ben came in acting as if he didn't know anything and said, "What was that about?"

"Carlton knows, I told him they were unaccounted for."

"Yeah, I tried calling but no answer, Avery. Hey, this sure looks suspicious. I hope it gets worked out and they find everything." He said, I should probably go ahead and call Robert Ashton so he can run this up the chain of command."

I walked out the shop door and noticed the bulldozer was back at base. I heard Timmy saying, "If I'm going down, everybody is going down."

Rocky and Crews told Josh and Timmy to shut up.

Timmy said, "I mean it."

I felt my blood pressure rising, they are going to try and pin this all on me.

After I left work, I went by to see Michelle, hoping to maybe bump into Teddy for some free legal advice. I went in and Michelle said, "Well hello, sir, may I help you?"

"Is your boss here?"

"He is here."

"Is he busy? I was hoping to speak with him."

"I will check and see," she said. She came back and said, "He would be glad to speak with you, Mr. Jackson."

I went into his office; he stood up to shake my hand.

"Thank you for seeing me, sir."

"Avery, you call me Teddy. I've told you that before."

"I know, sir, I mean Teddy."

"That's better, Avery. Now, how can I help you?"

"Well, Teddy, I've stumbled into something at work."

"Ah yes, Michelle said you loved your new job but things don't always add up."

"Well, I've seen a lot of illegal activities, fraud, theft of equipment and money."

"Well, Avery, can you prove any of these accusations?"

"Yes, some of this. I need more evidence before going to TPA and the authorities."

Teddy said, "Well, Avery, there's an old saying that has always held true and that's, follow the money."

"I do know this, Teddy, things are getting hostile at work and dangerous. Someone was tailing Michelle on her way home and bumped her car and it could have been much worse. My friend at work calls it a mob mentality." I got up and said, "Thank you for your time, Teddy."

"You be very careful, Avery. I'm here for you if you need help or find yourself in need of a lawyer."

I thanked him again on my way out the door.

Teddy was right, I've got to get into that office to search for some hard evidence. I thought about it, and made the decision, I'm going tonight to find the evidence I need. I mean, I have keys, so it's not breaking and entering. I thought about my plan of execution. I would arrive at base tonight at 22:30 hours, enter the fenced-in area, then lock myself inside. Then enter the building to find the evidence I need.

I parked down the street at the library and drove Michelle's car not to draw attention. I then walked down the street wearing a hoodie and some clear safety glasses just to break up my facial features. I got to the gate looking around making sure the coast was clear then used my keys, opened the gate, and went inside. After I was inside the fence, I locked myself inside. I then went to the shop door, unlocked it, and went inside locking it behind me. I went into the office and went to Carlton's desk. I opened the drawers looking for anything interesting. I didn't see much in Carlton's desk drawers which worried me. I looked over to the five drawer filing cabinet and opened the top drawer. It was the hiring packets we all filled out in the hiring process. I saw my packet in the very front. The second drawer had MSDS sheets. Material, Safety, Data Sheets explain how to handle and store chemicals. These were important with herbicides, pesticides, and storage of these chemicals or storage of flammables. The third drawer had receipts, order sheets, invoice sheets, vendors, sales representatives, equipment warranties. The fourth drawer had billing accounts, charges, billing receipts, credit card statements and receipts. The fifth drawer was all R.E.R. bids and charges to TPA. Hours, equipment, fuel, locations and itemized bills, payments. I took pictures of everything I saw. I made as many photocopies as possible that I could of all Ferrell Brothers Investors statements, deposit slips. Anything that had to do with bank accounts, bank deposits, bank statements. The whole time I was snaping pictures and making copies, I was trying to figure out why R.E.R. was billing TPA. Hoping this was the evidence I needed. I left everything as I found it raising no more suspension. If the evidence is in these photos they are also on this hard drive. Should I take it now and alert the authorities or wait. I can always come back after Michelle and I go over these photos of these records.

I got home and she was waiting with the evidence board and coffee set up on the kitchen table. We spread the copies all over the table and started going through them when we heard a knock at the door. I looked at Michelle confused.

She said, "I called in reinforcements. It was Mary Catherine and her boys. We laid out job locations, dates, then accounts billed, then accounts paid.

Michelle said, "Do you understand, Avery what is going on here?"

I said, "Yes, I think so."

Mary Catherine said, "Hell, Ray Charles can see this. But, It's pretty good, pretty smart system they got going on here."

We worked for hours doing our best to decipher Carlton's bookkeeping and accounting. We worked into the morning hours drinking a lot of coffee and Mary Catherine smoking like a freight train. We put everything into a file folder and Michelle and Mary Catherine went to Teddy's to make copies of the photos I took. We made three sets of everything we had. They then locked one set in Teddy's safe. I would send a set to TPA and another set to Ken Katel when the time was right.

After Michelle and Mary Catherine ran some of the numbers, they determined this had been going on for almost ten years. They estimated the total so far to be 2.8 million could, be more but not less. This is so much more than the theft of a few pieces of equipment. TPA employees do all the work using TPA's man power, equipment, fuel. R.E.R. then turns around and charges TPA, it's one hell of a scam. The subcontractor doesn't exist but they are getting paid by TPA for work never done. Then R.E.R. uses that money to buy large amounts of TPA's stock.

Part Two

Monday was a normal routine everyone was in good spirits as if nothing were out of the ordinary. Carlton was back and said he had a great vacation. I asked him about the equipment that I was questioned about.

He said he had already spoken to the police about it.

I was relieved but didn't know if I trusted him completely. It did seem things had cooled off. There was not as much tension in the room. Everyone seemed unsure of one another or just me.

My day went very smooth. I wasn't going to say or do anything to tip my hand. I felt like we were playing a game and I was in control. After work, I went by to look at a few things I had asked Michelle about. I had asked if what R.E.R. was doing, buying up TPA stock, was considered Insider Trading.

It was not. It's perfectly legal for a subcontractor to buy any stock they choose. R.E.R. was a subcontractor on paper at least.

We were sitting there reading, and Mary Catherine was straightening up in the office when all of a sudden the big bay window in front of the office exploded when a brick crashed through it and landed on the floor right beside Michelle's desk. We all were in shock trying to gather our composure. I felt blood trickling down my left cheek, luckily I was on that side because it shielded Michelle from getting hit by flying glass. I jumped up ran out the door seeing someone in a black ball cap turn around backwards running down the street looking back. I ran after them as fast as I could. They turned the corner and I was gaining on them. They ran into an alleyway and came to a four foot chain-link fence and had trouble getting over. Being closer I could tell they were about 5'5" in height. Me being 5'11" I jumped and hurdled the fence jumping again tackling them from behind.

"Whoa, whoa bruh, hold up" in a soft voice. I then realized it was a female. "Get yo hands off me dude tryin' to man handle me."

I was surprised to say the least by how spunky she was. I could hear sirens in the distance closing in fast.

"Why did you do that?"

"Do what? I ain't did nothin'."

"You threw that brick through the window at Winston Law Firm."

"Wasn't me!"

"Tell me, I'll let you go."

"You let me go?"

"Tell me the truth, and I will."

"Some old guy with a beard and he had on overalls. He paid me twenty bucks to throw the brick."

"You telling the truth?"

"Yeah, the man had TPA on his hat. I seen him good by the gas station."

I knew exactly who it was she was talking about. Sirens close I could see the lights flashing and I got up off of her. Looking back I told her, "Get on outta here." She was gone like the wind. I met the cops at the end of the alley. I gave them a description of her. Height, weight, light skin, teardrop at the corner of her right eye. They seemed to have an idea who she was.

I walked back to the office telling the girls what I had found out. The cops stopped by to take pictures just as Teddy had arrived. Michelle and I both apologized for the damages.

Teddy said he was just glad we were all safe. Teddy reiterated how this seems to be becoming more dangerous. Mary Catherine got her things and was on her way home. Michelle told her to call letting us know she made it ok.

That night Michelle asked when I would go to the authorities. "They are acting more aggressively now."

"Soon, I promise," I told her tomorrow I would talk to Steven and tell him to speak to his father, and let him know what was going to go down. I need to let someone know about that five thousand. I want no part of their dirty money, something they can hold over my head.

The next morning has played out in my mind a million different times. We were in the pow-wow finishing up our safety meeting. I had mentioned I had a slight headache. Probably stress from all that's going on. I went to the medicine cabinet that was mounted on the wall.

I didn't see anything for a headache and told Carlton he needed to order more Ibuprofen for the box on the wall. He had on rubber gloves putting new ink cartridges in the printer.

He looked up and said, "You not feeling well, Avery?"

I said, "I had a headache, it could be sinuses."

He said, "Here, I have a bottle of Aleve there on my desk." He got the bottle and pitched it to me.

I opened it and said, "There's only two inside." I told him I didn't want to take his last two.

He said don't worry he had another bottle in his car.

I put them in my shirt pocket and went outside to help Steven fuel the equipment from the big diesel tank. We got into the truck and we were off to the microwave towers just out of Pegram. There were three microwave towers we had to go mow and check supplies inside. I had put that bottle on the dash of the truck. My headache had eased up and almost gone after a cup of coffee opened up my sinuses. I went inside to open the computer room there at the last microwave tower to check the restroom. I came out and Steven was on the ground unresponsive beside the truck his lips were blue. I grabbed my phone and dialed 911.

"Steven, stay with me, buddy, Steven!! Come on buddy."

"911 what is your emergency?"

"Hello, yes my friend is out of it, he's going in and out of consciousness, his lips are blue, his skin looks pasty."

"Where are you?"

"Off forks river road just out of Pegram inside the fenced in area of the TPA microwave towers."

"Help is on the way, sir. What is your name?"

"Avery."

"They will be there in a few minutes. Avery, do you know CPR?"

"Yes, yes I do!"

"Does your friend have a pulse? Ah, two fingers on the wrist or neck."

"If he does, it's very faint. Steven, Steven wake up buddy! Can you hear me, I slapped his face a few times. He's gurgling, he's gurgling! I'm going to lay him on his side."

"Yes, do that, Avery so he doesn't get choked."

I could hear sirens.

"Avery," in a low whisper I leaned my ear by his mouth.

I yelled, "Steven! Come on, buddy you can make it. Don't let them get you too!"

The ambulance flew in behind the truck and both men ran to us opened a bag and began working on Steven. I stepped back to give them room. I said thank you to the operator and she told me it's all going to be alright now. I hung up and called Ben.

"Hey, get me that new stuff, the ah Naloxone," one of the medics said.

"He's got pinpoint pupils. Yeah, opioids I'm thinking."

Two police cars arrived. They were asking questions about our work. "Hello, sir, what is the victim's first and last name please."

"Steven Benson." One asked if Steven was on drugs or used drugs.

I said not of which I was aware. We had taken a drug test a few months back and he didn't seem worried about it. They put him on a stretcher and was working on him inside the ambulance.

I was still answering questions in front of the police car when one of the paramedics walked up to one of the cops and shook his head saying they did all they could but he didn't make it.

"Steven didn't make it? Is that what he just said?" I was in disbelief.

"I'm sorry, buddy we did all we could for your friend."

"I know you did; I know. Thank you both."

The officers, Jordan, and Davis were both with the Cheatham County Sheriff's Department. They were asking me questions. One taking a statement, writing down my answers the other looking through the truck.

Davis said, "Earlier, I asked you if your friend used drugs. You said no, not of which you were aware."

"Correct, he was always very alert, sharp, nothing like this."

"Do you know if he was allergic to any of these chemicals?"

"I don't think so, he's worked here for probably six years, it would have shown before now. It's just Pine sol, and bleach. He didn't even touch any of that today. I went inside, and checked the bathroom. He stayed in the truck."

Officer Jordan picked up the Aleve bottle on the dash and shook it. I saw him and I froze focused as he threw it back on the dash not hearing the two pills inside. My mind and heart were racing because I knew I didn't take them. But, where were they? There was only one answer. Steven had to have taken those two pills.

A truck pulled In, it was Ashton and Ben. They walked up speaking to the cops. “Officers,” nodding, “I’m Robert Ashton and this is Ben, we are with TPA. I’m the Regional Supervisor and Ben is the shop foreman. Both Mr. Jackson and Mr. Benson work with us. This is a terrible loss to our tight-knit work family. We have known Steven for six years and a great guy, and an excellent employee. We have nothing but good things to say about Steven. We have notified his family. TPA security, they too, are on the way coming to fill out reports and a statement.”

As he spoke to the cops, I couldn’t help but think my friend was no longer there and his body was on the way to the morgue. The medical examiner just finished up his paperwork and they are transferring the body to a regional forensic center to perform an autopsy.

“Avery, Avery, do you have any more questions to ask?”

“No sir, I don’t have any.”

TPA security arrived and asked me a few questions, and Jordan and Davis told TPA security they would, and didn’t mind sending their statement and report. I called Michelle telling her about Steven passing.

“Oh baby, I’m so sorry to hear that. I know you and him had grown close. Do you want me to come get you?”

“No, Ben and Ashton are here. I’m sure Ben will drive us back to base.”

The ride back to base was long it seemed, for just an hour and a half. Ben didn't know I knew all I knew but he was very nice to me.

"Yep, Avery, the good book tells us tomorrow's not promised. We just never know."

"Uh huh, you're right there Ben, you just never know." I also thought it says Thou shall not steal too. Now I have to get a look at that bottle. I have to see if I'm wrong about not hearing those two pills rattling around in there or was it empty, like deep down I believe it is. If it's empty, it was what killed Steven, and they are trying to kill me. Is that what Steven was telling me? When we pulled back into base, everyone was gone except Carlton. We parked and Ben got out and I took a napkin, picked it up, and my suspensions were correct. The Dang bottle was empty. I wrapped the bottle in the napkin, and put it back in my pocket.

I felt sick, angry, sad, so many mixed emotions. I told Ben I'd see him in the morning and Ben put his hand on my shoulder, "Avery, go on take the rest of the week off. I'll make sure you are paid. Go home relax, process everything and just relax."

Ha he didn't know shit about what all I was processing at the very moment. Someone tried to freakin' kill me!!! I looked at Ben and said, "Thanks. I will see you Monday. Let me know as soon as you hear anything from the autopsy."

Ben said, "Sure will Avery."

Ashton pulled through the gate, rolled his window down, and said, "Sorry about your friend, Avery. You ok to drive home?"

"Yes, sir, thank you."

I got home to be greeted by Michelle and Rosie at the front door. Michelle hugged me for several minutes. Rosie sitting on the floor looking at us trying to figure out what we were doing. I had thought all the way home about whether I should tell Michelle or not. She was already a little skittish with the brick and the truck following her.

"He seemed like such a nice guy. I sure hated hearing this but do you think?"

"I don't know what to think, I don't want to think it could be something else."

"But, it has crossed your mind, right?"

"Yes, but that's a whole different thing. It's a whole different thing I don't want to think about until I know for sure. Which will be in a few short days when the autopsy results come back. Here's what I know. I'm off work until Monday and I don't even want to think of that place or those people. So let's order a pizza, light some candles, find a good movie and a hot shower."

"Together? Oh great Idea we can save water," Michelle giggled kissing me. I lay there in bed after Michelle drifted off to sleep thinking of everything, even though I said I wasn't. I really couldn't sleep Rosie nudging my hand with her nose wanting me to rub her, which I did.

The next thing I knew my alarm clock was going off. I hadn't turned it off from not going to work but I did so then so it wouldn't wake me in the morning. I could smell the coffee so I got up.

Michelle was dressed for work finishing off her cup of coffee before taking off.

"What are you two getting into today?"

"Not much, just hanging out."

"Good, then you can take Rosie to her veterinarian appointment." She handed me a card that said, Rosie Jackson 8/12/13 10:30. On the back it said Veterinarian's Promise Animal Care. "We Treat Your Pet Like Family." I looked down at Rosie wagging her nub tail. So, we had our coffee and breakfast, eggs with smoked sausage. Then I got ready got Rosie's leash and we were off to the vet. We pulled into the parking lot and I saw a Black Corvette Stingray with a license plate that read Hot Vet.

I went to the receptionist at the window and she said, "Rosie?"

"Yes, she is here for her six-month checkup." I sat down Rosie jumped up onto my lap laying down watching the other people and dogs in the room as if they were peasants sniffing each other's butts. I looked up on the wall to the bulletin board that read Welcome Dr. Rebecca Ashton we are so glad you are part of our team. I thought Dang I can't get away from these people.

A young lady came in and said, "Rosie, we are ready for you." She took her leash and they walked down the hallway to a digital scale to get her weight. We then went into a room and she shut the door.

The Veterinarian came into the room from the back door and said, "Awe, Rosie Jackson, and her daddy, Avery Jackson." Well, she opened a folder reading, "7.8 pounds, she needs her rabies shot is all I see. What kind of food is she eating, hard or soft?"

"Hard, she eats when she wants."

She looked at her teeth, inside her ears. "Had any problems with ticks or fleas?"

"No not at all. We use the preventive medication drops."

"You have here, Safelife?"

"Yes." Rebecca was feeling her ribs and leg joints.

She said, "Here, feel this," taking my hand and putting it under Rosie's chest. "You feel that?"

I said, "Yes," she was rubbing the back side of my hand and said, "She has such a strong heartbeat. You might want to switch up her food sometime. I'm sure eating the same old thing all the time gets so boring. You know what I mean don't you, Avery? Something different every now and then."

The young lady from earlier opened the front door, and I pulled my hand away.

"Ah no, no I don't." Rebecca laughed and said, "Ms. Rosie gets her a rabies shot and she's good to go, Casey."

She said, "Yes ma'am, and see you soon, Avery."

About that time the back door burst open another young lady ran in. "Dr Ashton, there's an emergency out back! Brad Thompson's prize-winning breeder bull ran through a barbed wire fence!!"

"Get my bag," and Rebecca ran out of the room into the back of the building. I saw her grab a bottle of something off a shelf and a needle and go out the rear exit.

Casey and I looked out the window and a bull was going crazy. Casey said, "That poor thing is hurting." The bull was gonna tear the trailer apart. Rebecca drew a syringe quarter full, and got close and the bull kicked sideways, almost kicking her in the head. She got closer, and then jabbed the syringe into the bull's hip and it was almost like a switch went off.

I asked Casey, "What was that?"

She said, "A really strong sedative for pain. It's the strongest we got."

Rosie and I went and paid our bill and left. On our way home, a song came on the radio. Every time it came on, Steven would turn up the radio and sing along. He said he loved the song. It's called Blackbird, Blackbird by Anna Anawalt. He said, "Blackbirds are the messengers, protectors.

I had asked him, "Is that why you have that tattoo?"

He said, "Yes, those are my girls, I got that tattoo when they were born. They watch over me."

This song feels like and sounds like Bluegrass, and Americana to me but, now that I listen to the words, it sounds like Steven. I will find out who killed my friend.

It was Sunday afternoon and the phone rang, it said, "Dickson County."

I answered and heard a man's voice say, "Avery?"

"Yes, it is. Who am I speaking with?"

"This is Elliott Benson, Steven's father."

"Hello, sir. I have been meaning to contact you to give my condolences to you and your family. Steven was such a great person."

"Thank you, Avery. I want to ask you something Avery."

"Yes, sir what is it?"

"Do you think Steven was messing with drugs?"

'No sir. I don't. I never noticed or detected anything out of the ordinary. He was always straight, and a sharp thinker. I enjoyed our conversations. I confided in Steven on things."

"Yes, I spoke with him as well. I told to him watch out and be careful with that bunch."

"I'm very sorry for your loss."

"The toxicology report came back and they said Steven died of an overdose."

"What?"

"Yes, overdose. I talked to the medical examiner and he said Steven had enough opioids in his system to kill a horse."

…

Monday morning back at work was a stressful day knowing I wouldn't see my friend Steven there ever again. Our routine of jumping in the truck heading out to do our work, and our conversations which I will miss the most. It didn't feel right, I felt a heaviness on my chest. Guilt, knowing it was my fault, knowing it was meant for me.

After work, I went straight to Teddy's office to speak with him. I told him what I thought and how I believed it was meant for me.

He said, "Do you know what you're implying, Avery?"

I said, "Yes."

He said, "It's murder."

I told Teddy what Steven's father said the toxicology report stated and what the medical examiner said about the opioids in Steven's system. I also let him know I had the bottle the pills were in and where I had gotten them.

He said, "Good job, Avery, give it to me." The bottle was still wrapped in the napkin and in a zip-lock baggy. He said, "I've got a friend In Nashville I can send this to and have it analyzed to confirm or deny your suspensions. He has helped me out on a few of my cases. He's very good with the drug identification processes and variants of other drugs. If this confirms your suspensions then there is a killer out there. We will have to go to the authorities before there is another victim, possibly you, Avery. It will take a few days. Now I think I will deliver it myself instead of sending it. This is very interesting indeed," he said.

Michelle said, "We should listen to Teddy, he's seen and heard it all over the years but this has him very intrigued." I still had not told her about the events leading up to Steven's death and how I was given those pills or who by.

The next morning, I walked in the door at work and overheard Timmy saying, "I knew he was on drugs. I never liked him anyways."

I walked into the conference room looked at Timmy and said, "He never liked you either."

Surprised, Timmy said, "How's Robin?"

I said, "How's your wife's boyfriend, the one she's been seen banging in the parking garage at Dickson General."

Timmy got up out of his chair lunging at me, "You son of a Bitch!!"

I laughed and said, "Since you know so much, you should have known that for sure.

Ben told Timmy to knock it off. "Both of you!"

I sat down and winked at Timmy as he starred me. He turned and went out into the shop slamming the door behind him. I thought quickly and knew I had never told anyone Robin is Michelle's first name. They all just smirked and smiled acting as if nothing were wrong, as if I didn't notice they were trying to get under my skin, trying to run me off, scare me away, using my wife for intimidation.

That afternoon Michelle called and said I was going to have to take her car and fill it up with gas. She told me her card wasn't working. Every time she tried to use her card; the transaction was denied. She called the bank but they were closed. She said she would order her a new card, hers was looking old and scratched. She told me they had chips in the cards now.

I thought wow, that's pretty cool. I told her I would pick up a pizza from the bowling alley. I know how much she loves their pizza, and so do I. I called, placed our order, and was going to run by and pick it up. I went in to pay and handed the young lady my card and she swiped it and it was declined. I said try it again and it was declined again. With the line backing up behind me, I pulled a folded-up hundred dollar bill from the inside pocket of my wallet for emergencies only. I got home and told Michelle what had happened. She then called the number on our card to check our balance to find out our bank account was wiped out.

We were upset and angry just not knowing what the hell happened to all our money. Michelle called the twenty-four-hour number on the card to report fraud. The lady with the bank assured us they would refund any stolen funds. Call the main branch first thing in the morning to report the stolen funds. We felt some sense of relief knowing our funds would be reimbursed. I told my wife this was not a coincidence it was done intentionally.

She said, “You don’t think they’re behind this, do you Avery?” Michelle seemed to get louder, “I mean, how the hell?”

I said, “Wait a minute. My hire-in packet has all my information. I also had your whole name as my contact in case of emergency.”

“Those bastards,” Michelle said angrily now.

I told her I didn’t put anything passed them. I was just waiting to see what Teddy’s friend could find out to see what actually killed Steven for sure.

The next day at work, I was at the base using a blower, cleaning leaves, grass trimming, and debris off the parking lot when I felt a vibrating in my chest. I cut the blower off, removed my ear plugs, and heard my phone ringing. I knew the number; it was Teddy’s office.

"Hello, beautiful."

"Well thank you, Avery."

"Oh, excuse me, sir, I saw the number and thought it was Michelle."

"Ah yes, I understand. I have some very interesting information, Avery, I think we need to speak in person as soon as you can."

"Ok, I'll be there at 5:15 this afternoon, is that good?"

"Yes, that will be fine."

"Ok, see you then."

I stayed in touch all day with Michelle while she was working with the bank on our missing funds. They did exactly what the lady on the twenty-four-hour line said they would and reimbursed everything. I guess it was the inconvenience, and how easy it was for someone to just take from us. Something we worked so hard for. But, it happens so easily every day to so many being taken advantage of.

I got to Teddy's office that afternoon. I was very anxious to find out what exactly Teddy's friend had found out about the bottle and what had been inside that bottle. I walk in seeing Michelle first thing.

"Well hello, sir," she said smiling.

"Hello, pretty lady, how are you today?"

"Fine," she replied.

I told her if we keep meeting like this someone's going to think we got something going on. Mary Catherine laughed you two better quit. I told Michelle I had an appointment at 5:15 with her boss. I asked if he was alone, and she said yes, picked up the phone, and called back to Teddy. "Avery is here, Teddy, are you ready to see him?"

"Yes, dear send him on back."

She smiled and said, "He's ready."

I went into his office, Teddy said, "Hello, Avery, close the door there behind you. Please, sit down, we have a lot to talk about. I received word from my friend today, that he had the results of the test he ran on the bottle you gave me to be tested. I must say his findings are very interesting. The bottle had very strong traces of Fentanyl residue inside and still very deadly."

"Is that an opioid?" I asked.

"Yes, it is." Teddy was reading notes he had scribbled on scattered all over the top of his desk. Pharmaceutical fentanyl is a synthetic opioid approved for treating severe pain, typically advanced cancer pain. It is 50 to 100 times stronger than morphine. Fentanyl can come in several forms such as pills, powder, liquid. I've never heard of this stuff. Many haven't but it was developed in the late 50's. To be exact 1959 then introduced in 1963. It's legally manufactured and distributed in the United States. Two milligrams of this stuff can be lethal," he said. "I guess depending on one's body size." Teddy looked at me and said, "Hell, that would be like 10 to 15 grains of table salt." He also said, "The Centers for Disease Control and Prevention, (CDC) reported in Kentucky a 207% drug overdose increase in 2010-2013 due to laced heroin with fentanyl. And the bad thing," Teddy said, "was here in the United States we have two types, pharmaceutical, and Illegally made fentanyl."

I was in shock. Steven died from a fentanyl overdose. I asked Teddy why the toxicology didn't say fentanyl.

He said, "I asked my friend the same question. He said they have to specifically test for that drug. This is some very strong and dangerous stuff, Avery." His eyebrows narrowed and he raised his voice. "It was meant for you, Avery."

"Well, Teddy, what is my first move?"

He said, "You are going to need an attorney."

I took in a deep breath and exhaled. I said, "Do you know any?"

He shook his head and said, "This is murder! If we do this correctly, Avery, you may not need an attorney. You didn't give Steven those pills. Someone gave you those pills. But, we do need to report this very soon. You should talk this over with your wife."

"Michelle wanted me to do this sooner. I just wanted to be sure before I pointed any fingers."

"But, you know where you got those pills and exactly what they were."

That night I told Michelle everything I knew, and to say the least, she wasn't happy. I hadn't told her everything about the pills and how I got them. She was very upset to think things could have very easily ended differently. We talked about everything trying to figure out this mess. Who was responsible for Steven's death?

"Carlton tried to kill you, Avery!!"

"I knew it was time. But, what scared me was the fact that the fentanyl that killed Steven was in my possession. The police would say it was mine. Where had it come from? Carlton would just say he didn't know anything about it. Right, or would he? I needed to get him to admit it to me before I went to the cops or he would deny it all, and I'm the one left holding the bag or the bottle for murder."

The next day I thought of how I would put my plan into motion. So, after work, I went to Teddy's office to run my plan by him, and he agreed.

"Brilliant, Avery!" he said. "Get him to confess, and yes, it clears you, otherwise, it's just hearsay." He said, "I've got just the thing," opening his desk drawer. "It's a small recorder and a wireless microphone, you can put it inside your pocket. Press play the red light means it's not recording yet, and green means go."

This is awesome, I thought. That evening I told Michelle my plan to get him recorded to clear my name if they try to pin this on me. She too agreed and went to the kitchen drawer and got fresh batteries for the recorder.

So, the next day I called in and said I wasn't feeling too well, and may be in late. Later that morning I went in around 9:30 thinking everyone would be gone and I could speak to Carlton alone. I came into the parking lot and saw no TPA trucks there and knew I was going to have some time alone with him. I went into the building, stepped through the door, and pressed record on the recorder and a green light came on. I put it in my pants pocket and the wireless microphone in my shirt pocket. Carlton was there at his desk typing away on his keyboard.

He looked up, "Avery, hey buddy. I didn't think you were going to be in today."

"Well, I feel somewhat better, it's a toothache."

Carlton asked if I needed anything. Inside I laughed thinking, not from you. "No, I'm good. Hey, did anybody talk to you yet?"

"About what?"

"You know, they said Steven died from an overdose."

"Yeah, I heard that. I just wouldn't have picked him for a drug user."

"Carlton, he wasn't. He took those pills that you gave me in that Aleve bottle the day I came in here telling you we were out in the medicine cabinet. You threw me an Aleve bottle with two pills in it that he took later that afternoon."

"What?"

“Oh yeah, they were fentanyl. You son a bitch, you tried to kill me,” as I grabbed him by his collar shaking him.

“Avery, Avery no I didn’t!! I would do nothing like that to anyone. I’m not a killer!! I had just come back from vacation, remember? It was my first day back. They were there on my desk for a week or two before I left. I promise, Avery I wouldn’t do nothing like that.”

I stopped, and gathered myself thinking I’d gotten this all wrong. I fixed his collar we were both breathing hard.

“Don’t lie to me, dammit.”

“No,” he said, “I promise,” he was almost in tears.

“Hell, someone is trying to kill me!”

“I had no idea when I gave you those pills.”

Did I believe him, I don’t know. But, he gave me everything I came for.

“Avery, it’s Robert, he made me do all this.”

“All what?” I asked.

“Let me see your phone.” I showed him my phone. “Sit down,” he said. He wanted to see if I was recording him. “Ashton has been paying me to do this for years. He tried to kill me so I wouldn’t say anything.”

We both heard a truck pulling through the gate. Carlton jumped up and ran toward the bathroom. “Don’t say anything, Avery! I will call you.”

I looked out the window, it was Robert Ashton and Ben right behind him. I went out the door as they were getting out of their trucks.

“Avery didn’t think you would be in today,” Ben said.

“Yes, just came by here to ask Carlton about our dental insurance. I’m on my way to the dentist. I will see you tomorrow,” and walked onto my jeep.

Ashton asked Ben, “Has he come around yet? I think he’s getting there.”

“Good, we don’t need any trouble.”

I went straight to Teddy’s office. Teddy, Michelle, Mary Catherine, and I listened to the recording and were all surprised to find out there’s more involved here.

Mary Catherine said, “Boy, he sounds scared.”

Teddy said, “Wonder what else he wanted to tell you, Avery?”

Michelle spoke up, “How much more can there be?”

I told them I needed to find out. Later that afternoon I called Carlton and asked to meet somewhere.

He asked, “Where?”

“Let’s meet at the lake in front of Tella Co. It’s way out away from everything.”

He said, “OK, 8:00.”

“Ok, I’ll be there.” I checked my batteries and was ready to get the whole story. We met up at 8:00 p.m. on the dot. I took a twelve pack of beer to ease the tension and make him feel more comfortable. I had been there waiting for twenty six minutes before I saw the old brown escort drive by real slow and keep on going. I had the recorder in the console and the mic above my sun visor. I pressed record. Then I saw the escort come back by and looped around and pulled behind me and came and got into my jeep.

He looked around as If he were followed. “I kept seeing lights behind me,” he said.

“I’m sure, it’s dark outside.”

“I’m serious, Avery,” he said.

He acted as if he had already been drinking. I couldn’t tell if it was alcohol or paranoia. “Let me see your phone.”

“It’s turned off completely.”

“Lift up your shirt.”

“I asked him, “What the hell is this?”

He said, "Just do it," and I did.

"Do you think I'm wired up or something?"

"I don't trust anybody."

"Yeah, tell me about it."

"If something happens to me, Avery, Robert Ashton done it or had one of his goons do it."

"You want a beer?"

"Yes, thanks." We both opened our beer and took a drink.

"Mind if I smoke?" he asked.

"No, not at all go ahead."

He lit the cigarette, took a long draw off it cracking the window. "But, why?" I asked.

"He has stolen a lot of money from TPA."

"How?"

"He has a fake company charging them for work that really doesn't get done or we go do it with their own equipment and everything then is charged to them. It's been done that way for at least ten years, maybe longer. Then computers came into play and that's where I came in."

At that moment It just came out. “Did you screw around with my bank account?

“Yes,” he said, “but, I had too. They made me do it.

“Who made you?”

“Ashton and Ben, and those goons.” He finished his beer off fast and got another. “Some of the stolen equipment was sold. They get paid, and insurance buys a new tractor. Some take it to their homes and do work. That equipment that’s missing, they sold it. Ashton pays everyone!! Is that what was in the envelopes? Yes, he pays everyone.”

“Bryan Funt in on this?

“No, I don’t think so, he believes everything Ashton tells him. He approves all the financial reports and payments Ashton sends him. He could be in on it, or he’s an idiot.”

“What about R.E.R., Ashton’s company?”

“He said, “Yes, I believe so.”

I knew he wasn’t being completely honest.

“What part does Rebecca Ashton play?”

“I don’t know,” he said.

He was getting fidgety. I knew I had struck a nerve.

He said, “It’s getting late, I’ve got to get home.”

I asked, "Who followed and bumped Michelle's car that night?"

He said, "Josh used Ben's truck." He got out and asked if he could have another beer.

I said, "Yes, take the rest." I watched him get into his car and crank up as I pulled off. Michelle was waiting at the door when I got home. We sat down and listened to the recording. She clapped her hands together scaring Rosie when she heard him say he hacked our bank account.

"That despicable bastard! I knew they were behind it!"

The next day Michelle took the recording to work so Teddy could listen to it. She said he was floored hearing everything as it's unfolding like it was.

I went into work as usual and went out to Vanleer with Chris that morning. We had some windshield time together and he stays clear of the bull shit.

He told me he was sorry to hear about Steven's death. He too liked Steven.

He said, "I just come in here, do my job, and go home to my girl."

I thought to myself I'd ask a few questions feel him out. "They do a lot of work out at Ashton's, don't they?"

"Yeah, they told me to go down there a few times to work on equipment for him. I went but didn't like it cause I didn't know where we were going until I got there. Timmy drove, then I was there nothing I could do. If I say something they will find a way to fire me. So, I do what I'm told."

I asked him, "Why not report it?"

"To who?" he said, "TPA? They bumbling idiots. They would cover it up to keep people at the top from finding out."

Chris's phone rang. It was Ben, he told us to get on back to base he had some things he wanted to talk about with us. We pulled in and parked and there were three Dickinson County Police cars there. I immediately recognized two faces in the crowd, Lieutenant Forrester, and Detective Allen.

As I got out and walked up to the door, I was told to turn around and place my hands behind my back. I was handcuffed, and read my Miranda rights. They told me I was being charged with the murder of Steven Benson. Then the detective put me in the back of their police car and taken to the police station for booking.

In the car I asked the lieutenant who was pressing charges.

"All I know is I have a warrant for your arrest signed by Judge Simpson and District Attorney Elliott Benson. Seems some new evidence has turned up."

"Is that right? You will learn more when we get to the station."

We got to the station where I was fingerprinted and my picture taken for my mugshot. Now I'm sitting in a holding cell that smells like puke with six dudes. I have to wait to get my phone call. I will call my wife and she will be frantic. I had thought about the bond thing. I know it's 10% from reading the sign on the wall there by the phone. I will have to get a bondsman for bail depending on whether or not I even get a bond. I sat in the cell for an hour before finally getting my phone call.

"Baby ah, listen. I need you to come down to the police department."

"What?"

"Yeah," I was breathing hard. "I've been charged with murder of Steven Benson."

"Holy shit, Avery! I'll be right there!"

After I hung up the phone I thought I was going back to the holding cell. I was taken back to an Interview room for questioning. I went in and there sat Elliott Benson.

"Hello Mr. Jackson."

"Mr. Benson, what's this about?"

"About? About? My son, that's what this is about, Avery. You haven't been completely honest with me, Avery. Have you?"

I felt lieutenant Forrester's piercing blue eyes starring right through me, through that two way window.

"You knew about those pills!!"

My mind was racing. Carlton is playing both sides of the fence obviously trying to save his own hide blaming this all on me. "Wait a minute, Mr. Benson."

A knock at the door and Teddy walked right in. "You can't Interview Mr. Jackson without his lawyer present, Elliott, and you know that."

"Wasn't aware he had a lawyer, Ted."

"Ah well, now you know. It will definitely not be you questioning anyone Elliott. You will recuse yourself immediately!"

Elliott responded sharply, "I'll do no such thing, Teddy!"

"I will make a motion to have you recused on the grounds you are unqualified to perform legal duties because of a potential conflict of interest or lack of impartiality."

"That won't fly, Teddy!"

"For God sakes, Elliott! I know it's your son and your upset and hurt, seeking justice for him and I don't blame you. But it has to be done by the book."

Mr. Benson sat down and started to cry. He turned and yelled at me.

"You killed my son!!"

Teddy put his hand on Mr. Benson's shoulder. He got up and left the room.

Teddy said, "Avery, I will find out what your bail is and Michelle and I will have you out soon."

"Thank you, Teddy, thank you."

Later that afternoon my bail was set at half a million dollars. I knew that was fifty thousand. Two hours after I left the interview room, a jailer came and took me back to booking to get all my things. We went up front and I went through a door where Michelle was there waiting for me. I could tell she had been crying.

I said, "How did you pay for this?"

She smiled and said, "I have a really good boss."

On the way back to Teddy's, she told me he made my bail and paid it in cash. I was so thankful but nervous, angry, scared, I felt drained and my emotions were on overload.

We got to Teddy's and went in and Mary Catherine gave me a big hug and said, "honey are you alright?"

"I am fine, Mary."

"It's gonna be alright, Avery." I noticed Mary Catherine was crying as she hugged me. "Teddy's really good at what he does."

"I know, and I'm gonna go thank him again in just a second."

Michelle hung up the phone and told me to go on back. As I was leaving the room, I heard Mary Catherine say to Michelle, "I remember when I walked through that front door one night. I was cold, wet, hungry, and crying, beat up, bruised, my shoulder was out of place, and I had no insurance to see a doctor. I decided he beat me for the last time. I came through that door with three dollars to my name."

Michelle said, "Oh Mary, I'm so sorry."

"Oh, I had had enough and he wasn't going to lay a finger on my boys, that's for dang sure. I came in dripping wet, and Mrs. Betty got up and took the blanket off of her lap and wrapped it around me and got a towel and dried my boys off. She went into the kitchen and she and Teddy came back with coffee for me, and hot chocolate for the boys and some pie for us. I told Teddy I couldn't pay them, he said, 'don't worry about it. Everything will be alright now.' He may have said don't worry about it but I did. I wanted to repay them for their kindness. I was forever indebted to them. I knew how to type and help out, anyway they needed me too. I went to their home and cleaned to help Betty." Tears still falling, she said, "I was with them when she passed. I loved her, I them both."

As I walked into his office, he casually said, "Avery, so glad you made it. Now we must talk about your case."

I said, "Sir, Teddy, I will be honest. I don't have the money to pay you for this."

"Oh nonsense, Avery."

"No, seriously I don't."

"You need not worry, Avery we have already covered our bases. Of course Carlton will deny everything but we have his confession. He admitted giving you that bottle and those pills. Mr. Benson is very upset, as he should be. But, his hurt and anger are making him act irrationally. He knows the law as well as I. But, he doesn't know what we know. And that, Avery, is the truth. Like the old saying, Avery, the truth will set you free!!"

"Thank you again, sir."

That night Michelle and I lay in bed exhausted from today's events. "I believe Teddy has got this all figured out."

"You thought you did too, Avery."

"Yeah, didn't see this coming. Someone's playing dirty, very dirty."

Michelle drifted off to sleep first. I will admit deep down I was scared. I couldn't imagine not being here like I am now hearing her breath as she sleeps. Our lives torn apart by lies.

The next thing I know is my alarm clock going off for work. I called in and Ben answered the phone.

"Ben, this is Avery, I won't be in today. I will use this as a vacation day. I guess I will use them until I return to work."

"Do you think you'll be back, Avery?"

"I could have come in today, if I had wanted, Ben. I've just been charged, but not convicted of anything, Ben."

"Oh Avery, is there anything I can do?"

"No Ben, everything is fine."

"Ok, we'll see you soon."

I'm very sure when he hung up they busted out laughing. Probably cracking jokes about my arrest and how much vacation time I have. Probably not going to be enough vacation time for where you're going. Well, I've got a few surprises in store for them as well.

Teddy and I had to be in court Thursday morning for a preliminary hearing. We went into the courtroom and I saw Mr. Benson and an assistant district attorney sitting there. Teddy and I took out seats at the defense table. The judge came in.

"All rise," the bailiff said as the judge entered the courtroom.

"Good morning everyone, I am Judge Anthony Simpson and I am assigned to this district." The judge put his glasses on reading the file, slowly looking up occasionally. "This is a preliminary hearing for Avery Wayne Jackson who is charged with first degree murder of Steven Benson with drug overdose of fentanyl." The judge looked at the prosecution's table. "Mr. Jackson, how do you plead?"

"Not guilty, your honor."

“We will be back here Tuesday morning for jury selection 9:00 a.m. sharp. Do not be late to my courtroom.”

Teddy closed his briefcase and we turned around and exited the courtroom. We got out into the hallway and Teddy asked if there was anything I may have forgotten about?

I said, “Absolutely not. I’ve told you everything.”

“Good Avery, then we have nothing to worry about.” It was crowded but I thought I saw someone I recognized. “What is it, Avery?”

“Nothing Teddy, I thought I saw someone I knew.” I looked again but couldn’t be sure. Not that it mattered. They think they have me I thought to myself. Teddy said to come by his office tomorrow so we can talk more making sure we have our ducks in a row. I told him I would be there. He said around 11:00 am.

…

“Yes, sir.” I went home and took one of the three packets we put together with all the evidence we collected. I got it ready to be mailed to Ken Katel the reporter. I thought about calling TPA security and make an anonymous report of theft and fraud but, I questioned their competency since no one is actually accountable in this department. I mean why not expose them for their corruption, this is a story that should be told. Steven would say let’s blow the roof off this bitch!

I told Michelle things were going to get a lot more interesting. A news anchor on Channel 5 reported Avery Wayne Jackson has been charged with the murder of Steven Benson.

The story aired last night on the 10 o'clock news. We both had called and talked with our families about what was going on, assuring them everything was fine. It would be big news and gossip around town.

My mother said she would pray for us and put us in her prayer group at church. We thanked her for that. Dad asked if we needed any money, or food. They told us if we needed someone to talk to, just call day or night.

I thought that night and had another idea. The next day I did mail that packet, with the evidence I had collected to:

WTVR-TV
News Channel 3
Bell Town Road.
Nashville, TN 37209
Att: Ken Katel.

Dear Ken,

I found this all very interesting the theft and embezzlement of millions involving TPA and shell companies such as R.E.R. buying large amounts of TPA stock and a murder to cover it up. This Is *One Hell Of A Story*. A story like this gets you moved up to Prime Time. You're Welcome, Avery Jackson, a secret source.

I knew this would blow the roof off of it. I also had another idea. What if Rosie just wasn't acting or feeling herself today. So I walked into the lobby of Veterinarian's Promise. The young lady asked If I had an appointment and I told her no. She smiled petting Rosie in my arms. Rosie just doesn't seem to be acting well.

She said, "Oh no, poor baby we will get her in to see Dr Ashton as soon as possible." She asked what would it be listed under.

"Avery Jackson."

"Oh, yes, here's Rosie."

I sat down for a few minutes and noticed some stares. I'm sure after last night's story, I'm going to be a celebrity around town. Casey came down the hallway smiling at Rosie. Yall can come on back she's ready to see you now. We went into the room, Rosie up on the table looking at me nervously. I whispered sorry girl you're going to have to take one for the team. Casey went out the backdoor of the room and left the door open. I could see vials, medicines, needles, rubber gloves. I could see the vial Rebecca drew from the day I was there last time. It was turned and I could make out Citrate. I told Rosie to stay and I walk out the back door to get a closer look. I looked and saw no one. I could hear Rebecca two doors down talking to someone in the room.

I stepped close and heard Casey say, "Mr. Jackson you're not supposed to be back here."

"I'm sorry, Casey just looking out the window. Casey, remember that day I was here last and that bull was out there going crazy."

"Yes, that was scary. It's ok now though."

"Yeah, I saw Dr. Ashton give it a shot of this, wasn't it? You said it was the strongest y'all have in the building."

"Yes, it's this Fentanyl Citrate. The vial said Fentanyl Citrate injection, USP 500 mcg/10 ml Intravenous or Intramuscular."

I took my phone out and snapped a picture. I turned and stepped back into the room where Rosie sat patiently waiting for me. I heard a door in the back shut. I pressed record then shortly our door opened.

"Oh what a treat this is to see Rosie and Avery back so soon. What seems to be the problem today Miss Rosie?"

I said, "She's acting as if she doesn't feel well the past few days."

She looked at her chart and felt around on her then checking her temperature. I could tell Rosie wasn't happy about that at all.

"You know animals can sense things such as stress, anger, worry. Are you worried Avery"

"No I'm not worried at all. Why should I be?"

"I just know you have a lot on your plate with that investigation and all. Such a terrible thing. Steven was such a great guy. And drugs involved I hear. Avery you are a wild one, I just wouldn't have imagined."

"I bet you are a wild one." I looked into her eyes smiling and said, "I have some secrets just waiting for the right time to be revealed."

"Oh, I bet you do Avery," she said in a low almost whisper.

I said, "Your friend Carlton has opened my eyes to a few things."

"Carlton, oh yes he's opened more than my eyes for years," she said.

I was at a loss for words. I hadn't seen this scenario playing out in my mind.

"Oh Avery, I see the surprised look on your face. And I can understand why. Believe it or not Carlton has such a big heart." She giggled a sinister laugh and said, "that's not all. That's where I was coming from the night you saw me in the hallway at the lodge. I was just sixteen almost seventeen when we met. My father brought him to our home to do some work setting up his computer and security system. I saw him there for a few days. I was at the pool laying out. Golden brown skin and very well developed," looking down and smiling. "You know what I mean, don't you Avery?" In that low whisper again very seductive. "I could see him; I could feel him staring at me. I went inside to get a drink from the fridge, he came up behind me, I turned around and he kissed me. He took me in my bedroom floor. He was my first. I was a young girl and he took something from me, he stole my innocence. My virginity!! Something I was saving for my husband. He hurt me!"

I felt bad for her in a way.

"You see Avery," laughing, "he was not my first. Not at all," laughing, "but dang, it felt like it," as if she were recalling on an old memory as she continued laughing. "But, with that lie, I have him for forever and for whatever I want. I told him if he ever crossed me I would tell my father he raped me. I would tell everyone that he raped me. He thinks my son is his child. I don't know and could care less. My father took him from me, raised him. Hell, he named him. Yeah, my father, he's something else. I hate that man. He blamed me for my mother's death. He would get drunk come to my door cursing me, calling me names. Then calling her name, drunk and crying in the hallway passing out. The next morning know nothing at all or acting as if he didn't. So, Avery you bet on Carlton if you want, but I own him, I control him and don't you forget that. He will deny anything he may have said to you, or just not remember.

She said, "You know Avery, Carlton could just be the mastermind behind everything going on here. Whatever it may be." She picked Rosie up in her arms, "right miss Rosie, awe." She then turned handing Rosie to me and said goodbye Avery touching my hand as she walked out.

I left and was on my way home thinking. What the hell is going on here? And I'm the one charged with murder!!! I knew they were all too confident. I had to rattle them all. I looked around on my dash then in my console. There you are, a card. Lieutenant Jo Ann Forrester, Dickson County Police Department 1-615-224-8231.

I called Teddy and told him my plan and asked if we could meet there at about six this evening.

He said, “Absolutely.”

I detected a bit of excitement in his voice. I dialed the number and there was an answer.

“Lieutenant Forrester Dickson Co Police Department.”
“Hello lieutenant, how are you today?”

“I’m good I guess, who am I speaking with?”

“Avery Jackson.”

“Mr. Jackson, the question is, how are you today?”

“I’m ok under the circumstances.”

“How can I help you?”

“That missing equipment, have you had any luck?”

“No, I haven’t, do you have something you want to get off your chest, Mr. Jackson?”

“Yes, lieutenant I believe I do.”

“Well, how do you want to do this. You want to come in to talk?”

“No, let’s meet somewhere.”

“Where do you have in mind? Would my lawyers office be ok?”

"Yeah, sure I don't see why not."

We were there in Teddy's office when they arrived. Michelle called back said they were there and led them back. They came in and Teddy greeted them asking if they would like something to drink. He told them he had some very good coffee if they were interested.

"It is okay if my partner attended this meeting, right?" the lieutenant asked.

"Yes, of course."

Detective Allen said, "Ok, what do you have for us."

"You can find several pieces of that missing equipment at the home of Robert Ashton just out south of Milledgeville, TN on 22."

"How do you know this?"

"I saw it with my own eyes. I could actually see it from the road. Well, with binoculars."

"Milledgeville that's uh, uh, Hardman County?"

"No, that's Hardin, Chester, and McNairy County TN. I believe," Teddy said.

"You are right," the lieutenant said.

"Some of this equipment has been missing for years," detective Allen said looking over other lists of missing property.

I said, "I bet you will find other things that belong to TPA there as well. Also, you should search Ben Adams' place and Timmy Mason's home."

"We will have to contact Hardin County Sheriff's office since it's in the county, and TPA security."

"No," Teddy said, "Call them after you go in and make your findings. Just in case there are some loose lips."

"Yes, I agree," the lieutenant said.

"When will this take place?"

The lieutenant and detective looked at each other. "For sure Monday, if we get a judge to sign off on the warrant, maybe tomorrow. Oh, well judge Mark's is from down that way. Surely he knows a magistrate in the county who can issue a search warrant. A Saturday morning surprise might be interesting."

That next morning bright and early, the Hardin County Sheriff's office executed a search warrant of Mr. Robert Ashston's home where they found several pieces of missing equipment that belongs to the Tennessee Power Association. They also found computer equipment. Some of the equipment wasn't on the list but had TPA stamped or engraved on the equipment. In the barn they found several boxes of herbicide and pesticides that I'm very sure was purchased by TPA. Robert Ashton was in his pajamas cooking breakfast when they knocked on the door. He was actually in his pajamas when Sheriff Hank Harrell placed him under arrest and he was taken to jail. Robert Ashton was charged with theft of the Tennessee Power Association's property.

I wish I could have been there to see his face sitting in the back of that police car. I received a call from Lieutenant Forrester who thanked me for the information which aided in the recovery of the missing equipment and lead to an arrest.

I asked about the tractor. She said, "The 5000 Ford?"

"No, the Kubota M7040 4×4."

She said, "No, it wasn't there. But, they did have a lead out of Missouri on possibly one of the tractors that had been stolen."

I told her, "They moved it. I saw it a while back and took pictures of it there."

"Get those to me when you can, that might come in handy. We are going to question Ben Adams and Carlton Rogers soon. They both may be charged as accessory to theft and fraud, bid rigging, anything else I can think of."

"Ok, thanks for keeping me posted on this. Lieutenant, I didn't kill anyone and can and will prove it."

"I do believe you, Mr. Jackson."

"Call me Avery."

"If I can help you, Avery, let me know. There's more to this story I just wanted to get their attention. I will contact you again soon, lieutenant. You have a good rest of your day."

Teddy called me and was also happy with the news. He said, "Avery, I am going to reach out to the judge and the DA's office for a meeting to present them with the evidence we have to get these charges against you dismissed."

"Thanks again, Teddy, I appreciate all you have done for Michelle and me."

I really don't believe Robert Ashton spent any time behind bars. His bond was extremely low and just a formality. He was released with a court date in no time. Rebecca was there waiting for him to make his bond. I'm sure phone calls were made and favors called in. This was the definition of the good ole boy system if I had ever seen it. Everything was being kept extra quiet, not for these criminals, but for TPA's image. TPA sure doesn't want to alarm shareholders or the public to know the rates are high because of criminals. Ben was called into the police department for questioning, which he denied knowing anything and claimed he was just doing what he was instructed to do by his boss, Robert Ashton. The rest of the crew also had amnesia when it came to the equipment, chemicals, admitting they just followed instructions. Carlton had been called also to come in for questioning but every call went straight to voice mail. This itself made me nervous. I had to be sure I had enough to clear my name. I had thought about this and knew I needed more evidence. I had to be sure and I knew what I had to do before TPA security raids this place and locks it down once I expose the whole truth.

That night I went back to the TPA maintenance building. I followed my same steps as before, locking the gate behind me as I went through. Opening the back door and going inside the building locking it to behind me. I went straight to Carlton's office, unhooked the hard drive from the monitor and keyboard, when I heard something. It was coming from upstairs. Then I heard the creaking as if someone were coming down the stairs. I froze not knowing what to do I squatted down beside the filing cabinet. Hoping not to be seen. I heard the shop door open and footsteps coming my way. I felt my heart racing. I was looking into the reflection of the window not moving. I saw the reflection of a man standing there using his flashlight on his phone to see. I swear it looked just like Timmy in boxers and a t-shirt. He stood there looking for a minute then turned and walked away. I didn't move a muscle. I'm surprised he didn't hear my heart beating as loud as it sounded to me. I waited what seemed an eternity. Then I heard the stairs as someone was going back up and I could hear them walking right above me upstairs where all the supplies are. Then it was quite again.

I waited for 20 minutes and thought all I have to do is get out the door quickly then unlock the gate, get out and lock it back, and run like hell!! I stood up and tiptoed to the hard drive. It was already unhooked, ready to grab and go. I tiptoed into the conference room and gently picked up a folding chair and then another and put it in front of the shop door. They will pull the door open towards them and run through the door tripping over the chairs. I noticed something else that I thought would be interesting. I got the bottle of dishwashing liquid and squirted it all over the floor, coating it really good. I saw Carlton had a big plastic jar of thumb tacks on his desk. Had to have been a thousand or more. I grabbed the jar went out into the hallway squatted down not to make any noise and slung them out all over the floor. I then tiptoed over and unlocked the door. I had it in my head to try and lock it behind me to slow them down. I hoped this might give me enough time to get out the gate and lock them in. I'm betting they won't have shoes on or have their keys with them. Well, I pray they won't. Here goes nothing. I picked up the hard drive and tiptoed to the door. I heard nothing. I was ready to hit the Panic Bar on the door and run out and to the gate. I held the hard drive under my arm and dug my keys out silently. I slowly opened the door and slowly closed it behind me. But not completely to not make a sound and took off running to the gate maybe twenty yards. I reached for the chain and lock sticking my key in turning the key, unlocking it, and going through the gate, locking it behind me then I took off running looking for the finish line.

I heard a loud thud, sounded like someone tearing the building down and yelling, "I'm going to kill you!!!"

I ran faster than I ever have. Laughing so hard when I got back to my jeep. After I got in, I yelled from the excitement. I called Carlton's phone it went to voice mail. I called it again, voice mail. I was ready to get home. I laughed out loud thinking about Timmy slipping and falling all over the place on those tacks. I had called Lieutenant Forrester to ask if they had heard or had any leads on Carlton's whereabouts.

She told me they have been unable to find him, but still looking.

TPA security notified division supervisor Bryan Funt about Robert Ashton's arrest and the charges pending against him for the theft of TPA property. Bryan contacted division director Tom Shepherd. Tom Shepherd told Bryan to stay on this and keep him posted daily.

First thing Monday morning, Robert Ashton went and got himself a lawyer. Not just any lawyer, but one of the very best lawyer's in Tennessee. Brandon Perry was a young, smart lawyer out of Jackson, Tn. His commercials were always on the TV when we were in the conference room for our morning safety meetings. Ashton also filed for his retirement. He and his lawyer laughed at the charges.

"He hasn't stolen anything; he was still employed at TPA. He just had the equipment parked there at his residence because he was transporting it from base to base," Brandon Perry said. The computer equipment he used for work and he planned returning it when he no longer needed it. These are false allegations made, made by a person who is charged with a terrible crime. The crime of murder by Avery Jackson. To take the focus off of himself," Perry said smiling for the camera's. As Ashton and Perry walked away from that interview held at the Hardin County Courthouse in Savanah Tn., he told Ashton, "I got this, you have nothing not worry about, sir."

Later that day Teddy called letting me know the DA wanted to meet to discuss the evidence that we had. Teddy and I went to Mr. Benson's office where Lieutenant Forrester was there as well. We presented the tapes of Carlton Rogers admitting he gave me the bottle of Aleve which contained the Fentanyl laced pills. He then said on tape someone was trying to kill him obviously but he didn't know who. I told Mr. Benson and the lieutenant that Carlton thought it was Robert Ashton. They both looked and responded for the missing equipment.

"No, I don't think so. I think there is much more to this story." Teddy and I had discussed what they were going to listen to. I Let them listen to the first tape. We were not ready for them to hear the second tape. That was definitely coming soon enough. Teddy looked at Mr. Benson and asked how he felt about dropping the charges against me.

Mr. Benson replied, "As soon as we authenticate this recording and verify it was Carlton Rogers."

Lieutenant Forrester said, "We will ask Carlton as soon as we find him who he believes poisoned those pills, and why."

Elliott Benson said he would contact the judge and fill a motion to dismiss all charges against me. He didn't know if the judge would want to discuss all this in his chambers. He told Teddy he would contact him later that afternoon when he finds out.

Mr. Benson apologized to me several times.

He said, "Avery, I guess I'm like you just trying to find out the truth. Trying to find out who killed my son and bring them to justice."

He held out his hand to shake my hand and I gave him a hug. I could see the hurt and desperation in his eyes.

I stepped out into the hallway and called Michelle first thing telling her the good news. I could hear her telling Mary Catherine and Mary yelling, "praise the Lord!" I told her Teddy was good and not to worry.

"I've got a few things to take care of before I go home. I'll call you back in a little while."

"Ok baby, love you."

"Love you too." I caught up to Lieutenant Forrester.

"Hey," I said, she looked at me smiling.

"You were right, Avery. Well," she said, "I guess you knew all along."

As we walked I said, "You got a second?"

"Sure, what's up?"

"You remember when you said if you could help you would. Well, I have something about which I was wondering."

"Well, that depends on what it is."

"Do you know a really good computer guy? And I mean good."

She said, "At the department we have an officer in the tech department who is pretty good. Officer Marty Zimmerman. And he has a friend we call Vinci."

I said, "Vinci?"

She laughed and said, "I'm guessing like DaVinci."

I said, "Yes, I got it now. He was arrested a few years back for computer hacking. He has crazy skills one of the best!! He said the computer screen is his canvas, his keyboard was his brush and paint. He could do or be anyone or anything he wanted behind that screen. They offered him a job and clean slate to work for us. I heard his grandmother was so proud he had a real job. It kept him out of trouble and on a tight leash serving his probation and house arrest here with us. He has cracked several child porn cases."

I spoke up and said, "By checking the hard drive?"

She said, "Yes, exactly."

"Well, that's exactly what I need."

"Where did you get this hard drive?"

I froze for a second. "No one knows I have this hard drive. I'm holding it for someone. They told me if anything happened to them this will tell the story or will help untangle the web so we can understand the story."

She said, "Avery, did you obtain this hard drive Illegally?"

"I don't want to answer that. But, we need to look inside this thing soon."

I received a call from Teddy and he was very happy to inform me the charges against me were dropped. After Mr. Benson spoke with Judge Simpson, and with the overwhelming evidence we had gathered, they felt it best in this situation. Michelle was so happy, relieved things had worked out in our favor. She was on the phone making calls letting everyone know the great news that I was cleared.

Lieutenant Forrester called me on my way home and said, "Hey, you can bring the hard drive by? I will take it in and have them go through it carefully and download the information for you on a thumb drive. The guys will look for any firewall's or worms, whatever it is that destroys the information on there. We should recover the data, unless it's been wiped clean.

I said, "Wow, you sure know a lot about this stuff."

She laughed and said, "I just listen."

I said, "Thank you very much. I will have peace of mind knowing it's safe and secure. I believe you will be needing all this information soon."

She looked very puzzled, "I'm not going to ask any questions."

"Thanks again! It's been a long day I'm headed home to my wife." She smiled and said, "Lucky lady."

"We both are, see you soon."

It had been a long day, very long day.

My phone vibrated in my pocket as I pulled in the driveway. Chris Williams showed up on my caller ID. I answered, "Hello."

"Yeah man, how's it going?"

"I'm good," I replied.

Chris said, "Man, it's been crazy at base."

"Crazy, what do you mean?"

"Carlton hasn't been to work in over a week now and no one can get in touch with him. His grandmother filed a missing person's report today. Someone tried to break in a few days back. Looks like they tried to pry the back door open it's bent up. Bryan Funt has been there all this week. TPA security has been questioning everyone. Yeah, that's why I called to give you a heads up. I think they are fixing to call you in."

"Thanks man."

"Robert Ashton is retiring. I heard his paperwork has been approved. I heard TPA dropped the charges on him."

"What, really?"

"Yeah, not enough evidence. They going to have a press conference tomorrow. You know TPA gonna cover it up. They don't want to look bad."

"You got that right."

"I heard your charges were dropped too. Man, that's great!"

"Yeah, I was relieved for sure." I didn't go into detail. Wasn't going to let anyone know too much. "It's still an ongoing investigation."

"Well, man just thought I'd holler at you for a minute."

"Hey, thanks Chris. I will keep in touch man. Keep your ears open. See you buddy, bye."

I shook my head thinking of something Teddy said. "You have to pick your battles, Avery." I guess he's right.

Michelle and I enjoyed an awesome home cooked meal that night. Candles lit, music playing, we had the fake fireplace flickering. Rosie stretched out asleep at my feet.

It was very relaxing. The best I had felt in a long time. We sat there talking about the way things were playing out. I told her, "I'm probably going to dig my resume back out soon and start thinking about a new job. When all this mess hits the fan, we all will be let go, I'm guessing."

We sat there enjoying the peace and quiet until about nine when we got a call from Mary Catherine yelling, "Turn on the news! Turn on the news!"

"What channel?" I asked.

She yelled, "3!"

I flipped the channel over to 3 and it said, Breaking News, I thought *oh no*, here we go! Yep, it was Ken Katel on location live at TPA headquarters in Nashville.

"I'm Ken Katel live at the Tennessee Power Association headquarters in Nashville, Tn. I have received information from a confidential source about millions of dollars embezzled from TPA by a shell company by the name R.E.R., a company that works for TPA as a subcontractor. This has been going back ten years, possibly more. The stolen money then used to buy large amounts of TPA's stock." Ken's camera was in a man's face blinding him as he responds.

"I know nothing of this to be true. I have never seen this man before. Get out of my face!" he yelled at Ken Katel. Mr. Victor Rourke, Vice President of the Tennessee Power Association.

The camera pans back to Ken. "So, you have nothing to say about any of these accusations? Sir, I've looked at the evidence, and you have problems in your house. Problems that are costing the tax payers of Tennessee and neighboring states lots of money. Are you afraid the government could get involved? Mr. Rourke, are you afraid that charges may be pressed against this company, or you yourself, by the Securities and Exchange Commission for fraud and theft, and bid rigging?"

Mr. Rourke walked faster to his car while a driver opened his door and he jumped in the back. Ken began banging on the window. "When will we get a statement from the President of the Tennessee Power Association?"

The car sped off very fast. The camera following the taillights into the darkness. The camera came back to Ken. "Ladies and gentleman, we will keep you posted on this story as it develops. I just want to say, in all my years of reporting, this is an amazing story unfolding. A story that leads to the murder of a young man. I'm afraid there are a lot of questions to be asked, and answers to be answered. Reporting to you live, I'm Ken Katel News Channel 3."

Michelle and I were speechless. After a few minutes, I laughed and said, "Steven would be proud. He would be yelling, 'hell yeah, hell yeah Baby!'" I also thought about the looks on their faces in the conference room in the morning for sure. And

I imagined the looks on Robert and Rebecca Ashton's faces about right now. We turned the TV off and uncorked a bottle of wine to celebrate.

Michelle said, "I'm very proud of you."

"Proud of me? Why?"

"For not being like them, Avery." We sat together for a while longer listening to some more classic rock slow song's. Michelle and I went to bed with a feeling of relief. She drifted off to sleep in my arms. I lay there listening to her breathe, grateful.

I was awakened by Rosie growling I raised up in bed listening, Rosie looking at the door. I thought, someone was in the house. I knew I locked and deadbolted the front door.

Michelle touched my arm. "What is it baby? And about that time I heard something break on the front porch and saw flames. We both jumped up I ran towards the laundry room to get the fire extinguisher. Michelle called 911 and they were on their way. I knew not to open that front door. Michelle grabbed Rosie and her purse and we went out the backdoor.

We ran around to the front I pulled the pin on the fire extinguisher and sprayed it on the fire. Michelle grabbed the garden hose and sprayed water on the roof.

Our neighbor, Kevin, ran over yelling, "You guy's alright?" He also had a fire extinguisher. The fire department arrived really fast putting out the fire in no time. Dickson PD showed up, and the fire marshal also had arrived and was looking at the broken bottle they threw at the front door to start the fire.

Michelle and I held each other with Rosie in our arms. We all were pretty shaken but we knew it could have been a lot worse. A car came screeching up and Mary Catherine jumped out in her nightgown running to us. A policeman tried to stop her as she ran under the crime scene tape. She threw his hand off her shoulder, "Watch it mister, I got to check on my people."

She hugged us both. "Are y'all alright?"

"Yes," we both replied. Dang them bastards!" she bellowed." "Y'all can stay with me and the boys if you need to."

We thanked her kindly. The fire captain and the fire marshal both said other than the smell of smoke and very little water damage inside, it looked very good thanks to our quick thinking and efforts in putting out the fire. The fire marshal said, "Do you know who may have done this?"

I laughed as Detective Allen was walking up. "Avery."

"Hello, detective."

I looked at the fire marshal and replied could be a number of people with this investigation going on. The fire marshal said he would send this bottle into the lab for fingerprints, placing it into a plastic bag marked evidence. I was going to go in and take a look. I had already called our insurance representative and reported this. I spoke to Detective Allen; he was writing up a report while Michelle and I were giving him a statement. I looked at him and said, "Getting' a little crazy around here, detective."

"Molotov cocktails, Fentanyl, Murder. I can tell ya one thing, you will have two murders if they hurt my wife or my dog."

He looked at me, and I said, "I mean that, with every ounce of being I am."

"I don't blame you, Avery." He said, "You know this is what happens when people feel the rope tightening around their necks. Let's hope they get fingerprints off that bottle. I will have a patrolman paying very close attention to this area, your home specifically."

"Thanks, we are going in now to see how bad the damage is."

We thanked the fire department and fire marshal as we walked by for their fast response and hard work putting the fire out quickly.

Mary Catherine said, "Well, if y'all are alright, I'm gonna get on back home."

We thanked her for coming and checking on us.

I looked around, all around our neighborhood, and I just felt like they were watching us.

Michelle said, "What is it, Avery?"

Looking around, I said, "Nothin' baby, nothin'. I won't lie, I almost broke down as a feeling of helplessness rushed over me. But, I knew I had to be strong for her, for us to see this through. We went to the back porch walked in and looked around. Michelle said, "It's not bad at all, a little water damage on the furniture, curtains by the door got a wet dry vacuum. She started opening windows letting it air out. She said, "You know I was ready for some new furniture and paint in the living room." We laid towels down and got a lot cleaned up on our own. We drank coffee and watched the sunrise from our dining room table. We turned on the TV around 9:00 a.m. to see the press conference at the Hardin County Courthouse where the charges of theft and fraud against Mr. Robert Ashston were fixing to take place.

Brandon Perry and Robert Ashton stood together in front of the Courthouse in Savanah. Brandon Perry spoke smiling into the cameras. "We are here today thankful we live in a country where you are innocent until proven guilty. My client, Mr. Robert Ashton, thanks the court for seeing his innocence and dropping all charges against him. Mr. Ashton, do you have anything you would like to say?"

"I just want to thank everyone for knowing and believing in me and my innocence. Thank you."

Michelle said, "Just look at those two smiling like mules eatin' briers.

Then I noticed a couple of familiar faces in the crowd. I yelled, "Look, look there's Detective Allen and Lieutenant Forrester." As soon as Brandon Perry said we had nothing more to say, Savanah PD and Detective Allen grabbed Ashton by the arm putting handcuffs on him.

"What the hell are you doing? The charges were dropped." Perry yelled, "I'll have your badges for this nonsense."

Lieutenant Forrester said, "Step back, Mr. Perry, or you'll be joining your client."

They read him his Miranda rights as they were walking him to the police car to be taken back to jail. Perry said, "What's his charges?"

"Embezzlement, fraud, theft, bid rigging to start."

The TPA spokesperson was right there with them answering questions. "We do have evidence linking Mr. Robert Ashton to R.E.R., a shell company that has embezzled money from the Tennessee Power Association.

The cameras were still filming. Perry yelled, "This is harassment against my client!"

"No," the lieutenant said, "This is a different charge."

Perry yelled, "Don't say anything, Mr. Ashton, nothing."

Mr. Perry said to the cameras, "Seems the police department is upset they screwed up the first investigation now they are trying to pull another stunt. This is double jeopardy!!"

Rebecca Ashton was furious, to say the least. She was finishing up her yoga class when he called. "Yes, I will be right there Dad!" She left her yoga class going by her bank Farmers First Bank Of Dickson closing her checking account and withdrawing it all in cash. She then hurried to the police department to make her father's bail once again.

TPA called Ben Adams and instructed him to turn in his fuel card, credit card, and keys, he had been terminated. TPA also notified Bryan Funt and told him to bring his truck, computers, fuel card, credit card, and keys to TPA headquarters because he too had been terminated. Carolyn Murphy was appointed by Tom Shepherd as division supervisor. They put a new lock and chain on the gate and TPA had a security guard posted until the investigation was finished, and we would be notified when to return to work. Robert Ashton again made bail and was on his way back home in a few hours. Rebecca told Robert on the way to her house, we have to move or withdraw that money before they freeze the account.

Robert looked at her surprised. "Can they do that?"

"It would be hard on an offshore account but I'm sure it's possible. I'm also sure they will do their darndest to find out who owns the account. They will want their money back. But, we can move it. Move it so many times, they can't find it or prove anything. Carlton, the mastermind, set this whole thing up before he left."

Robert said, "He sure did, that SOB." Rebecca laughed as they pulled into her driveway.

I knew TPA would be head hunting but I wondered if I could find out any information to shed some light on what's going on. I reached into my pocket and pulled out my wallet. I found the card Tom Shepherd had given me and dialed his number. It rang a few times and a recording came on. "Yes, you have reached Tom Shepherd with Tennessee Power Association, I'm not in the office right now, leave me a brief message and a callback number, and I'll get back to you soon, thanks again." Then I heard the beep.

"Hello, this is Avery Jackson. Tom, if you could give me a call back, I have information about this investigation going on. My number is 1-615-224- 5150. Thanks, Tom.

Robert and Rebecca Ashton had just logged onto the page of Cayman National Bank And Trust Ltd. Using Rebecca's laptop. They had the account set up where it couldn't be accessed unless both passwords were entered. Neither knew the other's password, neither could open, or in this case, close without the other. Robert sat down putting his glasses on and entered his Evelyn-Lynn1969. Rebecca entered WindRunner1$. A horse she had when she was ten. She said he was fast as the wind. Betting a dollar once he could run 60 mph and she won clocked by radar.

And at that very moment with the push of a key, a key on a computer keyboard, they closed the R.E.R. construction banking account in the Cayman Islands. They then opened a new checking account in Bermuda. At the Bermuda Commercial Bank and Trust Ltd. The checking account was opened under the names James Redmond and Lynn Cassidy. Robert entered his password first same as before, Evelyn-Lynn1969 then got up and went into the kitchen. And on the screen it popped up save password, she pushed yes. She then entered her password HotVet2014. She then opened a drawer and removed a small lockbox. Inside were four passports and two pay as you go phones still in the packages. One was Robert Ashton, the other was James Redmond, and another was

Rebecca Ashton, and the other was Lynn Cassidy. Fake passports so real you couldn't tell them apart.

"He did good work, didn't he?" as Ashton came into the room. She emptied everything into a handbag and they were ready to go. They then got back into her car and went to his house. They went into the den and he opened his safe to get some things out.

Tom Shepherd called me back around three that afternoon. "Hello, Avery how are you doing?"

"I'm alright today, sir. How are you?"

"Well, I'm like many others around here wondering how bad this storm is going to be. How much do you know about this, Avery?"

"I know everything, sir, I kinda got this ball rolling."

"Why didn't you call me, Avery?"

"Well. I didn't know how deep into TPA this all went. Still not sure. But, my good friend was murdered, I think I was the intended target. Someone tried to burn my house down last night with a Molotov cocktail. I know and have proof of embezzlement of several million dollars by Robert Ashton. Equipment theft, bid rigging, fraud. My friend who was murdered compared this bunch to the mob. I turned over pictures of stolen equipment used in private residential work. Everyone was getting paid and taking bribes for their silence."

"Avery, this is all just unbelievable."

"Yes, sir I agree, you should have been in the middle of it," I replied.

I'm so sorry you have been subjected to this type of behavior, Avery. You said everyone was paid, did you get paid Avery?"

"I did, but that money is still in the building because I refused to be part of that behavior. I opened my locker one day and five thousand dollars was in an envelope inside. The envelope is still there inside that locker."

He told me he would be in touch and he would get back with me real soon for more firsthand information.

Michelle had already met with the insurance agent and home repair services for picking out paint colors. Now she is extremely excited about new furniture. Rosie doesn't know what to think. I'm just happy we were all OK and still have a home.

Robert Ashton was removing things from his safe. Rebecca was in the bathroom changing her hair color to match her new passport photo. Rebecca had a box that said high lift to lighten hair 45 minutes. She also trimmed her bangs. She came out to find her father laying in the floor unresponsive. She saw him on the floor and ran into the den to check on him. She checked to see if he had a pulse. He had no pulse, he was gone. She sat there beside him looking at him and how peaceful he looked. She did cry remembering the few good times she could recall. She then got up wiping her face and said the show must go on. She found his fake passport cutting it into tiny pieces putting the tiny pieces in a plastic baggy and placing it in her passenger's seat. She then got her handbag going throughout the house placing anything of value she wanted into her bag. She wiped down the bathroom putting any trash in a bag and then in the trunk of her car. She drove home stopping at a rest area on Interstate 40 throwing all the trash away. She then got back on 40 going home. She rolled down her window and reached over opening the plastic baggy hanging it out the window blowing all over the road for miles and miles. She laughed and smiled and thought to herself now no one will ever find James Redmond.

Later that evening sixteen year old Tommy Ashton came in and found his grandfather, Robert Ashton, laying in the den in their home unresponsive. Tommy called 911 and the Hardin County EMS responded.

He also called his mother's phone and no answer straight to voice mail. He then called his aunt, Darlene Ashton, Robert's sister. Before Rebecca left her father's home she had placed his will, life insurance information, and notes where it could be easily found there in his safe leaving the door partially open.

Robert Ashton was pronounced dead by the medical examiner there in his home.

Rebecca returned home and had finished packing the rest of her things in two suitcases and a handbag. An hour later a car pulled up and she put her luggage in the back and her handbag in the backseat and the car drove off and Rebecca Ashton was gone.

Lynn Marie Cassidy strolled casually into BNA in Nashville Tn then boarding a flight to New Jersey's Newark

Liberty International Airport then to Palermo, Italy. Lieutenant Forrester and her team, along with TPA and their teams were combing through the hard drive and meticulously going over the records of R.E.R and the fraudulent billing of TPA.

Lynn Cassidy landed in Palermo, Italy and checked into a hotel. After getting settled in, she opened her aptop and tried logging into her bank account. She entered both passwords but was denied. She entered the passwords again and it said Access Denied.

She began to panic when she couldn't log into her bank account and see that her money was there and safe. She thought it was just a technical issue. She had a lockbox with a combined total of $612,000.000 from her bank account and her father's safe.

Back in Tennessee, the corner concluded Robert Ashton had died from a massive heart attack. Sheriff Hank Harrell contacted Lieutenant Forrester. "Hello lieutenant, how are you today?"

"I'm doing fine, Sheriff, and what do I owe this pleasure?

"I don't know if you've heard but a suspect in an ongoing investigation is now deceased."

"What?" But, she knew in her mind that he, being with the Hardin County Sheriff, knew who it had to be, but waited to hear him say the person's name.

"Yes, ma'am, Robert Ashton has passed from a massive heart attack."

She responded, "Yes, Sheriff, I do appreciate you contacting me and letting me know this news. We will be in touch, thank you again, Sheriff." Lieutenant Forrester hung up shaking her head then contacting TPA with the news she had just received. They discussed their options and concluded they needed to find and bring in for questioning both Carlton Rogers and Rebecca Ashton.

The contractors were well underway on the renovations on our home. Michelle was on top of this project picking out everything from new flooring, colors, curtains, trim, a new front door, and anything of which she could think. We had just returned home from the furniture store when Fire Marshal Eric Quezada called. He told us they did not find any finger prints on the bottle the arsonist used to start the fire. He believes the arsonist wore gloves the whole time, and the accelerate was kerosene. I thanked him for the information. He said he would send his findings to the police department and insurance agency. He asked who he might question first if he were going to question someone?

"Timmy Mason, and Josh Stanford." I replied, "That would be a great place to start." That got me thinking of Chris and thought I'd give him a call and did. "Hey man, what's up he asked?"

"I told him, not too much."

He said, "Dude, I was meaning to call you and see if you heard."

"Heard about what?"

"Sit down man, brace yourself."

Laughing, "Ok," I said.

He said, "Robert Ashton is dead!!"

In shock, I said, "What the hell?"

"Yeah, his grandson Tommy came home and found him lying in the den dead."

"No, man, I hadn't heard about any of that news," I said as my mind hit overdrive.

"At that press conference, Ashton's lawyer, Brandon Perry said Carlton Rogers was the mastermind behind all this."

I said, "I don't know Chris, this all sounds shady to me. Seems everyone is turning up dead."

He asked if I was looking for a new job yet. I told him, "No, not just yet." I didn't mention about the arsonist trying to burn my house down.

He then said, "Well did you hear about Timmy being in jail?"

"No!! Hadn't heard that one either."

He said, "Crews told him that Timmy was arrested for domestic violence and assault on some doctor at Dickson General Hospital. He caught his wife with him. She had kicked him out. Robert Landry said he was sleeping upstairs at the maintenance building."

"Wow, I had no idea," I said.

"Yeah, you never know what someone is going through."

I thought to myself if you only knew.

"Well, man I'm gonna get off here."

I told him, "Keep me posted if you hear anything."

"Ok, Chris, take it easy man." I hung up the phone and sat down. Michelle could tell something was going on in my head.

"What's wrong, baby?" she asked.

They found Robert Ashton dead at his house a few nights ago."

"What?"

"Yeah, that's what I said."

"What from?" she asked.

"Chris didn't say. They may not even know yet. I will make a few phone calls and find out if anyone knows anything."

She looked at me with a strange look. I asked her, "What are you thinking?"

“Probably the same thing you’re thinking.”

“What, fentanyl?” She said could be suicide.

“Could be, I guess,” I told Michelle I was going to call Lieutenant Forrester and see if she could tell me anything at all.

I called her number and someone answered but it wasn’t her. “Detective Allen speaking how can I help you?”

“Hello, detective, this is Avery Jackson, I was calling to speak with Lieutenant Forrester.”

Mr. Jackson, yes, I was just talking about you. Well, I was talking to the fire marshal, Eric Quezada about the arson investigation.”

“Oh yes I spoke with him earlier today as well.”

“He said they were unable to lift any finger prints. Said the arsonist more than likely wore gloves. He also said you gave him a couple of names.”

“Yes, I gave him a couple. He won’t have to go far; one is probably still there in custody.”

“Oh really?” he said.

“Yes, Timmy Mason was arrested for domestic violence I heard.”

“Let me give booking a quick call. Hold on.” He said.

I held it for about five minutes. He came back and asked, "You still there, Avery?"

"Yes, sir."

"Man, talk about timing, he was just fixing to bond out. Yeah, I told them to put a hold on him for me."

Inside I laughed and told him, "Well detective, take your time he's a real asshole."

The detective said, "Oh yeah. I might get to him tomorrow, I don't know, he sure ain't goin' nowhere soon."

"Oh yes, Lieutenant Forrester, I wanted to ask if she's heard anything."

He said, "Well, she will be back later this afternoon. I think she's checking cell phone records."

"Ok detective, thank you again."

"Ok, bye-bye."

Tommy or his aunt had not heard from Rebecca in days and drove to her house. Tommy used his key to go inside. Her car was in the garage and nothing at all was out of place. They continued to look around seeing nothing to alarm them. They could hear sirens wailing headed towards them and it was getting louder when a cop car came screeching up. Two cops got out and walked up to the door.

"Dickson PD!!" Tommy and Darlene Ashton heard them and opened the door. "Show us your hands, show us your hands."

Darlene yelled, "What the hell's going on?"

Officer King said we got a notification from Watchdog security an alarm was going off at this residence. Tommy said, "Shit, I forgot to enter the code on the keypad."

Darlene yelled at Tommy for cursing. "I'm Tommy, this is my mom's house."

And I'm Darlene Ashton, this is my niece's house. We came up here looking for her. We called her phone but no one answered."

"Do either of you have any identification?"

"Yeah, sure do," Darlene said handing them her driver's license. Tommy was glad to give his learners permit to one of the officers.

"I'm Officer O'Neal and I will write up a report."

Tommy looked at her and smiled. Officer King asked when was the last time they tried calling her? Darlene Ashton said, "On our way up here about an hour ago, see." She handed officer King her phone.

"May I?" he asked before pushing the call button. Darlene said, "Yes, of course." He pushed the call button. They all heard a noise coming from the kitchen. Tommy ran in there followed by the officer, and Darlene Ashton. It went to voice mail but the mailbox was full. He hit the call button again and they heard the vibrating phone in a kitchen drawer. They opened the drawer Tommy started to grab it and Officer O'Neal pulled his arm away.

She said, "Nobody touch anything else. Let's all walk out of here and call this in."

Darlene and Tommy both knew Rebecca wouldn't go anywhere without her phone. They knew something wasn't right. Darlene yelled, "Oh my Lord," but trying to be brave for Tommy just losing the only father figure he's ever known.

Darlene said, "Uh yeah, I do want to file a missing person's report. I can after twenty-four hours and it's been that."

Officer's King and O'Neal called Dickson PD to open a missing person's investigation.

Marty Zimmerman, a corporal with the Dickson County police department works as an Electronics Technician. He informed Lieutenant Forrester that they could see cell phone data where Carlton Roger's phone pinged off a cell tower in Madisonville, Ky.

"Where in the hell is Madisonville, Ky?"

"Why would Carlton be in Madisonville? Wait, is he still there?"

"As far as I can tell."

“Call Madisonville, send a picture, send a description of his car, hell send somebody if we need to. Find Carlton Rogers, people!!!”

Among the chatter of people’s voices you could hear a phone ringing. “Dickson PD, Officer Marrow.”

“Yes, Detective Allen, she’s right here, yes.”

“Lieutenant, it’s Detective Allen, wants to speak with you.”

“Jack, hey what you got?”

“Well, well,” she replied, “the plot thickens.”

Detective Allen said, “You know dang well this is not just coincidence. So you found nothing out of place?”

“No, nothing. Her phone was in the drawer. King and O’Neal called it in on a disturbance call they responded to after a notification from Watchdog security. Her son, Tommy, and Aunt Darlene were there looking for her. They did locate her phone her in the kitchen drawer. Said no dang way she would leave without it. It appears it was left on purpose. I mean everything is here toothbrush, makeup, curling iron, blow dryer, clothes, suitcases in the closet. Her dang car’s in the garage.”

“Bring that phone to me.”

“Marty just told me Carlton’s phone pinged up in Kentucky. Jack, take pictures, seal it off, keep everyone out. I will also come by and look as well.”

Part Three

He said, "We have the pieces to this puzzle, we just have to try and put it together, lieutenant."

"You're right, detective, keep your eyes open. Get me that phone so Marty can get in there and maybe unscramble some of this."

"I'll get that to you ASAP." Lieutenant Forrester yelled, "Get me a dry eraser board in here now, please."

Michelle had gotten up and went into work this morning. She was very pleased with the progress the contractor was making and knew another few days and the job would be complete. She left Rosie and I there to keep any eye on things. She also knew she had files and paperwork to catch up on at work. Teddy and Mary Catherine were glad to have her back and excited to hear all the details of her remodeling adventures. She also filled them in on both investigations, the arson investigation, and R.E.R. Investigation. She also had a copy of my resume to make a few changes. We both knew I would be needing it soon.

Lynn Cassidy was checking on property in Sicily which was about 73 dollars a square foot. A person would need about 300,000 dollars to retire there. Lynn Cassidy wanted to open her own veterinarian office. Italy is so beautiful and she has always loved its culture. She had thought she would wait a few days before trying to access her bank account again. Not to raise any suspicions. Her realtor had several places to show her and some with spectacular direct ocean views. She felt good about the start of her new life.

...

Later that day, I'd say it was about 11:00 a.m. my phone rang and it said TPA and I answered. "Hello," I said.

"Hello, is this Avery?"

"Yes, it is. Who am I speaking with?"

"This is Tom Shepherd."

"Oh, sorry Tom, I didn't catch your voice "

"Ah listen, Avery, do you have time to meet with me at the maintenance building?"

"Yes, Tom I can, when would you like to meet?"

"How about now? I mean 11:30?"

"Yes, no problem." I pulled into the parking lot and stopped at the locked gate where a car was parked and Tom got out.

"Hello, Avery good to see you."

"Yes, sir, how are you doing?" I asked.

"I'm ok under the circumstances."

He had a key to open the new lock that had been placed on the gate a few weeks ago. He unlocked the lock we walked inside then we walked toward the building. "Avery, the investigation is moving along, and TPA, along with authorities, are untangling this web of lies that has cost Tennessee Power Association a large amount of money. But, thanks to you, Avery this has been brought to light. We wanted to thank you for having the courage to come forward." We stopped and he unlocked the door. "We also understand you and you're wife suffered damage to your home at the hands of an arsonist. I myself suspect it was due to this investigation" he said sadly. We went in and it was eerily spooky being so quiet. We walked to the office were Ben and Carlton shared the space and then the other office which was Robert Ashton's. We walked a few more steps to the right, the conference room, where in my mind I could still see everyone like the very day I walked in.

"Avery, we have a proposition for you. Would you be interested in running this department? This would be your base station. You would have full control over everything that goes on here. You would be the new regional supervisor."

"Well, I don't know sir if the others would like me."

He interrupt me, saying, "There are no others, Avery. You are my number one. Everyone else has been sent termination letters with their last paychecks. You hire anyone you wish."

"I don't know what to say, sir."

"Just say yes, Avery, we need someone like you, someone we can trust, someone I can trust." He looked around, we stepped into the kitchen area and could see the lockers. He looked and said, "where is your locker, Avery?"

I pointed and said, "There sir," reaching and grabbing the lock with the broken key still inside. "Do you want me to get the bolt cutters, sir."

"No Avery that won't be necessary."

"When would I start?"

He responded, "How about Monday morning?"

"Yes, sir, that sounds great!" He told me to come in and call him first thing then he handed me the key to the new lock.

He turned as he was walking to the door and told me to lock up as I left. He said, "Go on in there, Avery, and straighten up your new office," and he left.

I was by myself. I was in shock, so surprised. I almost wanted to cry with all the emotions I was feeling. I couldn't wait to tell Michelle the great news I had just received. The first thing I did was get a scraper and remove the name plate on my new office door that read Irishman. I then straightened up the place. Cleaning the desk inside and out. Post it notes with phone numbers. Carlton had dates, combination lock numbers, messages and dates, pin numbers for different credit cards, passwords. Several post it notes to call Ray, call Art, I then moved to the conference room cleaning the tables off. Then cleaning the bathroom and mopping the place, even finding some of the tacks I had previously thrown down. Yes, I laughed out loud. I went into my office and called Michelle.

"Hello, Ted Winston Law Firm, Michelle speaking, how may we help you? What do you have on?"

"Who is this?"

"A secret admirer."

She giggled and said, "I hope my husband doesn't find out."

"I was told to call this number for a good time."

"Avery, you crazy thing, why does the caller ID say unidentified number?"

"Well, guess where I'm at?"

"At home with the contractor."

"No, I'm at work."

"Where? Did you get a new job or something?"

"Yes, you are talking to the new regional supervisor of the Tennessee Power Association." I heard nothing. "Hello, hello."

"Oh my goodness, Avery, are you serious?"

"Yes, dear. Tom Shepherd called me to meet with him here at the maintenance building and offered me the job."

"Won't the others get mad?"

"No, there are no others, just me. I decide who works here now. I will hire who I want. I'm in my office at my desk right now."

"Oh Avery, this is just unbelievable!"

At that very moment, my cell phone was ringing as well. "Honey, I'm going to have to let you go, it's Dickson PD. I'll see you when you get home, love you."

"Hello, Avery Jackson?"

"Yes, yes it is."

"This is Lieutenant Forrester calling you back. Detective Allen said you called earlier."

"Yes, I did. I was just checking to see if you had found out anything."

"Well, yes I have. We got a ping on Carlton's cell phone."

"That's great," I said.

"But, it's in Madisonville, Ky. We have called and sent two officers up the to try and locate him. I have some more news. Robert Ashton is dead." I told her I had heard that. She said, "There's one more thing, Rebecca Ashton is missing as well. Her son and aunt went to her house and found her cell phone. Nothing else was out of the ordinary."

"How did Robert Ashton die?" I ask her.

She said. "The medical examiner said heart attack."

"Are they sure? I mean, did they check for fentanyl?"

She said she would call them and have them to check for that specifically. There was silence. I was trying to prosses everything that was going on with this investigation. Lieutenant Forrester said, "If you think of anything, let me know Avery."

"I will, lieutenant."

I made it home before Michelle and brought her favorite home. Pizza from Skyway, the bowling alley in town. Everything at home was looking spectacular. I have to say her choices made our house look better than before. Rosie was so glad I had pizza; she loves the crust I throw her. Michelle was also impressed with the work the contractors had gotten accomplished today. She rang the doorbell; Rosie went crazy trying to see who it was. I asked who it was, looking out the peep hole. She said special delivery. I opened the door and she jumped into my arms kissing me very passionately.

You must have the wrong house. We laughed so hard. We ate and drank wine listening to music enjoying the looks of things. She told me about her day and really enjoyed seeing Mary Catherine and Teddy. We talked about the new job and who I might be thinking of hiring. I told her Chris Williams would probably be my first choice. We talked more about how Carlton and Rebecca may have gotten away with the murder and the money.

She said, "Be positive Avery this is far from being over. One of our favorite songs came on the radio. Michelle had a surround sound built into the house. Into The Mystic never sounded so good. We slow danced, grateful for one another.

Lieutenant Forrester had her dry eraser board with a group going over the facts. Here in the center we have TPA and straight up above that we have R.E.R. and above that we have Robert Ashton to the left we have Rebecca Ashton and to the right, Carlton Roger's. Here above Robert Ashton 2.8 million dollars, let's put an X on top of Robert Ashton. So now we have a straight line. Rebecca Ashton, 2.8 million, and Carlton Rogers.

Officer Brett Vandiver asked the question everyone else was thinking. "Lieutenant, was Carlton Rogers and Rebecca Ashton anything other than business partners?"

Vandiver said, "it's strange but they are both missing with 2.8 million dollars. That's not a coincidence to me."

Lieutenant Forrester said, "Let me make a quick phone call."

My phone rang at 8:49 that evening. "Hello, Avery this is Lieutenant Forrester, I'm sorry to be calling so late but we have a question. How well did Carlton and Rebecca know each other?"

I said, "You mean like, romantically?" I said, "Yes, I thought I gave you the tape of her telling me about them. They were an item for years and may still be. I was just telling my wife; they may have pulled this whole thing off."

"It has crossed our minds here at the station as well. I will record it and send it to you."

"Ok, Avery, thank you so much."

The lieutenants came back into the room. "Ok, we do have conformation they have been romantically involved and may still be. So this could be a motive, for murder."

Officer Vandiver said, "Oh yeah, I'd say 2.8 million is motive for murder."

...

Lynn Cassidy had just purchased a beautiful 1900 square foot home in Sicily. A two story villa style with a small gated front yard, landscaped with roses. So close to the water the realtor claimed that when she slept with her windows open at night and she awoke the next morning, that she would taste the salt from the Mediterranean sea on her lips. White with aqua blue shutters and enough room to add on or convert a space for her veterinarian office. She loved being so close to the turquoise water. Her skin golden and kissed by the sun. She was already buying furniture and had thoughts of sitting out on her patio drinking her coffee listening to the waves gently roll in as the sun rises to start another beautiful day.

...

Back in the United States early Thursday morning, Lieutenant Forrester was determined to find the two people who could answer the who, what, when, and where in her investigation. She had come in early that morning feeling refreshed, drinking on her first cup of coffee.

"Lieutenant," Officer Vandiver yelled across the room. We just got a call from Atkinson train yard in Kentucky. They just found a cell phone that is believed to be Carlton Roger's cell phone. A yard engineer was walking by a train car heard a phone ringing. Looked around and found it taped to the train car."

She yelled, "Yes! Get those two officers there now! Get that phone, take pictures," she yelled, "tag and bag everything, that tape too! There could be fingerprints on it. Have them search the train yard thoroughly!"

Vandiver yelled, "Yes ma'am."

Lieutenant Forrester yelled, "Let's go people!!"

I called Chris that morning and asked if he was busy. He said he wasn't and I asked if he could meet me today.

He said, "Yeah sure, where at?"

"TPA maintenance building."

He told me he could be there at eight.

"That's great!" I said, "see you then." Michelle had gone in to work earlier and the contractors were almost finished. So I left Rosie in charge and I left for the shop to meet Chris. I got there first and unlocked the gate and went on inside and parked next to the building. It wasn't long after Chis pulled in parking beside my jeep.

He came in and yelled, "hello."

"Hey man!" I yelled back, "come on in."

He came in with a puzzled look on his face. He said hello still looking unsure of what's going on. He sat down and said he had gotten a termination letter in his last check. He said he had talked to Josh and he too had been terminated for lack of work it said.

I said, "Yeah, I heard everyone did."

He said, "Man unemployment around here was not going to cut it." He then told me some good news he was very proud to announce that him and Mitzy were expecting their first child. I congratulated him and asked, boy or girl, he said they didn't know just yet. He said he was going to fill out a few applications. He said he heard the highway department was hiring. He also told me his cousin might could help him get on there. He said Mitzy was on him about insurance and everything for the baby. He looked at me and said, "Hell, I'm nervous.

Then out of nowhere he said, "Were you working undercover for TPA?"

"What?" Catching me off guard, I laughed. "No! Why on earth would you ask me that?"

"Well, Timmy and Josh told it. Said TPA sends out undercover people into departments to spy."

"Oh, well no, I hired in like you and everyone else. My file is probably in that cabinet like yours."

"Oh, sorry Avery. What the hell are we doing here then?"

I shook my head understanding his question more now. "Tom Shepherd called me a few days ago and had me meet him here too. He asked me if I'd be interested in a job here."

Chris perked up. "Wow, Avery, that's awesome man."

I looked at him in his eyes and said, "I'm going to need some help."

He said, "I will help, tell me how."

"I will need a new shop foreman."

'Well, what about Ben?"

"Everyone is gone, Chris. It's just me, and if you accept, you, buddy."

"Holy shit, Avery, are you serious?"

"Absolutely, I'm serious. Be here first thing Monday morning, regular time. I will add you two hours for today on next week's check. We can discuss more on Monday after I call Tom Shepherd and let him know you are my choice for shop foreman."

"Thank you, Avery, I won't let you down."

"I hope not, buddy or we will both go down in flames. See you Monday!" I yelled at Chris as he went out the door.

Detective Allen and a forensic team had searched and fingerprinted Rebecca Ashton's residents and found nothing but her and her father's fingerprints. Nothing out of the ordinary. They called the Veterinarian's and said she had been gone a week now. She left one afternoon and never returned. They checked with her bank, Farmers First Bank Of Dickson and they too confirmed she came around 9:42 on 8-15-2014 and closed her checking account and left. Her Yoga instructor said she received a phone call around 9:00 a.m., she remembered they had just finished up and she left in a hurry. He told Lieutenant Forrester that was the same day we arrested her father Robert Ashton. She did make his bail and they left together. Then it's like she vanished. I think her and her boyfriend Carlton took off with the cash.

Lieutenant Forrester said, "You may be right, detective. I will have Marty and Vinci run through the phones and find whatever they can in them."

Lynn Cassidy waited until that evening to try and access her bank account again. She entered both passwords exactly as they should be and access was granted. She pushed the key and there was her money all safe and sound. She felt a sense of relief and thought it's just me being paranoid but, she also thought you can never be too careful.

Seeing all was good, she signed off the account. She exhaled, closed her laptop, and poured herself another glass of wine. With the ocean breeze blowing slightly in her hair and her feet up on the patio handrail, she could feel the warm sun on her face as it slowly started to set and the day would turn to night as one by one the beautiful stars would appear.

Marty Zimmerman and Vinci were having no luck with the phone of Rebecca Ashton. It was as if it had been wiped clean inside and out. Everything had been deleted except for messages and calls from her son Tommy from the time Rebecca's father died until they went to her home and discovered she was gone. There was nothing that tied her to Carlton Rogers at all in that phone. And that's exactly what Marty told the lieutenant. He said she had to have had a burner phone.

"You may be right, Marty," the lieutenant said. "That would explain how they were communicating." They were still waiting for the two officers to return with Carlton's phone.

As soon as Lieutenant Forrester found out that Robert Ashton was dead, she contacted TPA to let them know. They had to plan their next move and that move would be to press charges against both Rebecca Ashton and Carlton Rogers as Coconspirators.

TPA wasted no time filing a claim against the estate of Robert Ashton. Lieutenant Forrester contacted Elliott Benson and after hearing the evidence, and knowing everything was tied in with the death of his son, Steven, he gladly issued warrants for the arrests of Rebecca Ashton and Carlton Rogers.

Detective Allen went into the interrogation room number three. Josh Stanford sat there waiting very impatient, nervous, and agitated.

"Good morning, Mr. Stanford, how are you today? My name is Detective Jack Allen and we are investigating an arson."

Josh said, "Yeah, well what's that got to do with me?"
"Well, Mr. Stanford, your name came up."

Josh replied, "I have no idea what you are talking about."

"Do you know a Timmy Mason?"

"Yeah, I know him. I work with him."

"Are you two related?" the detective asked.

"Yeah, we're cousins down the line."

"Where were you Wednesday night the 22nd around 10:30?"

"I was home in bed."

"You sure about that?"

"Yeah, I'm sure detective." Josh had smirk on his face as he answered the question.

"Well, I've got a witness that says otherwise. Here's the deal Josh, you seem like a good guy with your whole life ahead of you, I hate to see you take the fall for this. I mean twenty-five years for arson, mandatory day for day, no parole, you'll be an old man when they let you out."

"I ain't done shit!"

"Well, let me go talk to Timmy. I bet he throws your ass under the bus to save himself. You know, work everything out with his pretty little wife, live happily ever after while you're away for twenty-five on vacation at the cross bar motel." The detective got up, looked at Josh, and said, "Let me go next door." He left the room, goes to interrogation room four, which was empty, opens and slams the door on purpose. Motions for officer Vandiver to open the door come inside and talk loud. Next door Josh could hear the voices not able to make out who or what was being said but did hear his name.

The detective knew Timmy Mason was downstairs in a cell and told Officer Vandiver to go get him walk him down this hallway and knock on the door as he comes by. The detective slammed the other door then walked back into the interrogation room Josh was in and said, "Yeah, you are lying. Timmy said, it was all you, Josh."

"Bull shit!" detective. A knock at the door.

The detective yelled, "There he goes, free as a bird!"

"Look out the door."

Josh got up opened the door seeing Timmy going down the hallway. You son of a!

The detective slammed the door. “You see, Josh, he played you. He said you did it all.”

“That’s not true!!”

“Then you tell me now what true is then.”

“He did it!! All I did was drive. Crews told us how to make it and then we made them. But, he is the one who threw it.”

“So you had more than one?”

“Yes, we got a jug of kerosene from work and found a couple of glass bottles.”

“That’s right, Josh, now don’t you feel better?” Detective Allen told him. “take this piece of paper and write down everything you know and remember, and sign and date it. And Josh, don’t leave anything out. This is your life we’re talkin’ about here.”

After signing the confession, Josh Stanford was read his Miranda rights and charged with arson as was Timmy Mason and continued to deny any involvement.

The detective got up and left the room as they were taking Josh to booking. Lieutenant Forrester had been watching from behind the two way window.

“Good work detective, good work. I will let District Attorney Benson know we have an arson confession on the Jackson residential home fire investigation.”

The detective responded, “Why can’t they all be this easy, lieutenant? Heard anything back on the duct tape from Carlton’s phone?”

She said, “No, not yet but the lab is working on it as we speak.”

That evening I was just getting out of the shower when I heard Michelle saying, “Oh thank you so much detective, Allen, that is great news! Thank you for all your hard work, detective.” She hung up and looked at me and started stomping her feet in a happy dance yelling, “They got those little bastards!!” She said, “They confessed, they confessed!”

I yelled. “Who?”

She said, “Timmy and Josh!”

I yelled, “I knew it!!0

She said, “Yes, yes, they confessed!”

We hugged and were so happy that those responsible would be held accountable for their cowardly actions. Later that night we were watching the news, Channel 17 to see if they mentioned the arson case. It was right after the weather forecast, the news anchor reported ‘two arrests were made today in Dickson County Tn. Timmy Mason and Josh Stanford were both charged and awaiting trial for arson. Both were out on bond.’

...

Tommy Ashton and his friend Bradley Childs had just cut the 40hp engine off on their 16' Jon boat they were in fishing on his grandfather's lake early that Saturday morning as the sun was rising. The water was still and looked like glass as Tommy skipped his plastic worm across the water. You heard the buzz of the line coming off the reel when Tommy and Bradley cast hoping to hook a monster bass. They fished, enjoying the peace and quiet, laughing and cutting' up like teenage boys and best friends do. They hadn't fished here since it had been dug out and made several acres bigger by his grandfather which had taken two years to finish. They fished along using the trolling motor to ease around the shoreline trying to find that right spot. The fish finder they had mounted themselves was a hummingbird piranha max 4. It worked really well showing the contours, drop offs, water temps, depth in the new areas of the lake. Bradley had saved up his allowance to buy it for the fishing tournaments He and Tommy were planning to enter and win all the big prizes. They had it all planned out.

Bradley said, "dang it."

Tommy asked, "What is it?"

"I don't know but the anchor is hung."

Tommy leaned over looking at the depth finder. He said, "It's big, it has a…"

Bradley said, "What is that?"

"I don't know what it could be."

"We are in the new part of the lake, I guess it could be a rock."

"Well, it's a dang boulder if it is," Bradley said. "It's about forty feet down it shows, and big. I can cut the rope I guess."

"Bull shit," Tommy said I'm ready for a swim. I'm goin' in to see what we got down there and free our anchor. I will just follow the line down." Tommy jumped in holding onto the boat breathing deep then exhaling, breathing deep then exhaling. Tommy told Bradley, "I'll be back In a few minutes. If I tug on the rope pull me up."

"Ok," Bradley said.

Tommy grabbed ahold of the line taking a deep breath and was gone. The water was murky and very hard to see as he pulled his way down toward the bottom of the lake. He pulled and pulled then he felt something that was flat. He could make out that it was a cab. He held on pulling himself around the cab and knew it was a tractor. Some of the glass was busted out on one side. He found the anchor wrapped around the door handle and unhooked it. When he did the door opened, fish and turtles were swimming around. His blue jean belt loop got hung on the door handle. He was running out of air and starting to panic.

Bradley was starting to worry Tommy had been down there for what seemed to be an awfully long time.

Tommy was getting cold he saw something in the seat that caught his eye, something glowing, he reached and grabbed it, and then a hand came toward him. He realized what it was! It was a watch on someone's arm with skin hanging from the bones! Tommy yelled but there was no sound, just bubbles. Scared, he pushed off with all his might ripping the belt loop freeing himself, swimming back to the surface kicking as hard as he could.

Tommy came up breaking the surface, gasping for air as his lungs were burning from lack of oxygen. Exhaling and breathing hard, taking in deep breaths, trying to catch his breath and calm down.

He yelled at Bradley to call 911 as he held onto the side of the boat getting his breath.

Bradley said, “What Tommy?”

‘Call 911, there’s a dead body down there in a tractor!”

“Are you sure?”

“Hell yeah, I’m sure!!”

Bradley dialed and spoke to a dispatcher. He asked Tommy the address Tommy yelled, “Robert Ashton’s residents on 22!!” Bradley helped Tommy in the boat giving him a towel and a hoodie to put on and get warm. Tommy untied the anchor and tied a life jacket to the rope to know exactly where the body was. They then headed to shore to wait on the police to arrive.

Lieutenant Forrester had just gotten word that the tape used to secure Carlton Roger’s phone to the box car was tested positive for blood and fingerprints. The lab technician said the tape had Robert Ashton’s fingerprints all over the tape. And yes, there were specks of blood all over it. The blood was tested and was type O positive. She wondered if anywhere in the files she had if it told what blood type Carlton Rogers was. She had on her board a copy of Carlton's driver's license but blood type is not on the Tennessee driver's license. She then looked at his TPA file looking for something, anything that might tell his blood type. And there it was, there it was on his birth certificate and indeed it was O positive. The lieutenant said out loud, "bingo. We need to get a forensics team back out to Robert Ashton's home and search for blood. Carlton Roger's blood to be specific!!"

Lieutenant Forrester yelled across the room, "I will be reaching out to Sheriff Hank Harrell ASAP!!!"

...

Hardin County Sheriff's deputy Stanley Carroll arrived at the Ashton residence to speak with Tommy Ashton and Bradley Childs and take their statements. Sheriff Hank Harrell pulled up and spoke with the boys asking Tommy what exactly he saw down there. Tommy told him he saw an orange cabbed tractor and a watch glowing and then saw the watch was on someone's wrist. I took a life jacket and tied the anchor rope to it and marked the spot. The Adamsville volunteer fire department and a local towing company arrived. Sheriff Hank Harrell was talking with the tow truck driver and thought it best to bring another truck with more winch cable to assist with the recovery. West Tennessee Dive Rescue and Recovery team arrived and talked to the sheriff before backing their three boats to the water's edge ready to be launched. The medical examiner was called to be there for extraction from tractor, certify the death, then transporting the body to the morgue when the body is in a safe location. Sheriff Hank Harrell met with everyone there and insured that everything was done safely, and correctly since this could be an accident or possibly crime scene.

The sheriff said, "We all have hand held radios and are operating on channel 5 so everyone is on the same page. Let's all be professionals and respectful, by that I mean let's not be posting pictures on social media. The last thing we need is hundreds of people down here looking for missing relatives."

As a matter a fact, the sheriff changed the channel on his radio. "Sheriff Harrell to any available unit."

"Go ahead, sheriff."

"Barlow give me a call on my cell."

"10-4 sheriff." Sheriff Harrell's phone rang.

"Kent, hey post 'keep out' there at the gate at Robert Ashton residence on 22 while we're recovering this body. I don't want everybody and their brother out here hindering things. Don't let anyone in unless they're legit. Sorry folks but as I was saying, we have someone deceased who may have family worried about where they are. We want to recover this body to give a family closure Let's be safe out here and watch each other's backs. If you see something, say something. Oh, and watch for snakes it will be getting dark soon!! Hopefully, we will be long gone before dark."

West Tennessee Dive Rescue and Recovery launched their three boats and headed out to the dive site which was about one hundred ten yards from the shoreline. One of the rescue boats pulled the two cables out to the dive site, radioing back to pull out an additional thirty feet. Two divers, Clyde Thompson and Gene Mackie entered the water checking the intercoms in their mask before going under. The depth of the tractor was forty one feet deep. They followed the line Tommy and Bradley left for them and it was a great help and an excellent idea. Sheriff Hank Harrell's cell phone rang about that time.

"Hello, Sheriff, Hank Harrell speaking."

"Yes, oh hello Lieutenant Forrester, I was just thinking of you."

Lieutenant Forrester said, "Sheriff, this is business," they both laughed.

He said, "Well, lieutenant, right now as we speak I've got divers in the water on a recovery here at the residence of Robert Ashton. They are getting ready to hook cable up to a cabbed orange tractor with a body in the driver's seat. The call came in today from Tommy Ashton. I meant to call you sooner."

The lieutenant said, "Sheriff, you sure know how to talk to a girl. Sounds exciting, can I come help?"

Sheriff Harrell said, "I thought that might get you going."

She said, "I'm already in the car. Thank you, Sheriff."

Lieutenant Forrester hit the blue lights headed that way in a hurry. She figured she could be there in an hour or so.

After thirty minutes at the dive site getting equipment ready, a mic sounded off.

"Come in topside, come in topside."

"Yeah, go ahead Gene."

"Checking com's."

"Come up Clyde. Go ahead Gene."

"This water is murky and hot."

"Yeah, I thought that too." They followed the line down to the tractor. The door still open, Gene said, "Fish and turtles been eating good."

"Gene this is Bobby, topside, see if the tractor is in neutral or in gear."

"It's in gear, topside."

"See if you can take it out of gear."

"10-4 topside." Clyde hooked the shackle and both cables up to the drawbar getting it ready to winch it out the same way it went in. Clyde said, "Pull pressure topside." Clyde then felt the cable tighten up until all the slack was gone and the cable was tight. "Hold that topside."

At the front gate with blue lights flashing, Lieutenant Forrester pulled in and was stopped. "Yes, deputy I'm

Lieutenant Forrester with Dickson County Pol ce Department, Sheriff Hank Harrell is expecting me."

"Yes ma'am, go on through, follow the paved driveway to the back of the house, turn right by the barn, and you'll see the lights." She drove through and followed his instructions. It was dusky dark and she could see the lights flashing very well.

Sheriff Harrell waved at her as she pulled in putting her car in park getting out. "Lieutenant," Sheriff he smiled and said, "You are just in time, we are getting everything ready to winch this baby out and see who we've got in there."

"Topside we are clear, ready when you are."

Sheriff Harrell and Lieutenant Forrester walked over to see everything going on. The tow truck drivers throttled the truck engines up increasing the rpm's to turn the massive winches. Both trucks hooked to the tractor began to pull and the outriggers digging in.

"Topside, we got movement, everything looks good."

"Slow and easy topside. I'm going to straighten the steering wheel, get the front wheels straight."

"10-4 Gene, let us know if we're going too fast."

"10-4 topside."

Sheriff Harrell could see the highway and could see a string of headlights starting to gather. Sheriff Harrell changed his radio channel. "Come in dispatch."

"Go ahead, Sheriff."

"Send me another unit toward Robert Ashton's residence and tell them clear that road. Write tickets if we need to. I don't need a bunch of lookie lou's causing a wreck being nosy."

"10-4 Sheriff." He laughed, changed his radio back to channel 5.

The lieutenant said, "What is it?"

He said, "Those crazy rednecks gonna cause a dang wreck." The engines roared as they towed the tractor back to shore.

"Topside, everything is moving smoothly, we are almost there." Everyone was waiting for the cab of the tractor to break the surface. Lights were set up and facing out into the blackness, the blackness of the water. As everyone stood there waiting for the cab of the tractor to break the surface, a big barn owl flew around landing on the light bar of one of the tow trucks. It was looking at all the people hooting loudly as if he was agitated because they were disturbing its hunting.

Lieutenant Forrester said to Sheriff Harrell, "I don't know if he's pissed or all the lights have him disoriented."

The sheriff said, "Probably both." Then they all heard the water splash from the cab breaking the surface slowly. As the tractor was pulled back up onto the land, the lights were all pulled back and fixed on the orange Kubota M7040 4x4 tractor. The water was draining from the cab slowly. The door was closed before being pulled backwards through the water to secure the cab in case there was any possible evidence left in there.

If this turns into anything other than an accident, the sheriff looked at Lieutenant Forrester and said, “I hope you brought your boots.”

“I do have some hiking boots in the car with good tread.” The lieutenant went and got her boots, feeling like she was being watched. It was a very eerie feeling. She looked up, and saw the owl staring right at her. She froze in its gaze feeling like it was staring right through her like it was trying to tell her something.

“Lieutenant, Lieutenant Forrester.”
“Ah yes.”

“Are you ok?”

She looked back toward the owl and it was gone. “Yes, sheriff, I’m alright.”

“Come on over, I didn’t want to open the doors until you were here.”

“Thanks, Sheriff, let me also grab this camera too. When they got back over to the tractor, several people were already gathered to see what they could see. But the windows were coated with mud. The sheriff opened the left side then the right side, muddy water drained out with several fish and a few turtles. The body was slumped over held in the seat by the belt.

"Hard to tell much at all other than it was a male." The lieutenant got up on the steps taking pictures of her own. Then a sheriff's deputy also took pictures. Lieutenant Forrester checked the serial numbers and it was a match. She then called the Tennessee Power Association security letting them know she was looking at their missing Kubota tractor. She took more pictures of the serial numbers sending them to TPA's security personnel. The medical examiner got up in the tractor taking some pictures for his report.

Then came the gruesome task of getting the body out of the tractor. The medical examiner unbuckled the seat belt. It took several to get the body out because it was stiff from being in a seated position. They put the body on the stretcher and more pictures. The medical examiner noticed something in the pocket of the dead person.

Sheriff Harrell and the lieutenant had an evidence bag, the medical examiner opened the pocket and used tweezers to remove the item which they all concluded was a passport. All the pages were destroyed except one, which was laminated.

The name on the passport page was:
David Ethan Carter. US Citizen
Surname David E. Given name Carter
Place of birth Fort Smith, Arkansas USA
Date Of Birth 03 Feb 1968 Sex M
Issued on 10 /15/2012 expires 10/15/2022

"Well, this is very interesting, isn't it lieutenant?

"Yes, Sheriff, very. I'm going out on a limb here but I don't think this guy looks like a David."

"Oh no, lieutenant?"

The Sheriff asked, "What's he look like to you?"

She looked and said, "I'm thinking more like a Carlton. Carlton Rogers to be exact."

The medical examiner looked at her and asked, "Someone you're looking for?"

"Oh, yes sir, we are."

He said, "Well, the dental records will be our best bet with the terrible condition he's in."

"Well, I think we've seen enough," Sheriff Harrell said, and they loaded him into the ambulance.

"Well, Sheriff Harrell, you sure know how to show a girl a good time. I'm sure TPA will be here first thing Monday morning checking numbers for insurance purposes."

The sheriff said, "We will wrap this evidence with police tape and I'll have someone patrolling this area pretty heavily."

She opened her door and thanked him again and said she needed to be making her way home it's getting late.

He told her to call if she needed anything and if he could help in anyway. She smiled big, "Thank you. I'll be in touch Sheriff Harrell."

...

Sunday's at the Jackson house had always been very relaxing until the fire, but since the remodeling and new furniture, things were definitely getting back to normal. Michelle and I slept in until Rosie decided it was time for everyone to wake up and play. Then it was coffee, easy listening rock on the sound system, pajamas, tee-shirts, bra's optional, and house shoes. A little housework, laundry, maybe a movie in the afternoon or football and comfort food. We loved our Sunday's.

Michelle said, "Sunday, fun day!!" Lounging around suited everyone just fine, even Rosie.

It was around one when my phone rang and recognized Lieutenant Forrester's number.

"Hello."

"Hello, Avery, how are you doing today?"

"I'm fine, Lieutenant, and you?"

"I just wanted to keep you up to date on what's going on with the investigation. I received a call from Hardin County Sheriff Hank Harrell and they have recovered the Kubota tractor."

"Wow, that's great."

"Well, that's not all, Avery, I'm asking a favor of you here keep this piece of information just between us. We found a body in the cab of that tractor."

"Oh man!"

"Yes, Avery that's what I said."

"You said we?"

"Yes, Sheriff Harrell called me and I got down there before they got it on shore."

"Well, who was it?" Avery asked.

"The medical examiner was very sure it was a male. We are all waiting for those dental records. There was a passport in his pocket and the given name was David Ethan Carter."

"Never heard that name," Avery said.

"I haven't either, so I ran the name through our data base and nothing came up."

"So, it's a fake? Well, do you think it's Carlton Rogers?"

"The body was in very bad shape. We are now just waiting on those dental records to confirm if it is him," she said. "If I had to bet, I think it's definitely Carlton Rogers," she added.

"So, where is the elusive Rebecca Ashton?" I asked.

"Avery, we are looking high and low for her. It's like she vanished."

"Yeah, seems she has lieutenant." Later that afternoon I saw on my New Channel 3 app on Facebook reporter Ken Katel has a News 3 exclusive tonight about the scandal involving Tennessee Power Association, taxpayer's, and shareholders at 6:30. I told Michelle it was sure to be interesting.

Lynn Cassidy was overseeing the construction as the workers were finishing for the day. They had made great progress working on the office building being added to her home. Lynn, being the businesswoman she was, also knew the extra square footage would increase the value of her home. She had drawn sketches and was working closely with the dark-haired handsome owner and architect Pollo Gianni. She flirted with Pollo sometimes even calling him Apollo, with a lot of unnecessary touching. She thought the young architect looked like a Greek God with the sun glistening off his golden brown skin and his sculpted abs. He was over the project and Lynn knew he was also into the flirting. He assured her the veterinarian's office would be very nice. She could see his lips moving but wasn't hearing much he was saying, almost drooling. Pollo proudly showed her the hand painted glass with the name of her office she had picked out. *Fur Babies R Us*, Lynn Cassidy Veterinarian's Office. She was very impressed with Pollo's work. Lynn was trying her best to stay focused and keep it professional because he was married. Then she laughed to herself, she knew she didn't give a rat's ass if he was married or not.

...

Tennessee Power Association a News Channel 3 exclusive investigation brought to you by News 3's own Ken Katel. I yelled at Michelle, "Here it is come on!" Ken Katel was standing at TPA's headquarters. This story was brought to you first by News 3 a month ago. Tennessee Power Association, like many other large companies, doesn't want you to know about this fraud, theft, and embezzlement. This story started with the embezzlement, theft, and fraud within the Tennessee Power Association by some of its employees. But, this story quickly evolved into murder!! I have to say, I have received death threats since reporting on this story. A whistle-blower sent information of the crimes being committed by employees who work for TPA.

Michelle came and sat down beside me handing me a bowl of popcorn.

That employee himself has been targeted with physical violence, even arson. These companies don't want the public to know because it's you, the taxpayers, who are left paying the bill literally. When the thefts occur, your rates increase, and stockholders lose money. Who pays for that loss? You, the taxpayers. I'm not talking about paperclips or staplers. I'm talking about equipment, industrial equipment. Tractors, industrial lawnmowers, skid steers, riding lawnmowers, excavators, fuel, manpower, Where is the accountability? How did TPA not know? The embezzlement you asked, 2.8 million, possibly even more. The murder, possibly two individuals innocently caught in this web of lies and deceit. I obtained photos from the property of former TPA regional supervisor Robert Ashton's residence in Hardin County where the authorities recovered a piece of Tennessee Power Association's equipment at the bottom of a lake. Not only did they find a tractor that belonged to the Tennessee Power Association, but a body was also found inside that sunken tractor. The body is presumed by authorities to be that of Carlton Rogers. The medical examiner will use dental records to confirm the identity of that body. But, as I said earlier, these large companies, don't want you to know the truth. That truth cuts into their profits. I have requested an Interview with TPA's president and still, they refuse the people of Tennessee the truth. We will be following this story as it progresses. I'm Ken Katel with a News Channel 3 exclusive.

The news anchor said, "Thanks Ken this a very interesting story for sure.

I looked at Michelle and she looked at me and we both sat there in silence. Amazed at the work and great job Ken had done reporting this story and being on the inside knowing there was so much more to be told. Ken couldn't name Steven by name because it's still an ongoing investigation. The truth will come out, it always does.

The following morning It wasn't long after Lieutenant Forrester arrived at work when she received the phone call she had been waiting on. The Deputy Chief Medical Examiner, Calib Neal was on the phone telling the lieutenant his findings.

"Lieutenant, good morning."

"Good morning, sir."

"I just got off the phone with Sheriff Hank Harrell and he told us it was you who thought this was Carlton Rogers. We followed that lead and it saved us lots of time and your suspensions were correct. This person sent to us was indeed Carlton Rogers."

Lieutenant Forrester said, "It's sad but at least the family will have closure. Deputy Chief Neal, were you able to determine the cause of death?"

"There was too much damage to the body you know to positively decide."

"Well, again thank you for the speedy results, Deputy Chief Neal, you have a good day."

"And you too, Lieutenant Forrester."

Lieutenant Forrester walked over and placed an X on Carlton Rogers's name just as she had done Robert Ashton's name. The only name left was that of Rebecca Ashton, and then there was one. Lieutenant Forrester told her investigators to contact the U.S. Marshals to get them on her trail. "We need her to find out the answers to several questions. I will get with District Attorney Benson on issuing a warrant for her arrest."

...

First thing Monday morning, Chris Williams and I went over the resumes for the future new hires. After speaking with Tom Shepherd we got a truck and trailer ready to transport the tractor back to the base after it is released from the Hardin County Sheriff's office. Lieutenant Forrester volunteered to go and break the news to Carlton Rogers' grandmother. The lieutenant arrived at the house of Mrs. Hazel Gallimore. She knocked and a Hispanic woman answered the door.

"Hello is Ms. Hazel Gallimore here?"

"No, she is not here."

"Do you know when she will be back?"

"No."

"Are you a friend to Ms. Gallimore?"

"Yes, I am her friend and house keeper, Gloria Mendez. Ms. Hazel is in the nursing home now for three weeks. Ms. Hazel she, she is 83 and has had a stroke and cannot take care of herself."

Lieutenant Forrester told Gloria that she needed to talk to her.

Gloria told her, "Ms. Hazel was unable to communicate and didn't know where she was."

"Oh, I'm so sorry to hear that."

"I have a number for her son, Ray. He is out of town working."

Lieutenant Forrester wrote it down to call him later. "Thank you, Ms. Mandez." Lieutenant Forrester then drove over to Whispering Oaks Assisted Living. She went in and walked down a hallway looking at names on the doors as she made her way to the desk and asked for Ms. Hazel Gallimore.

"Ms. Hazel, yes, she is right down the hallway here on the left," a black lady named Phillis Johnson said.

"I'm Lieutenant Forrester and we were investigating a missing person's report she had filed."

"Yes, I heard about that. She went down two weeks ago had a stroke." Phillis said, "I'm the shift supervisor and see Ms. Hazel every day and she just seems to be getting worse, I hate to say. She will hardly eat, don't move, or make a sound."

Can I see her?" Lieutenant Forrester asked.

"You sure can, come on." They went to her room, knocked on the door, and went in. "Ms. Hazel you have a visitor," Phillis said extra loud.

Lieutenant Forrester saw a little silver-haired lady in a wheelchair in front of the window. The lieutenant pulled a chair over beside her and looked out the window too. She could see a bird feeder with birds eating, hopping around drinking water from a small fountain. "Ms. Gallimore, I'm Lieutenant Forrester with the Dickson County Police Department. I wanted to inform you we have found your grandson." No response at all. "Ms. Hazel," the lieutenant took her hand and again she said, "We found your grandson," and at that moment a large bright red cardinal hit the window so hard its feathers went everywhere.

Ms. Hazel yelled, "Carlton, Carlton," jerking lunging forward falling to the floor.

The lieutenant still holding one hand, yelled for Phillis. Phillis ran into the room and another lady ran in.

"Ms. Hazel, what you doin' down here?"

She yelled again, "Carlton!"

Lieutenant Forrester moved back out of the way so they could get Ms. Hazel back into her chair. She then told Phillis and the other lady about the cardinal they all looked out the window seeing it was dead on the ground. They were all shaken by this all staring at the cardinal and then looking at Ms. Hazel in disbelief. The lieutenant told Phillis she was going to go now.

She told Ms. Hazel Gallimore she was very sorry for her loss and she told her goodbye.

She got in her car and ran his name through the database just being curious. She entered Ray Gallimore first into the computer no one of that name came up around here. The lieutenant then entered Ray Rogers and no one by that name came up around here. She thought to herself he could live somewhere else. She put her car in drive and made her way back to the station.

...

Lynn Cassidy was a few days from opening her new office. She was there in her new office looking at the work Pollo's crew had completed at the end of the day. The finishing touches were almost all done. She had advertised an opening the following week that would give her enough time to hire a receptionist and a helper. She already had two sisters from here in town with experience working with animals. Sophie and Petria had volunteered down at the animal shelter for several years both loved animals and thinking of veterinarian careers. They told Lynn they wanted a first chance at the opportunity for the positions. She was still waiting for the security service to come hook up and add more cameras to her existing system, tying the system together so she could monitor everything from her phone. She had planned on keeping it small, just enough to draw some income. She just wanted to blend in and not raise any suspicions.

The following morning Lynn Cassidy was on her balcony enjoying her morning coffee. She loved watching the sun rise and feeling its warmth. The warm air from the ocean breeze and waves calmly rolled onto the white sandy beach. She was still in her robe knowing she had another hour or so before Pollo and his crew arrived for a long day. She watered her flowers in her pots and her hanging baskets. She loved watching the hummingbirds drink from her feeders and the bright red, pink, and purple petunias. The geraniums are red, white, and pink. She prided herself on all her beautiful flowers. She heard the buzzer at the gate. She walked over pushing the intercom button looking at the clock, "Hello."

"Hello, Lynn it's Pollo."

Yes, come on in she fluffed her hair. She heard the door open and close. She yelled, "In here, be right out." She was still in her nightgown as she walked out to meet him.

"Good morning beautiful," Pollo said to her. She walked straight toward him and his eyes locked onto her toned golden brown body, her gown leaving nothing to the imagination. She walked straight into his arms, "Do you like what you see?" she whispered.

"Oh yes," he said, "very much so."

"She grabbed his hands putting them on her breast as their faces came together passionately kissing and ripping her see-through top off. They fell back onto the couch, after weeks of flirting, it was like a violent volcano eruption between them. Pollo could hear his heartbeat thumping in his eardrums. Lynn was wild with ecstasy losing all control. They both knew it was going to happen it was just a matter of time. This was exactly what Lynn and Pollo both wanted, rough hard sex. After they finished, Lynn got up not saying a word, and went to the shower.

Pollo caught his breath got up put his clothes on and left. She was in her shower feeling almost high from the sex she and Pollo just had. She was washing her hair and saw the silhouette of a man through the curtain.

"You back again for more? I'm ready if you are," Lynn giggled.

"He walked out of the bathroom went to her security system, turned it off, and removed the memory card, replacing it with a new one. He wore gloves, being very careful not to disturb anything. He placed her laptop and phone in his bag. He replaced the laptop with one he brought with him and replaced the cell phone as well. He went back into the bathroom.

She said, "I knew you'd want more and more," she laughed. He lunged grabbing her head and slamming it to the wall several times. The shower curtain ripped from the shower rings wrapped around her head. She was disoriented not knowing what was going on, "Pollo!" she yelled.

"I made you, Lynn!!" He then slammed her head into the side of the tub until a trickle of blood ran down the drain. She lay there her eyes wide open, but not breathing. He got up, and went to get his bag, walked to the window looked outside, looked around, and made sure no one was around. He went out the door locking it, closing the door behind him. He then walked very casually through the gate and down the street. He walked away as if nothing had happened.

Twenty minutes had gone by and Pollo was returning with two coffees and a box of pastries. He pushed the buzzer on the intercom and no one answered. He pushed the buzzer again. Pollo thought that to be strange so he sat everything down hopped over the gate and went and knocked on the door. No answer. He knocked again calling her name.

"My Bella Lynn, open the door, I have coffee and pastry for you." He heard nothing. He thought she cou d be downstairs at the new office building already. He went downstairs to the office building and he didn't see her anywhere. So, he unlocked the office to welcome his crew for a day of work. He figured he would see her later in the day with a smile or her face. Pollo tried calling about 10:00 a.m. and still no answer, straight to voice mail but it said the mailbox was full. Pollo again tried calling Lynn around 1:30 p.m. and still no answer. The back door in the office that goes upstairs was locked. Pollo used a screwdriver to open the door and yelled upstairs, "Lynn," he listened not hearing anything. "Lynn!" He proceeded up the stairs to the top. "Hello, Lynn." He stepped into the living room and saw the couch where hours ago Lynn and he had sex. "Hello," he yelled loudly. He walked into the bedroom and heard the sound of water running, his eyebrows narrowed curiously. "Hello, hello Lynn!" He pushed the bathroom door open enough and was in shock at the sight before him. He saw her blue eyes, but the same blue eyes he had seen earlier had lost their sparkle. He knew there was no life left in her body. He shuffled backward trying to get out as fast as he could he ran down the stairs to get his phone to call 113 the Polizia. He reported he had found the client he was working for dead in her house in the shower.

Lieutenant Forrester was on the phone with District Attorney Elliott Benson discussing the charges to bring forth against for Rebecca Ashton. The District Attorney knew with no evidence they couldn't charge her with the murder of Carlton

Rogers. The medical examiner's overview and the cause of death were undetermined on the death certificate. District Attorney Benson felt the embezzlement was more than enough for a warrant. He assured the lieutenant the U.S. Marshals would find Rebecca Ashton in no time. He issued the warrant and the call was made.

The polizia arrived at the home of Lynn Cassidy. Just as Pollo said, Lynn was dead in the shower, the water still running. Lorenzo Alvize, The Pubblico Ministero is the public prosecutor and Inspector Mattia Salvatore of the homicide division was in charge of the investigation. They were taking crime scene photos. They questioned Pollo Gianni about how well he knew the victim. Pollo answered he just worked for her. He said she was very nice to everyone. Lynn Marie Cassidy 5'4 blue eyes 34 years old from Milwaukee Wisconsin. Pollo said he believed she had lived there for four months. He said she was opening a veterinarian office downstairs.

The Body Removal Attendant arrived and waited to transport the body to the obitorio. Prosecutor Alvize and Inspector Mattia were very suspicious, taking pictures of the wall where several of the tiles were broken with blood and hair in the cracks of the tile. They knew this was no accident. They permitted the Transport Specialist to remove the body.

The Inspector told Pollo not to go very far In case they needed to speak with him further. They looked around while processing the crime scene, and both agreed, that this was a crime scene but nothing seemed to be amiss. They would know much more after the autopsy. Prosecutor Alvize said he would let the Bureau of Consular Affairs know to look for Lynn Marie Cassidy 34-year-old white female from Milwaukee Wisconsin.

The days were getting shorter and the leaves were changing. Michelle promised Mary Catherine we would go see the boys play their senior year. The Dickson County Cougars are undefeated this year 7-0. The best year they have had in a long time. Chris said he believes in state playoffs for sure. Many say it's because of Trevor and Troy. They are being recruited by some big-name schools. Mary Catherine told Michelle every day the mailbox is full of letters from schools wanting them to come play for them. We had gone to a couple this season and enjoyed watching them make the big plays. Tonight was a district game and they needed a win. Michelle had a head cold and wasn't able to make this one, so I went alone. The game was great!! The community came together to support our team. I sat with Mary Catherine yelling and cheering for the boys. The Cougars had the lead over the Henry County Patriots all night never looking back.

I decided to leave with 1:47 seconds left on the clock to beat the crowd out. As I was walking past the concession stand, I heard a voice yell, "Well, well, there's old Avery Jackson. Mr. do no wrong." I looked but already knew who it was. I thought I had seen him earlier. Timmy Mason was walking towards me. I turned around and kept on walking. "Hey, boy I'm talking to you." I could tell by the way he was slurring his words he was drunk. "Sorry 'bout your boyfriend, Steven."

He knew how to get me to stop and I did I turned around and looked at him and asked, "You say something?"

He walked up close and said, "You'll get yours, Jackson."

I laughed and said, "How's that wife of yours?"

He gritted his teeth and swung at me. I ducked and laid his ass out on the muddy ground where people had walked all night. People were circling us to see what was going on. Timmy was face down in the mud moaning. A Dickson police officer working security ran up and grabbed me.

"There will be no fighting here, mister, you are both going to jail," the officer said.

"He swung at me, officer."

"Don't matter, I ain't having any fighting."

They got Timmy up and handcuffed him first. He acted as if he was trying to come at me.

Then a voice spoke up and said, "I saw the whole thing, that guy started it and swung at him."

It was Detective Allen. "If you look, Mason, there seems to be a drunk and out on bond. Haul his ass to jail for public drunkenness to sleep off the alcohol."

We turned and walked toward the gate. "Thanks, detective, I didn't mean for any of that to happen."

"Hey, Avery you were just defending yourself from what I saw. Hey, good punch too."

I looked at him and asked, "Have you heard anything on the investigation?"

Detective Allen said, "Well, other than the captain breathing down our necks to find Rebecca Ashton, we don't know where she or the money is. You do know that was Carlton they found in that tractor, right?"

"Yeah, I had heard that," I told him in disbelief shaking my head. "Well, do you have any Idea where she could be?"

"U.S. Marshals are looking for her.

I told the detective, "She's a smart one."

"Yeah, well, Avery sooner or later life catches up to people, or is it that karma thing? Well, I gotta be going now."

"Yeah, thanks again, detective." I got to my jeep and headed home. I thought to myself it seemed so long ago when Steven was killed. And still nothing on his killer. Hell, it could have been me.

Inspector Mattia had been running the name Lynn Marie Cassidy through the AFIS database with the fingerprints that were on the passport. Lynn Marie Cassidy was a citizen of Milwaukee Wisconsin up until 1998. Lynn Marie Cassidy passed away in 1998 from an auto accident. This seemed extremely suspicious to the Inspector so he called the Prosecutor Lorenzo Alvize to try and understand his findings. After a lengthy discussion, they agreed to meet at the morgue to see what the medical examiner had found out. The medical examiner had found four linear fractures on the left side of her skull. Bruises around the back of her neck and right cheek in the shape of a hand. They were both present when her fingerprints were taken. They also took pictures of the two tattoos she had on her body. A band of sunflowers around her left ankle and a lightning bolt on her right ankle. The Inspector opened his laptop scanned the fingerprints and ran those through AFIS. The medical examiner gave them her blood type as well. Blood and hair for DNA were also taken for records. It was only a few minutes and a positive match came across his screen. He looked at the screen his eyes narrowed adjusting his glasses focused on the information he was reading and looked across the room at the Prosecutor.

"Hey Lorenzo," he said, "This woman is a fugitive from the United States. The U.S. Marshals are looking for her. Her real name is Rebecca Lynn Ashton, and she was wanted for embezzlement and questioning for murder times two. The Inspector took his glasses off, looked at the Prosecutor, and said, "She will not be answering any questions, I'm afraid.

Inspector Mattia said, "I will contact the U.S. Embassy when the examiner finishes his report and determination of the cause of death. They can notify the U.S. Marshals that we have their fugitive. We regret to inform them that the fugitive has died from foul play, murdered. When we conclude our autopsy we will notify her family for transport back to the United States. We will continue our Homicide investigation to find out what happened to her. She may be a fugitive but she is a victim and was killed by someone. The medical examiner had finished his report and ruled the cause of death was Blunt Force Trauma. He also informed the Inspector and Prosecutor there were traces of semen inside her vagina. This could have been sexually motivated. The examiner extracted samples for DNA testing. Rebecca Lynn Ashton's death was ruled by the Prosecutor Lorenzo Alvize as a Homicide.

Inspector Mattia called Pollo Gianni and asked him to come to the station to answer a few more questions.

Pollo arrived at the station an hour later and was led to a dimly lit room with a table and three chairs. He sat down and noticed a camera in the corner pointed down at him as he sat there nervously awaiting the inspector. He felt like they were watching him intentionally making him sit there and wait.

The buzzing of the fluorescent light was starting to get to him. He sat there hypnotized by the buzzing sound triggering a migraine.

He heard the door knob turn and the Inspector came into the room and sat down. “Hello, Mr. Gianni, how are you today?”

“I am ok.”

“Do you know why you are here, Mr. Gianni?”

“No, I told you all I know.” The door opened again and Prosecutor Alvize came in and sat down not saying a word looking at Pollo. He opened a file he had brought with him looking through the file then sliding a piece of paper to Inspector Mattia.

“I ask you again, Mr. Gianni, do you know why you are here?”

“I know I’m here because of the death of Lynn Cassidy.”

“How well did you say you knew her.”

"I told you I just worked for her."

Prosecutor Alvize spoke up asking Pollo, "You are married, are you not?"

"Yes, yes I am a happily married man."

"Ah, I see. So you're saying you and Miss Cassidy were nothing more?"

"I love my wife," Pollo said firmly.

Inspector Mattia yelled, "That's not what we ask you! You are lying to us, Mr. Gianni. We found your sperm inside her!! You came on to her, she rejected you, and you just couldn't take her rejection, and you raped and killed her."

Pollo slammed his fist on the desk, "No! No!! That's not what happened."

The Inspector laughed and said, "Then tell us what happened and stop lying to us."

"It was consensual. She had been making advances towards me for weeks. I pushed her away repeatedly. This morning I came here to discuss business, and she invited me in, then she seduced me in her see-through lingerie on the couch. Yes, I fell weak and we had sex. She got up and went to the shower. I left and returned, I say thirty minutes later, around 8:20. I buzzed the gate and no one answered. I jumped the gate and I knocked on the door several times. I thought she went downstairs to the office, and so I went down there but she was not there. My, guys showed up and we began working. You can check her security system.

Inspector Mattia said, “We have checked her security system and it wasn’t working.”

Pollo said, “They were supposed to fix the system.”

“Well,” Prosecutor Alvize said, “that is very convenient, wouldn’t you say, Mr. Gianni?”

Pollo asked, “Am I being detained?”

“No,” Prosecutor Alvize replied.

“I will not say anything else without an attorney. I’m leaving!”

Prosecutor Alvize nodded to Inspector Mattia. He knew they didn’t have enough to hold him until they confirmed the DNA results. Prosecutor Alvize asked Pollo if he would be willing to consent to a DNA Swab before he left. Pollo agreed stating he had nothing to hide and wanted to help any way he could to track down Lynn’s killer. A technician came in to do the buccal smear. The tech took a swab of Pollo’s mouth by taking the swab rubbing it on the inside surface of his cheek. The tech placed the swab into a small plastic bottle breaking the stick leaving the swab inside and closed the lid, placing a tape seal across the top. Pollo then initialed and dated the tape. It was ready to be shipped to the lab for DNA testing.

Pollo got up and was leaving. When he got to the door, Inspector Mattia told him, “Don’t go too far, Mr. Gianni, we will see you soon I’m sure.”

After Pollo left, Inspector Mattia told Prosecutor Alvize he didn’t know if he believed what Pollo had told them. The Inspector said he was going to go check the security from the pastry shop and ask some questions. Maybe see if anyone saw anything out of the ordinary.

The Prosecutor said, “Check the street cameras, they could have captured something.”

The Inspector went back to Lynn Cassidy’s home, standing in front at the gate and looking around. He didn’t see a street camera with a direct line of sight to her home. He turned a complete circle looking around for anything that might give him a lead. He did notice a neighbor had a doorbell camera. He surveyed the street, the surrounding houses and businesses and decided to go door to door asking questions. He went back to the bakery and spoke to the owner looking at the security tape of the exact time Pollo walked in, then timed it back to Lynn’s home. That gave him a very good idea of a timeline and the time she was killed. By his calculations that would have been somewhere close to 7:45 am. This would also help pull up any security footage in this timeline. He went door to door asking questions but he wasn’t having a whole lot of luck. He had the house keys in his pocket and decided he would go inside. Nothing looked out of the ordinary. He looked around and went out on the balcony. He took a deep breath, the sun felt good on his face, he closed his eyes taking a deep breath. He inhaled and exhaled, opening his eyes, and saw someone staring at him from the balcony across the street. A little old lady with silver hair, olive skin, and dark eyes. The Inspector waved at her. She just looked at him. Inspector Mattia waved again she waved back. He showed her his badge and asked if she remembered the lady who lived there in Italian.

She nodded yes. The little lady said she never wore much clothes. She said she saw a man in a jumpsuit, hat, and dark glasses, black hair slick back behind his ears, a little hair on his face, black shade. He was standing at her gate. I went inside and didn't see him anymore. His first break in the case. He checked the security tapes of businesses up and down both sides of the street. He was able to verify Mr. Gianni's story to and from the Bakery shop. But, as hard as he had looked, he hadn't found anything definitive. He got back to the station and went to the tech department looking at street cameras for anything out of the ordinary. Prosecutor Alvize came in and the Inspector told him he felt Mr. Gianni's story seemed very credible to him, and was checking out. He told the Prosecutor the story the witness had told him. Now he believes they are looking for someone else.

In Nashville Tennessee, a phone rang at the U.S. Marshal's Service field office. "Deputy Marshal Craig Whittaker, how can I help you?"

"Yes, this is Andrew Wallace with the U.S. Embassy and Consulates office in Palermo Italy. We are calling about a fugitive case you have posted."

"Ah, yeah whatcha got?"

"Rebecca Lynn Ashton out of Dickson TN for an embezzlement and murder Investigation."

Deputy Whittaker said, "Yes, do you have first-hand information about this fugitive?"

"Yes, we have positive DNA and fingerprint identification that matches your fugitive."

Deputy Whittaker said, "Great job guys, they have a lot of questions for her."

"Oh, I'm sorry to inform you deputy but your fugitive is deceased."

"What?"

"Yes, deputy, sorry but Rebecca Lynn Ashton was found dead at her home in Sicily. The identity she had assumed was Lynn Marie Cassidy from Milwaukee Wisconsin. The passport was a fake but of very good quality. Some of the best forgery work our forensic experts had have ever seen."

"Oh, man. Ok, Mr. Wallace, I will contact, ah let's see, Elliott Benson, he issued that warrant, and let him know that our fugitive, Rebecca Ashton, is deceased. Have them keep that place locked down. We may send someone to take a look at her things and see if there is any evidence for us on this end. Oh and let us know when your investigation is complete so the family can be notified."

Mr. Wallace told Deputy Whittaker the family would have to contact the Bureau of Consular Affairs also, and most importantly, they would have to have a Consular Report of Death Abroad. This is very important when the family is filing insurance claims on her estate. And that has to happen for transporting the body back to the United States.

Deputy Whittaker thanked Mr. Wallace, gave him his email address, and asked him to send that information to him in a file.

"Oh, and I don't know if I mentioned it but the Prosecutor and Inspector in charge of this investigation are Prosecutor Lorenzo Alvize and Inspector Mattia Salvatore in Sicily. The contact number is 011-39- 682-3894." Ok, ok, thank you again, Andrew. Let me know if you guys need anything."

"Sure thing man."

U.S. Marshal Deputy Craig Whittaker looked over the case file and then contacted Dickson County District Attorney Elliott Benson. DA Benson had just finished a meeting with a witness on another case he was prosecuting. He had just walked into his office and sat down when his phone rang.

He picked up, "Yeah, Brandy."

His secretary said, "You have a call on line 2 from the U.S. Marshals service out of Nashville, Deputy Craig Whittaker."

"Yes, hello this is District Attorney Elliott Benson how can I help you?"

Mr. Benson, this is Deputy Craig Whittaker with the U.S. Marshal's Service in Nashville. I just received a call from the US

Embassy and Consulates in Palermo Italy. They have your fugitive, Rebecca Ashton. All right, all right."

"I have some bad news though, Mr. Benson. She was killed at her home in Sicily."

"Sicily? Well, that might explain how she just disappeared."

"Yes, she assumed the identity of a deceased woman from Milwaukee Wisconsin. She was going by the name Lynn Marie Cassidy. She had bought a home there in Sicily and that's where she was killed."

"I see, deputy, that's terrible news."

They have an ongoing investigation underway working the case to find the person or persons who perpetrated this crime."

"Thank you for your help, deputy."

"Oh yeah, I told them to keep her place on lockdown in case you guys wanted to go look around for any possible evidence."

"Thanks again, deputy."

"I will also send you the contact information relayed to me by the Embassy in Italy."

"Again, thank you, Deputy Whittaker."

"Sure thing, Mr. Benson. Have a good day and if you need anything, just let me know."

"I'll do that, thank you, bye now."

Inspector Mattia had been going over the tape for several hours when he noticed something very interesting. He kept seeing the images of a man on several security cameras walking right past Pollo Gianni. This could be our man. The man was dressed in coveralls, a hat, dark hair, and sunglasses, carrying a black bag almost like a doctor's bag. He went past a clothing store just before getting to Lynn Cassidy's home. He could see him in a reflection but just couldn't see his face.

Prosecutor Alvize came in and Inspector Mattia explained his findings, wondering if it was just a coincidence. He passed the store at 7:35 a.m. then at 8:07 a.m. going back in the opposite direction. Prosecutor Alvize did indeed find this very interesting.

"Look, look, here he has on gloves in this photo. In the reflection from the story window from across the street he looks as if he comes out of her gate wearing gloves on."

"Zoom in, zoom in right there. Those look like Isotoner black leather driving gloves."

They looked at each other and said, "Maybe a stylish killer."

The Inspector, with a concerned look, said, "That would explain the lack of fingerprints." They were both positive this man was a person of interest. They nodded, both thinking, both knowing deep down, this was their man.

They tried using facial recognition but didn't have a clear enough picture. They used a sketch artist to draw a sketch and Mrs. Catory, the only person who saw our suspect, said that was the man she saw. They used the press releasing the sketch to the local newspaper and media as a person of interest in a murder investigation asking for any help on the date of 10/02/2014 around the time of 7:00 a.m. and 9:00 a.m. on Corso Umberto. Contact Inspector Mattia Salvatore at 011-39-682-3894 Any information could be imperative to this investigation. Any help would be greatly appreciated.

...

I was in my office ordering cleaning supplies when I heard a vehicle drive through the gate and looked out my office window. It was Lieutenant Forrester and Detective Allen.

They came in and I met them at the door greeting them like old friends and inviting them in. They sat down and I asked if they would like some coffee or bottled water. They declined thanking me for the offer. Lieutenant Forrester said, "We just wanted to come by and let you know the latest information on our investigation."

"Any news on the whereabouts of Rebecca Ashton?" I asked."

"Well, yes we do," Lieutenant Forrester replied. We do have confirmation of her location, but it's not what we wanted, Avery."

I could tell by her response this wasn't the good news I thought it to be. Detective Allen said, "They had found Rebecca Ashton dead in her home in Sicily Italy."

I shook my head in frustration but also in disbelief. Out of anger, I said, "Well, that sucks, we may never get the answers to Steven's death or even Carlton's death. She had those answers!!"

"Avery, I promise it wasn't because we didn't try."

"I understand that, lieutenant, but I just can't even think that the end justifies the means. It just doesn't seem fair. I think of Steven's father and how upset he will be when he hears this news."

Lieutenant Forrester said, "His secretary had called her. She said he was heartbroken and left for the day. She also would fax over all the information the Embassy was sending. They have an ongoing investigation to find who perpetrated this crime."

I thanked them for the information and asked them to keep me posted. Before they left the detective noticed the post-it notes on the filing cabinet, call Art.

He asked, "Who's Art?"

"I don't know," I told them. "This was Carlton's filing system so he wouldn't forget things. The lieutenant noticed, call Ray, on one of the yellow post-it notes.

“Have you met Ray?” she asked. That’s his brother, right?”

“I’m not sure,” I told her, “I thought his brother’s name was Art, well half-brother he told me once. I’m not sure how many brothers he had.”

Lieutenant Forrester said, “Someone named Ray was on the contact number at the assisted living home when I went to let Carlton’s grandmother, Hazel Gallimore, know we had found Carlton. I tried looking him up but couldn’t find him. Which is a good thing, I guess. I was going to call him and didn’t get around to it. I did have an officer call him and we did send the medical examiner’s report. It was ruled accidental.”

“What now?” I asked them.

“Well, now we will contact her family and the Tennessee Power Association. We have no more paths to follow. This will now be lawyers and lots of paperwork.”

Lieutenant Forrester said, “We may call everyone in who worked there, question everyone again, and see if we can jar their memory on what may have happened to Carlton Rogers.”

I asked them what they thought happened to him. They both agreed it was no accident but you have to prove it. I thanked them and asked that they keep me posted as they were leaving.

Detective Allen and Lieutenant Forrester said, "Now they were going to inform Tommy Ashton and his aunt, Darlene, his mother was deceased."

I had not met Tommy Ashton but I knew that within six months he had lost the two most important people in his life.

After leaving, the lieutenant and detective were discussing the case, and Detective Allen asked Lieutenant Forrester, "Do you believe in karma?"

"After receiving the information that Rebecca Ashton was killed, I can't say that. I mean, we don't know the whole story. Avery was right, we didn't get a chance to ask Rebecca the question to determine her involvement. Did Carlton mastermind this whole thing? Or were all three of them involved? Jack, it feels like this was a game but no one was ever going to win. A game with only the innocent left to pick up the pieces. You have Tommy Ashton left without his grandfather and mother now. Ray without his brother, Ms. Hazel Gallimore, went down from worry and will die with a broken heart. Elliott lost his son; Steven's daughters lost their dad. And for what? It all leads back to people and greed."

The detective said, "Money!! Money, lieutenant, it makes the world go round. Empires have fallen, civilizations have been wiped out, lives snuffed out, blood spilled in battle!! And every day it happens over, and over again. But, you and me, we're here because of who we are on the inside. Tryin' to make a difference. Make the world a better place. So don't get too wrapped up or down on yourself. We follow the clues. We have to play the cards we're dealt. We chose this game because we care. We have to keep playing the game, it's who we are."

Inspector Mattia Salvatore kept looking for a break in the case but it's been three weeks and the case is growing cold by the day. They are releasing Rebecca Lynn Ashton's body back to her family. He and his team are going back over any security footage looking for that one thing that could break this murder investigation wide open. They questioned Pollo Gianni again and Pollo remembered seeing the man on the street. They had footage of him and the man within feet of each other. The photos of the man were grainy and still no positive ID of this mystery man with slick back hair and stubble on his face. The last time Pollo Gianni was at the station answering questions, Pollo's wife had followed him, and as he was leaving Inspector Mattia and Prosecutor Alvize heard yelling and looked out the shades and through the window seeing Pollo and his wife arguing out front on the sidewalk. She followed him to the polizia station and found out why he had been there being questioned, He admitted he had been unfaithful to her. She told him never again and she was filing for divorce. Prosecutor Lorenzo Alvize and Inspector Mattia Salvatore both knew the longer an investigation goes the more difficult to solve. People forget things, memories fade, and people move on, They both agreed to keep running the sketch and description of the suspect/person of interest in the local newspaper and media local news outlets. They had gotten some great news from the tech department. One of the video technicians had made an important discovery reviewing some store security footage. The suspect has a small tattoo behind his left ear. The tattoo was of an A with a circle around it. Inspector Mattia asked what the tattoo meant. One of the technicians explained its meaning to him.

"The A surrounded by a circle is universally known as the symbol of Anarchism. It was established in global youth in the 1970s," showing him a picture.

"Yes, yes, I have seen this before. Good work, good work everyone!! This is a very important detail that we will not share with the public." He thought to himself and discussed it with prosecutor Alvize and they decided that it may be too easy to have removed.

Tommy Ashton didn't cry. As he sat there being told the last link to his youth was gone, the life he'd known was gone forever. Lieutenant Forrester told Tommy, and his aunt Darlene, the terrible news that his mother was deceased. Lieutenant Forrester and Detective Allen explained what details they knew. They too, were waiting for the file with the details of Rebecca's murder. Lieutenant Forrester told Tommy and Darlene how sorry they were for their loss, and told them if they needed anything to feel free to call on them. They left the contact information for the preparation and return of Rebecca Ashton's body and her personal effects. Tommy Ashton and his aunt Darlene had filed all the paperwork through the Bureau of Consular Affairs and went through all the other red tape to have his mother's body sent home. The funeral home his mother and grandfather used had served the family for many years. They had prearranged funeral arrangements with Hillcrest Family Funeral Home in Dickson. Tommy had been wrestling with the idea on seeing his mother before her cremation, but his aunt talked him out of it. She was worried what shape Rebecca's body would be in after being so brutally assaulted.

Darlene wrapped her arms around Tommy and told him to remember the good times, the laughs, and bedtime stories.

The trail rides, and driving lessons in her Corvette." (That Corvette is now his that he has driven to school twice with his friend Bradley Childs.)

After a week, Rebecca's body arrived back home in Tennessee. The family had a small ceremony with family and a few friends and her ashes were buried beside her father and mother in a small cemetery in Milledgeville. The same cemetery where so many other family members were laid to rest. A week later Rebecca's things arrived from Italy. Darlene and Tommy went through the things when they came across a King James Bible that zipped with Rebecca's name engraved on it. Tommy recognized it. His mother had read him verses from it when he was young. He unzipped it and a letter fell out. It was addressed to Tommy but hadn't been mailed.

Tommy was excited to see what his mother had said to him in this letter. Tommy grabbed the letter before his aunt saw it and went to his room to read it.

"Dear Tommy, Hey, baby I know you may be mad at me for leaving the way I did. I knew there would be a lot of things said that aren't true about your grandpa and me. I can't wait for you to see this place. I knew Aunt Darlene would take care of you just like she was there for me when I was growing up. I'm telling you baby; this place is beautiful. I have us a place here in Sicily which is in Italy if you're not studying your geography like you should. We are right by the sea. These girls here are all so tan and will think you're a little cutie pie. I miss my baby boy! A tear fell on the page as he continued. So as soon as school's out, you're going to come visit. We will keep this little secret between us. I'm sure those TPA people are mad about Grandpa Robert getting some of their money. He just hustled them like they hustle people every day. I can't wait for you to see this place. Hey, we can scuba dive, fish all day. I'm telling you; I can't wait to see you. I'm going to go now baby. I will write again when school is almost out to make our plans. Burn this letter after you read it so they can't find me. Love you, always and forever. Love, Mom. PS You can drive my car but be careful. Tell Aunt Darlene I love her."

Tommy wiped the tears from his face knowing things would never be the same again. The life Tommy had known was gone forever and that was hard on him. His aunt came to his door, knocked, and opened the door, and asked if he was hungry. She saw him crying and sat down beside him on the floor in his room.

Seeing the letter, she hugged him and said, "Baby, we gonna make it, we gonna make it. I'm here for you baby. I won't let nothing happen to you. I wish I could take your pain away but I can't. I can only love you, Tommy."

Darlene Ashton got up and asked Tommy if he would like a sandwich and Tommy told her yes he would, he was hungry. She went to the kitchen to fix lunch.

Tommy put his letter back in the bible and continued looking through it. He flipped to the back where the notes were. He always enjoyed reading the family history in back. You could usually find births, weddings, deaths, in bibles in the old days. He flipped back there and there was a small leather coin purse with two keys. He got the keys and went out to her things. He didn't see anything that required any keys. He started opening all the boxes then he found a boot box. He opened it a under the paper and boots, and found a lock box. He tried inserting one of the keys but it didn't fit. He then checked the other and it fit. He opened the box and was surprised at all the stacks of money inside. He closed it back, picked up the lock box, and took it to his room. He sat down on the bed looking back inside the box. He sat there and counted all the money in the box. There was one hundred twenty six thousand dollars in the box with some family jewelry, letters from his grandparents, the title to his mother's car and paperwork on her house. Tommy felt a flood of emotions and then thought this was all his now. He put everything back in there and locked the box and put the keys back in the bible and then went and had lunch with his aunt, trying not to think of it all. The thought of all that money made him nervous, very nervous, even a little nauseous. He was scared to say anything to anyone thinking they might try to take it like they did his grandfather's home.

Tommy thought long and hard about everything that night and decided he would take half of that money and open up a savings account in his name like grown-ups do. He got up and put half the money into a paper sack and went down to the Farmers First Bank of Dickson where his grandfather and mother had always done their banking. He pulled in and parked, went inside, and walked up to the counter.

"Hello, sir, how may I help you today?" the teller asked Tommy. I want to open a savings account.

The teller said, "You do?"

Tommy said, "Yep."

An older man saw Tommy through the glass window of his office and was watching him closely.

The teller said, “You will need to sit down and fill out some paperwork.”

He said, “ok, yes ma’am.”

The older gentleman walked to his doorway and the teller waved at him and pointed towards Tommy. The man came out and walked towards Tommy.

“Good morning, sir how are you today?”

“Alright I guess,” Tommy replied shaking his hand.

“I’m David Mills, Vice President of the bank. How can I help you today?”

Tommy said, “I want to open a savings account.”

“Alright, you came to the right place.”

Tommy said, “Yeah, I want to put this money I have here in this bag into a savings account.”

Mr. Mills looked at the bag and laughed. Tommy looked confused. Mr. Mills said, “I’m glad it ain’t got a gun in there.”

Mr. Mills continued laughing but Tommy didn’t get the joke and spoke up saying, “No sir, I’ve got seventy-five thousand.”

Mr. Mills laughed louder. Tommy wasn’t understanding, getting frustrated, reached down, and picked the bag up from the floor dumping all the bag's contents on his desk. Tommy said, "Here is seventy-five thousand."

Mr. Mills abruptly stopped laughing, immediately jumped up and closed his door, then closed the shades to his office. "Son, what's your name?

"Tommy Ashton."

"Tommy, Tommy, Tommy. I haven't seen you in several years. I don't know if you remember, but we went quail hunting back about six years ago at your grandaddy's place. I had that red truck with those two short-haired bird dogs."

Tommy was thinking and said, "Yes, yes sir I do remember those dogs, their names were Mo and Joe."

"Yes, that's right, that's right Tommy. Now where did you get all this money son? My momma's safe, and this is just half of it."

"Tommy, I was sorry to hear about your mother's death."

"Thank you, sir."

"You call me David from now on, Tommy, we're kin somewhere down the line. Tommy, you already have a savings account here with us, and have had since you were born."

Tommy looked very confused.

"You see, Tommy, your grandaddy opened it a long time ago. Now I wouldn't dare tell you what to do but, I would tell you like I would tell your grandaddy, take that money and put it back in your safe. Does your Aunt Darlene know about you coming down here?"

"No sir, I was going to surprise her."

"Well, Tommy, she is your Power of Attorney."

"What does that mean?"

"Well, son, she is here to guide you and watch over you and your finances until you are eighteen."

Tommy said, "Well, Mr. Mills I didn't know any of this."

"That's understandable, Tommy, so many people don't know. And it's not just young people, it's all ages. We deal with this all the time son. And I bet you will be your Aunt Darlene's Power of Attorney when you both get older. Do you want me to call her down here to discuss everything?"

Tommy said, "No. I will do what you suggested and take this back home and talk with her."

Mr. Mills put the money in the bag, Tommy got up, shook his hand, and walked to the door turning around before opening it.

"Well, how much is in my account?"

"Tommy, you have almost two million dollars and I need to speak with your aunt about the life insurance policy your mother left you. Actually Tommy you will probably have over two million in this bank when it's all said and done."

Tommy said, "Thank you again, Mr. Mills for helping me with this. I think I need to go talk to my aunt."

"Tommy, you call me or come by anytime you want. We can sit down here and talk about anything. Make sure you let your aunt know to call me."

"I will, and thanks again, Mr. Mills."

Tommy left the bank and went home to sit down and talk with his Aunt Darlene about the money he had found in the lock box and the money he found at the bank.

"Tommy, I was going to tell you when I thought or felt you were old enough or mature enough to understand all this mess." Darlene started to cry and she told Tommy they both loved you so much and wanted you to be taken care of if something ever happened to them. Your grandaddy wanted you to be able to go to any school you wanted, be anything you wanted to be, and I still want the same thing for you. You're going to be a great man, Tommy, and I'm here to help you. It's in your blood baby.

Tommy looked up and said to her with tears in his eyes, "I would trade all this money just to have them both back again."

"I know you would baby. Those people made some wild accusations against your granddaddy and mother, but guess what, they never proved a thing, did they? That Carlton Rogers is behind all of this. He is responsible for this theft. I think he felt guilty and ran that tractor off in the lake on purpose and committed suicide."

I had just gotten into my office after sitting in on a safety meeting with Chris and three of our new hires before they left base for the day. Two of the three were still in the probationary phase of their hiring. Chris was taking them around to some of the substations showing them how to enter the secure areas, also taking inventory on cleaning supplies. Chris and I were very pleased with the choices we made on our new hires. We will hire more in the spring as the mowing season picks up. I received a phone call from Lieutenant Forrester.

"Avery!"

"Hello lieutenant, how are you?"

"No time to talk, Avery, just calling to let you know Ken Katel and his news team are probably on their way over for a follow up on his investigation of the fraud and theft involving R.E.R and the Tennessee Power Association. I thought quickly and decided right now was not the time I felt like answering questions especially with an open ongoing investigation.

I thanked her, hung up the phone, ran out the door to the gate and locked it, then went back inside to call Chris giving him a heads up letting him know to take his time not arriving back to base until this afternoon. It wasn't long when a News Channel 3 van pulled up to the gate. Ken Katel stood in front of the locked gate and in front of him, a man with a camera recording every word.

"And 3, 2, 1… I'm Ken Katel reporting to you from the Tennessee Power Association facilities base here in Dickson County. This is a story of murder, theft, fraud, and embezzlement. I first reported to you five months ago after a whistle-blower exposed this unbelievable story, something you might read in a crime novel. I just received news that two of the persons of interest in this investigation are deceased. Carlton Rogers and Rebecca Ashton have both passed since the beginning of this investigation. It appears Carlton Rogers was involved in an accidental tractor accident. And Rebecca Ashton was found murdered at her home in Italy which is still an ongoing investigation. This is a terrible turn of events and like so many, such as myself, is wondering, "Where is the 2.8 million dollars?" These are questions we may never know. I'm sure stockholders are still scratching their heads in disbelief that such a thing could have happened. I have sent several emails and left several messages with TPA and there has been no response. The executive board of the Tennessee Power Association is still being very tight-lipped, only saying they will be happy to answer any questions when this investigation is complete. Remember friends, you heard it here first. I'm Ken Katel, WTVR News Channel 3."

"And that's a wrap," the cameraman yelled.

Ken looked at him and asked, "How'd my hair look?"

"Fine man! I would have told ya if it didn't."

They loaded up their equipment and headed back to Nashville discussing who was buying lunch. I watched out the window as they left and thought about how this all began. I thought about how much things around here had changed. I could still see myself walking through that same gate on my first day. I guess that's the thing about time, you can't stop it, you just have to go with it, and you have to live it. I guess that's what angers me most. It's people taking from others, taking things that don't belong to them to get what they want. Even if that means taking a life.

That afternoon I went by Teddy's, Michelle said he had something for me. I walked in and sat there at her desk smiling.

Mary Catherine said, "Hello there, Mike Tyson."

I laughed and asked, "What are you talking about?" Michelle had a curious look on her face. Mary Catherine said, "I saw you knock that guy out."

"What me? No, must have been someone else."

Michelle hung up the phone and asked, "What about knocking someone out?

Mary Catherine said, "No, Avery, it was you a couple of weeks ago."

Michelle yelled, "Are you two holding out on me?"

I acted as if I knew nothing at all about what she was talking about. Michelle, "He's ready to see you now."

I walked toward the hallway looking at Mary Catherine slyly, shaking my head. "Ah ha, yeah, I know what I saw."

I just laughed and walked down to Teddy's office. I knocked on the door and he said, "Come on in Avery. Please have a seat young man. Teddy, how have you been?"

"Good and yourself?"

"Things are great, seems everything is back to normal. Congratulations on your job promotion."

"Thank you, Teddy. Avery, I just wanted to give you all these copies of the charges that were filed against you and then dropped. I spoke with Elliott and he filled me in on the details about the death of Rebecca Ashton and the possibility we may never find out who killed Steven Benson. I thought about that myself. I even asked myself, 'Was there justice for Steven if we don't know the details, the truth?' I can't say, that would have to be one's personal opinion. I trust I will see you at the ceremony on Friday."

"What ceremony? Elliott is having a celebration of life for Steven at St Patrick's Catholic Church then in the cemetery there will be a few words before being entombed in the mausoleum."

"I didn't know they were catholic."

With his eyebrows raised and shaking his head, Teddy said, "Well, Elliott is, and Steven was sometimes." Teddy said, "That's his words, not mine."

I laughed I just couldn't hold it in thinking about Steven. Teddy said, "Well, I'm sure you will be invited, Avery, Elliott does know how much you thought of his son and how much he thought of you."

"Yeah, he was a good guy. Thanks, Teddy, for everything you've done for me, I'd probably be behind bars without your help."

"You're quite welcome, Avery. We all need help now and then."

"Thanks again, Teddy!"

That evening Michelle and I were home eating supper and my phone rang, and I saw Elliott Benson on my screen. "Hello."

"Hello, Avery, this is Elliott Benson."

"Yes sir, how are you doing this evening?"

"I doing ok, I guess, under the circumstances."

Yes sir I understand."

He said, "I'm sure you know by now about Rebecca Ashton's death?"

"Yes sir, I did hear that."

"It leads me to believe our last hope for finding the truth died with her."

"I have to say, you're right sir, it seems that way. As I said before, Mr. Benson, I'm very sorry for your loss."

"Thank you, Avery, and that brings me to the reason I called. We are having a ceremony of life for Steven this Saturday afternoon at St Patrick's Catholic Church. The girls said they wanted to release balloons for their daddy. I understand I'm sure it's been rough on them. It's like they say, tomorrow isn't promised. Will you be there Avery?"

"Yes sir, I will."

"Could I ask something of you?"

"Yes sir, what is it?"

"Would you say a few words, please?"

"Yes, absolutely, I'd be honored to."

"Thank you so much, Avery, thank you."

After I hung up, Michelle asked how that went, and I told her I thought it went well.

"He did ask me to say a few words."

"What did you tell him?"

"I told him I'd be glad to." Michelle hugged me and told me how proud she was of me. She knows I get nervous speaking to large crowds. But I think being put in a leadership role at work has helped me. Doesn't matter, Steven was my friend, and as I told his father I'd be honored.

After we got the table cleared and dishes washed up, I started working on some notes. After working on my notes, I went into the bedroom and slid into bedroom where Michelle and Rosie were watching TV.

"So, something you forgot to tell me."

"Something, like what?"

"Mary Catherine was very sure she saw you knock some guy out the other night.

"Well, I didn't want to worry you."

"But, Avery you can tell me anything."

"Well, there was no need it was over and done."

"Give me the details, or you'll be sleeping on the couch."

"Ok, ok, the other night at the game, as I was leaving, some guy got mouthy. And I knocked him out when he got in my space."

Well, who was this guy getting' in your space?" I laughed. Michelle, "I mean it, Avery."

"Ok, Timmy Mason was there, and as I was leaving he made some smart comments about me and Steven. He did come at me when I returned the trash talk. And he did get in my space and I clocked him."

"Oh, Avery! Well, did you get him good? Two hits, me hitting him, him hitting the ground. Face down in the mud baby!!"

"Oh well, don't be thinking you're tough around here, mister, I'll put ya in the headlock." We wrestled around, I held her down kissing all over her face, and Rosie helped, licking her face as well. We laughed thinking about Timmy going back to jail all muddy. She told me to be careful those people haven't forgotten how things went down. I laughed and said, "That's why I didn't tell you, so you wouldn't worry."

"Please Avery, just be careful."

Part Four

The Tennessee Power Association went after Robert Ashton's estate. They were having no luck finding their 2.8 million dollars. They worked hard following the IP address to the Cayman Islands then it disappeared. The account was closed just as it had twice before.

Officer Zimmerman said, "It's like following a ghost." He and Vinci had been following the breadcrumb trail until it ended. That is exactly why people use these banks to hide things, illegal things. Darlene Ashton wasn't going down without a fight. She was as tough as her brother Robert. Her way of thinking was that her brother may have been charged but he wasn't convicted of anything. She, like many others, believed Carlton Rogers was behind every bit of this. They made wild accusations but proved nothing."

She said, "Hell 2.8 million dollars don't just disappear." But, that's in fact what it had done. She called the attorney her brother had contacted before his death, Brandon Perry.

"Brandon Perry's office, Lauren speaking, how may we help you?"

"Yes, I would like to speak with Mr. Perry, please."

"May I get your name and number, and I will give him a message."

"Darlene Ashton."

"And is this a legal matter?"

"Yes, he was my brother, Robert's, lawyer before he passed away. "

"So, he was representing your brother. Ms. Ashton, can I get a number from you?"

"1-731-584-5309."

"Ok, Ms. Ashton, I will give him this message to call you. It may be a day or two, he is in depositions today for sure."

"That's okay, hun, thank you." Lauren then took the message she had just written down on a post it note into Brandon's office placing it on his desk beside the phone.

Darlene hung up, grabbed her lighter and a cigarette and lit taking a deep draw, and exhaled while looking deep into the smoke like it was a portal taking her somewhere else in time. She focused on the smoke, looking deep not moving. She heard the door slam. She remembered looking through the bars, her brother on the outside telling her, 'it's gonna be alright, Darlene, it's gonna be alright.' Darlene bruised up, black eyes, busted lips. Robert was talking to her but she was in a daze. 'I'm gonna get you out of here in a few hours. I've got a lawyer on the way it's Farese Law Firm outta Memphis. I'll be back here in a little while, going to talk to judge Grimes. I'll have you out in no time.'

The cell door next to hers slammed, and she jumped remembering hearing him kicking the door loud. 'Darlene open this dang door!'

'No Billy Lee, you been drinking again.'

'I'm gonna beat you ass when I get my hands on you girl.'

She whispered to herself, not no more, not no more, and pulled the hammers back on her daddy's o d double barrel shotgun. 'Billy please come back tomorrow when you have sobered up.'

Darlene was crying and pleading, 'I'm a good woman, Billy Lee, and I'm good to you, and I don't deserve this!'

'Dammit Darlene!!' He kicked and kicked the door until the frame splintered and he rushed in and charged toward her. She remembered pulling both triggers seeing a flame and smoke from each barrel smelling the gun powder. Darlene blew his ass right back out that door onto the porch. 'Not any more Billy Lee, not anymore.' She put the shotgun down and called the sheriff. Robert had her out and at their mother's home resting in her old room in just a few hours.

Mr. Farese put the doctor on the stand who had seen Darlene after she lost her baby due to a beating she received from husband, Billy Lee Hensley in a drunken rage after losing their rent money in a poker game. He said she was bad luck.

Fractured arms, stitches from where she ran into the door or just fell down for no reason.

Her preacher who went to her home to check on her after she missed several Sundays just to find her beat up and bruised with black eyes or busted lips.

She remembered the sound of that gavel when the jury returned with a not guilty verdict and Judge Grimes said in a thundering voice, 'not guilty!!'

She took care of her mother until her death. She helped raise Rebecca Ashton as her own pretty much, and will Tommy as well. She is a tough Southern woman who wasn't going to be run over by the likes of the Tennessee Power Association with a bunch of allegations that were never proven.

The silence was broken when the phone rang. Darlene was jarred back to the present with sweat trickling down the sides of her temples, she squinted her eyes trying to focus. The cigarette she lit was ashes on the table, the filter still between her fingers.

"Hello," she said answering the phone.

"Yes, this Is Brandon Perry calling to speak with Ms. Darlene Ashton."

"Yes, this is she."

"Hello, Mr. Perry I wasn't expecting to hear from you for a few days but thank you for getting back with me so soon."

"What can I help you with?"

"Well, the Tennessee Power Association has filed against my brother's estate, which I thought they might. But, here's the way I see it. They charged him, made all kinds of accusations, but proved nothing."

"Uh-huh yes ma'am I do see, and I do agree."

Darlene continued and said, "now Carlton Rogers was behind this whole thing cooking the books and everyone knows that."

"But, TPA's argument will be Robert Ashton's signature was on the billing, and he owned the shell company."

"Well, anyone could have forged his signature."

"This could be tied up in court for a long time costing both parties a lot of money."

Darlene said, "Exactly, Mr. Perry. We play the hand were dealt. More than likely, if they somehow prove it, they would liquidate everything then auction everything off for what they could get."

"Yes, that's exactly the process. But, as I said, Ms. Ashton, that could take a while."

She said, "I want to retain you, Mr. Perry, as our lawyer. You contact them and tell them to get their darg lock off of our gate by the end of the day or I'll cute the dang thing off myself. Mr. Perry, we want to play hardball, you understand?"

"Yes, ma'am! These big corporations like TPA will try to buy you out and try and get us to make the wrong choices and mislead us to get what they want."

Brandon laughed and told her that wouldn't happen.

She said, "I hope not. My brother chose you because your good he said and could tell you like the challenge."

Yes ma'am I do love the fight and I'll get started on this paperwork. You'll be glad you chose me. You have a good rest of your day ma'am, talk to you soon."

"You too, hun, bye, bye."

Lieutenant Forrester had taken down the dry eraser board removing everything, placing it in a file folder and in her desk drawer. She opened and looked at the file she received from DA Benson's office from the investigation of Rebecca Ashton's case. She looked and there wasn't much to go on at all. She knew there was a time difference but called the contact number on the file. Then Googled the time difference to find out it was seven hours. The phone made a tone sound several times, then someone did answer.

"Hello Inspector Mattia speaking."

"Hello, this is Lieutenant Forrester from the Dickson County Police Department."

"Yes, hello."

Lieutenant Forrester told him, "I found this contact number on the file sent from the U.S. Marshals Office."

"Yes, I'm Inspector Mattia Salvatore lead investigator on this case. The murder investigation of the American woman Lynn Marie Cassidy or as her real name, Rebecca Lynn Ashton."

"Inspector Mattia, have you had any other leads on the case?"

"No, we have not had any breaks in the case. We just had our one witness who saw a man with stubble on his face, black hair, coveralls, and a black bag. Our forensic technicians concluded his height to be about 5'9 180 lbs."

Lieutenant Forrester said, "Well Inspector, that's not much to go on." Lieutenant Forrester told Inspector Mattia they were still working on an investigation which Rebecca Ashton was involved in. She then asked him if he would send her copies of anything else he finds.

Inspector Mattia said, "Yes, sure lieutenant."

Lieutenant Forrester gave him her email address so they could have direct communication. "Thank you Inspector Mattia, you have a good day."

"Maybe you mean, good night."

Lieutenant Forrester said, "Yes. You have a good evening, sir."

"You too, Lieutenant, good bye now."

Lieutenant Forrester hung up the phone slowly shaking her head not knowing anything more than she did. Her captain was riding her to close the case asap for the statistics. Captain Daniel Wesley was a 28 year veteran of the department. He was all about the numbers looking good in the eyes of the public. So, when the press questions him about crimes, he has numbers and statistics to compare with other cities around the state or country. Lieutenant Forrester felt there had to be more. Her intuition, her gut, her 16 years of being a cop told her there was more.

I had been working on my notes getting them prepared for Saturday when my cell phone rang. "Hello, Lieutenant Forrester how are you doing today?"

"Not bad, I guess. And how are you doing Avery?"

"I guess I'm ok for the middle of this beautiful day."

"That's good," she said. "Hey, I was wondering if you recall Carlton ever running any equipment."

"No, they actually tried keeping him in the office as much as possible. He wasn't very mechanically inclined or coordinated. I remember him them telling he flipped a truck. I know the tractor he was on one day here at base took out a transfer and knocked out power to half the city. He said it jumped out of gear. You know what, I still have all the files here boxed up and I know his is in there. Yeah, yeah here is his file. TPA said to keep everything for two years, then shred it.

Yes, oh the stories were true alright. And another incident here he drove off in a vehicle that looked like the truck he was in. Highway Patrol arrested him for a stolen truck on Interstate 40. It was a misunderstanding Carlton claimed. Both Carlton and the other vehicle owner received warnings for leaving the keys in their ignitions.

“Wow,” she said. “I mean it could have just been bad luck.”

She asked me, “Do you think he ran off in that lake? Could he?”

“Yes.”

“Do I think he did? I just couldn’t answer that positively. Carlton told me once that Robert Ashton had saved his ass a few times. He needed him, of course he saved him. I can fax you the file if you like.”

“Yes,” she said “please, that would be great. Thanks so much Avery. Your help has been greatly appreciated.” Lieutenant Forrester looked over the information that was in the file that had been sent over and didn’t see anything out of the ordinary. As Avery said, Carlton had a few incidents over the years. She noticed his contact was his mother, Hazel Gallimore. Which was actually his grandmother, again, nothing out of the ordinary because she had adopted him. She placed the information in the file she already had and placed it in her desk drawer.

After I sent the paperwork over to Lieutenant Forrester, I continued working on my notes. I have been practicing reading notes to Michelle and Rosie. Tomorrow afternoon I will share my thoughts, display my feelings, and express my remorse with his daughters, his father, family, and friends. I'm nervous but It could have been me, and still to this day, believe those pills were meant for me. Saturday morning came and Michelle and I were up enjoying our coffee. She was talking and I was reading over my notes. She said something and I responded yes.

"Avery," she said, "I just asked you if you were wearing flip flops to see if you were paying me any attention. And you said yes! Baby, I know you're nervous but don't be. Steven would be so proud of you too."

It was a beautiful sunny day mid-seventies, very nice for an early November day. Detective Allen and Lieutenant Forrester were on their way to the celebration of life ceremony. They had known Steven but also knew District Attorney Elliott Benson for several years, working with him on several cases. On the ride to the St. Patrick's Catholic Church, detective Allen said, "Well, I'm sure you will soon hear the news."

Lieutenant Forrester, with a puzzled look, asked, "What news, Jack?"

"Well, lieutenant, I decided it's time I put in my retirement papers. I think Celest and I are ready to walk those beautiful beaches of Florida watching the sunsets in my speedo."

She snickered a little and said, "Dang partner, I didn't need all the visual."

They both laughed and she looked at him and said, "I'm proud of you! I'm sure Celesta and you will enjoy the beach walks and sunsets, oh and your speedo." They both laughed some more. She said, "Jack, it's been awesome working with you. You have taught me so much and I learned so much working with you. I'm going to miss you."

He said, "I will miss you too. Hey, you can always come and visit us on vacation."

She wiped a tear from her eye and said, "I'll still call for advice and your opinion on cases."

"You do that, lieutenant."

They arrived at St. Patrick's Church and there was already a crowd, a full house for sure. They recognized several people from the police department, courthouse, lawyers, city. Many were there because of Elliott Benson, who had a lot of friends. He had worked in the Dickson County and the surrounding area for more than thirty-five years. At one time it was thought he could have run for Governor and won with ease until his first wife Amy passed from breast cancer who was Steven's mother. He later married his present wife, Stephanie and they are now raising Steven's girls, their granddaughters. Michelle and I had gotten there early, she wanted to make sure we had good parking. She said there would be a several people there from what she had heard. Mary Catherine drove Teddy they were parked by us and going to sit beside Michelle and me.

After everyone arrived, we would have two people speak inside, then we would file outside to the graveyard and his father would speak. Then, I would say a few words before a dove release. It was either the doves or balloons and the girls picked the pretty white doves. I saw and spoke to several people before it started.

"Hello Lieutenant Forrester. Hello Detective Allen, it's good to see you two again. Lieutenant Forrester, Detective Allen, you remember my wife, Michelle."

"Good to see you too, Michelle, and you too, Avery."

Detective Allen said, "Wow, this place is packed."

Lieutenant Forrester turned and shook hands with Teddy.

Lieutenant Forrester was talking to Michelle about how pretty Steven's girls looked. We saw and spoke to Yolanda the lady who was with Steven at the Christmas party at Montgomery Bell State Park. Michelle and I made our way over to speak with her.

"Ylonda, hello I'm Avery Jackson and this is my wife, Michelle."

She smiled, "Yes, I remember you both from the Christmas party. So nice to see you again," she said.

We hugged her and could see she had been crying. I could also see what Steven saw in her. A very attractive woman with emerald green eyes and long black hair. And when she spoke, there was a German accent I could hear. She held my hand and told Michelle and me how much she missed him. She told me how much Steven talked about me and the stories he would tell about his days at work. She cried more and Michelle hugged her and asked if she wanted to step outside to get some fresh air. As they walked off I looked in the remembrance card and found her name beside special friend, Ylonda Vincent.

I went to go and speak to Mr. Benson. I had seen him speaking to another man walking down the hallway towards the back where they had refreshments. I walked that way and then turned into another room.

As I walked up, I heard Mr. Benson say, "You did good, Art."

I walked on by thinking, Art. I thought, that's strange because I had seen something like that. I remembered, 'call Art.' I walked up to a table, got a drink, and turned around watching the two men. The man took a sip from a flask he had taken from his jacket pocket and then offered it to Mr. Benson, and he too took a sip. I walked back that way being curious. I saw the man give him an envelope that he put in his jacket pocket. I could see them in the reflection of a picture of angels on the wall there in the hallway. I was just around the corner and could hear the men talking.

Mr. Benson said to the other man, "This will take care of my girls."

The man took another sip from the flask and said, "An eye for an eye."

Mr. Benson smirked and said, "A life for a life," they both looked each in the eye, and hugged, and slapped each other on the back.

They shook hands, and Mr. Benson said to him, "See you, Ray, good work."

I waited a second and came around the corner and almost bumped right into Mr. Benson. "Oh hey, Avery."

"Hello sir." I looked at him surprisingly and asked, "How you doing today, Mr. Benson?" I could see the black haired man walking down the hallway.

"I'm doin' pretty good, I guess. You know it hasn't gotten any easier. His girls ask where he is all the time."

I could see the tears swelling in his eyes, he looked away from me and said, "I miss my boy, I miss my boy, Avery."

I handed him a tissue I had gotten as I walked in. I did feel sorry for him and gave him a hug. He thanked me, took a deep breath then exhaled. "Oh my, Avery," he said with tears on his cheeks, "I'm going to wash my face and try and get it together."

I wanted to ask him who that was he was just speaking with but thought I should just let him go have his moment. I walked toward the front of the building, looked around to maybe get a better look at the dark-haired man. I didn't see him anywhere out in the foyer, but it was packed with people already. I looked inside the viewing room and could see Michelle already seated, along with about eighty other people, and many standing in the back. I just wasn't expecting this many people. I made my way inside and down toward the front and beside her on the pew. My eyes went directly to the urn at the front on a table surrounded by a floral arrangement with beautiful roses.

We had gotten a remembrance card as we walked in. I had read it several times looking at all the pictures inside of Steven and his life.

The first speaker to speak was Steven s priest, Father Arthur Jamison. He had known Steven all his ife. He stood at the podium and cleared his throat. It's a beautiful day to be here remembering our brother Steven. I have known Steven all of his life here on earth. You see this urn up here with these beautiful flowers. Those ashes are not Steven. He has gone on to be with our Lord. You or I can imagine the beauty he sees now. He is in heaven with the creator of all. I want to share a memory I have of Steven. I remember when his mother passed. I was explaining to Steven his mother was in heaven watching over him. I told Steven he would see her again someday. He said Steven looked up at the ceiling crying and said he wanted his mommy now. You could see Elliott Benson up there behind him wiping the tears. He too remembered that horrific time in their lives and how it almost broke him. Father Jamison told how he had to break up a fight after Sunday school between Steven and another kid. I sent the other kid, who was blooded up on his way, and I asked Steven what it was all over He said he was making fun of another kid because of his shoes and clothes. Steven was a kid with a big heart who grew into a man with a very big heart. He was a loving father who loved his girls more than all else. Father Jamison spoke loudly; let's all bow our heads in prayer. Dear Heavenly Father, we come to you today to thank you, dear Lord for giving us, allowing us the time we had with Steven before calling him home, Lord. We know, dear Lord we will see him again when we pass through those pearly gates. Dear Lord, forgive us for all our sins, forgive us for the many ways we let you down. Thank you for the many blessings you have bestowed upon us, even when we are not worthy of your love. We ask these things in Jesus name, amen. The piano player began to play amazing grace and there was not a dry eye in the in the room. As he turned and walked back to the pew to sit down, he walked past Elliott Benson who had stood up, and he hugged him and said, “I love you brother.”

“I love you too, Father.”

Mr. Benson turned and approached the podium. Elliott smiled as he looked out at everyone in the room. I said I wasn’t going to cry when I got up here, but If I do, please forgive me. I look out there and can still see my baby boy in my arms over there being baptized. Or him running down that aisle right there. I can still see him in that seat right there beside me holding me tight and crying so hard but trying to be so strong because he knew I needed him when his mother left this world. I can see him right over there sneaking into the back pew on a few Sundays after service had started. Or over there smiling so proudly when his girls were being baptized. I never thought I’d be standing up looking down at his urn. No parent should ever have to bury their child. Our holidays won’t ever be the same. This Thanksgiving and Christmas there will be an empty chair at our table. Steven won’t be there to see his girls at graduation. Lisa and Leslie won’t have their father to walk them down the aisle on their wedding day. When someone is gone, or taken in this case, it leaves a hole and it affects everyone. As Father Jamison said, I will see my son again someday. Because I know where he is. He wiped the tears from his face. I thought about my friend and could feel his pain. Elliott Benson’s voice was trembling as he continued to speak trying not to cry. I, I would like to thank you all from the bottom of my heart. For, for being here. Here with us celebrating Steven's life. Everyone heard one of the girls crying saying, 'I miss my daddy.' Elliott said we are going to go out into the cemetery where Steven's friend, Mr. Avery Jackson will say a few words, then Steven's girls, Lisa, and Leslie, will release the white doves in honor of their father.

We all got up and began to file outside to the cemetery, and Steven's final resting place. Elliott Benson carried his sons ashes. I could still see the tears streaming down his face. His wife, Martha, walked with him, and his two granddaughters holding hands. As we walked out the door, the air was cool and the sun was bright, but it felt so good to just exhale as we walked.

I looked up after I heard birds in the trees in and surrounding the cemetery. I laughed after seeing the birds, hundreds of blackbirds chirping hopping around in the trees. I said out loud, 'Only you.'

Michelle looked at me and asked, "What did you say?" Laughing, I said, "Nothing."

Holding hands, we continued to the cemetery. The blackbirds seemed to get louder as we went toward the cemetery. We all gathered in the cemetery There was a box on a stand where the birds were and then Leslie and Lisa Benson stood on each side of the box. There was a headstone that read Christy Allison Benson. Loving wife and mother born 1962 died 1985. On the other side of the stone, Franklin Elliott Benson born 1960. A three foot deep hole was dug beside his mother's grave where Steven was to be laid to rest. Elliott Benson walked up to the hole, got down on his knees, with tears streaming down his cheeks, and placed the urn into the hole.

I walked up beside him helping him back up to his feet and he hugged me almost in a bear hug. He turned to the crowd and said, “Now Avery Jackson, a friend of Steven’s, will say a few words.”

I faced the crowd noticing the blackbirds were louder than I thought. I started to reach for my notes but thought to myself, no I didn’t need them. I had practiced this speech a hundred times already. I looked at everyone staring at me and said, “Today we are gathered here to celebrate the life of Steven Benson. He was a good man, a good son, a good father and a good friend to me and many others here today. I looked at Michelle and she nodded and smiled at me as a sign of encouragement, reassurance. It did make me feel more comfortable and at ease. I looked up and noticed the blackbirds again and it made me think, and went totally off script.. “Steven had a tattoo I asked him about once. Two blackbirds on his arm. He said blackbirds were messengers, protectors. He said the two on his arm represented his two daughters. I can’t help but look around today seeing all the blackbirds and think it’s Steven’s way of saying, telling us, it’s all going to be ok.”

Leslie yelled, Lisa, because she had pulled the string releasing the five white doves. They flew up, wings flapping, everyone looked up and watched the beautiful doves take flight. The blackbirds in the trees went silent at once. There was an eerie feeling that came over me. The silence was broken by a loud boom, I knew it was a gunshot. The blackbirds took off all at once. Another gunshot exploded, everyone screamed and yelled with panic running trying to hide and take cover.

"You son of bitch!!" I looked in the direction of the shots to see Timmy Mason coming straight toward me.

Lieutenant Forrester yelled, "Shooter, shooter!!!"

I looked around for Michelle, seeing her and Mary Catherine grabbing Lisa and Leslie, and taking cover behind some tall headstones. People were running scared everywhere not knowing exactly where to run. Detective Allen pulled a revolver from his shoulder holster he had under his jacket. I ran right at Timmy looking right into his eyes. He looked possessed crazed, almost unrecognizable. The drugs had him wired up. His clothes were filthy.

He yelled, "I'm not going to prison, not now, not ever!! He shot again twice striking Detective Allen in the shoulder, then again in the chest. Ain't no fun when the rabbit's got the gun!"

Lieutenant Forrester returned fire hitting Timmy in the leg but he kept coming. He shot and hit Lieutenant Forrester in the side. I knew he had one shot left then he turned, bleeding profusely, and ran and hid behind a vault close by. I could hear sirens coming, lots of sirens wailing, headed right for us.

I saw Teddy. He said, "You're bleeding, Avery."

I guess I got hit by the first or second shot I didn't know. My left arm was bleeding pretty good. Teddy took his tie off and tied it around my arm

I said, "Thank you."

"He smiled and said, "I was a medic at Pearl Harbor. I'll fix you up, son." As soon as he tied it, I ran in the direction Timmy had run. I could see he had lost lots of blood. A man ran over to check on Detective Allen and then ran over to Lieutenant Forrester. He ripped his shirt, folding it, and put pressure on her side.

She said, "Jack, how's Jack?"

"He's fine!" But that was a lie, and he knew it. He said, "here put pressure, put pressure on this to slow the bleeding. Paramedics are on the way!" She applied pressure going in and out of consciousness. Teddy had crawled over to her to help her. Two patrol cars slid in sideways. Officers got out taking cover, looking for the shooter.

I yelled, "He went this way!!" The paramedics came in behind the church at a safe distance to start treating the injured. I pointed at the vault. The officers came up taking cover behind headstones. I recognized officer Vandiver and officers King.

Officer Vandiver yelled, "Come out with your hands up!!" There was silence. "We have you surrounded!! Come out with your hands up!" The tactical unit had just arrived and was approaching. I heard over the radio one male suspect armed possibly injured. Then again the silence was broken by another gunshot. A helicopter had just arrived and did a fly over above the vault checking everything out.

Over the radio, someone said, "Threat level four, threat level four! Approach with caution!!" The tactical unit confirmed all clear.

I heard someone on the radio say, one 10:15 deceased self-inflicted gunshot wound."

I got up, walked in disbelief, shocked at what had just happened. I heard something, my ears still ringing, and looked up to see a blackbird chirping loudly looking right at me. I froze in my tracks.

Tears started streaming down my face, I smiled seeing Michelle was ok and running towards me. I exhaled and said, "Thank you buddy, thank you."

She ran into my arms crying kissing me, and said, "Thank God you're ok!" She said, "Your arm, Avery."

I looked into her eyes and said, "It's just a flesh wound."

She laughed and said, "You're crazy, you're crazy, I knew it."

We walked toward the church; I saw a sheet had been placed over a body. As we got closer the paramedics were putting Lieutenant Forrester into the ambulance in a hurry. I asked one of the paramedics how bad she said they were having trouble stopping the bleeding and she was in and out of consciousness. She had asked about Jack several times. I looked at her, then turned around to the person on the ground then back to her and she said, "Yes, he didn't make it." She looked taking the tourniquet off my arm and gave me a gauze and said, "Apply pressure and you need to go to get Dickson General get that arm sown up. By the looks, I think It passed right through."

"Thanks," I said, "I'm on my way." They slammed the doors and took off in a hurry, there was several officers there taking statements. We checked on Mr. Benson and his family before saying goodbye to Teddy and Mary Catherine. The bleeding had stopped pretty much but my arm was burning pretty bad.

Michelle drove me to Dickson General Emergency Room. After an x-ray that verified the bullet passed right through, and seven stitches on both sides of my arm, a good cleaning, and some pain medication, Michelle and I were on our way home. In the car we were still trying to prosses what had happened, and how lucky we were not to have been killed.

We both could see the full moon, and I said, "That's about right," she looked and shook her head. She ask me if I knew if Detective Allen had a family. I told her I believe he was married with children and grandchildren. We had checked on Lieutenant Forrester before leaving the hospital and a nurse Michelle knew from doing her taxes told us she was in stable condition and resting.

We got home and Rosie was so glad to see us. I think she could tell how upset Michelle was and she was loving on me a lot as if she knew I was injured. Chris called and said he had heard about the shooting at the cemetery and asked if we needed anything. I told him we were ok but I probably wouldn't be at work Monday or Tuesday.

"Wow, that's some crazy shit!"

I said, "Yeah, it was. "I always knew that Timmy was a dang coward."

“Yeah, I have to agree. Anyway, he said, “Don’t worry, I have everything under control.”

“I know you do, buddy, that’s why you’re there. I told him I would swing by Wednesday for a few minutes, I had something I needed to pick up.”

He laughed and said, “Well, use your good arm. Ha, Ha,” and I did laugh out loud.

I then called Tom Shepherd explaining how a previous employee, Timmy Mason, had shot me and two others, killing one of them, and then taking his own life.

“Avery, take as much time as you need.”

“I assured him I would be back soon even if it was on light duty. I told him what an awesome job Chris Williams was doing.”

Michelle asked what it was I had to go pick up that was so important. I looked at her and told her my plan. I explained I had been thinking I was going to have a monument made and placed at Steven’s graveside.

She said, “That’s an awesome idea, Avery. And by the way I’m sure Steven would have been very pleased by all your kind words and thoughts and how much his friendship meant to you.”

I turned on the TV and it wasn’t long until the news anchor reported they had reports of a Church shooting in Dickson County with two injured and two fatalities. More on this story when we know further details. I shook my head and just turned the TV off still in disbelief thinking about it all.

"Hold pressure, hold pressure," she heard the man saying. She was trying to say something moaning loudly.

"Jo Ann, Jo Ann can you hear me?" Her eyes opened and she gasped for air with a strange woman standing over her.. "Just breathe, honey, just breathe."

"That man with black hair was telling me to apply pressure."

"There ain't no man here, honey."

"But, Doctor Mitchell has dark hair. Maybe you were remembering him in surgery. You wouldn't forget him, he's fine, you'll see, he's on his way to see you."

It had been three days before Lieutenant Jo Ann Forrester finally came to. She looked around the room confused.

The nurse said, "it's alright, you're ok."

She asked, "What day is it?"

The nurse smiled and said, "Tuesday."

Jo Ann said, "Dang, I'm sore."

The nurse said, "You should be baby, you were shot. You really needed to rest."

“All those flowers are so beautiful, who sent them?” she asked. There were several floral arrangements. Such beautiful flowers.

“I just came on shift; I’ll be your nurse for the next twelve hours. My name is Karen,” a short white lady with salt and pepper short hair. “If you need anything, press that button and someone will answer at the desk.” The nurse pulled the cards and the first said Get well soon, prayers for a speedy recovery, Love Dickson PD. There were four more cards, they read one from The Jackson’s, Elliott Benson and family, Mayor Augustus Brooks City of Dickson, and St Patrick’s Catholic Church.

“Oh man, that’s very sweet of everyone.”

“Yes, it is honey. How’s Jack?”

“I don’t know anything about anyone named Jack.”

“Detective Jack Allen, he was also shot at the cemetery.”

“Like I said, I just came on shift.” Karen smiled, “Hey, he could have gone to another hospital.”

“Yeah, I guess you’re right.” That worried her. She asked if she could have some ice.

Karen said, “You sure can. That pain medication makes your mouth dry.” Karen said, “All your things are in here.”

There was a knock at the door. Karen opened it, smiling, and said, “Yes Doctor, I called as soon as she woke up. She’s still a little woozy.”

"Yes, hello Jo Ann, I'm your doctor, Doctor Travis Mitchell. I was on call when you came in Saturday afternoon. I just wanted to come look in on you." Karen handed him her charts. "How do you feel?"

"I'm sore for sure."

"Yes, the bullet tore your stomach muscles, you will be in here for a few days, and we did have to remove your gall bladder, and appendix."

"What?"

"Yeah, but you will be fine without them. I'll give you some time to wake up, and I'll check back with you later."

"Thank you, doctor."

The doctor left the room and Karen looked at her, smiling, "I told you he was fine."

"Oh Karen don't make me laugh, but you were right about that though. Where are my personal things, especially my phone, both of them?"

Karen said, "Yes, hun, everything you had when you came in is here in this plastic bag locked in a drawer at the desk with your room number on it."

"Ok, thank you, Karen." Jo Ann was resting trying to get her bearings about her when she heard a knock at the door.

It was Captain Daniel Wesley. He came by after being notified by Dickson General that Lieutenant Forrester had awakened. “Hello sleeping beauty.”

“Don’t make me laugh, sir. I look terrible.”

“You look pretty good for someone who was shot a few days ago.”

“Thanks, what about Jack, how’s he doing?”

“Jo Ann, I’m sorry to have to tell you this, but Jack didn’t make it.”

“What?”

Captain Wesley saw the tears swelling in her eyes.

“He, he had submitted his paperwork for retirement. He and his wife Celesta had their plans to, to move to Florida and enjoy their days with their grandchildren.”

“Now Jo Ann, you knew Jack better than anyone, and he knew he died saving others. Hell, you both saved lives that day. The mayor is planning a ceremony for you.”

She glared at him with tears on her cheeks, angry. “Oh I’m sure you and the mayor would love that. A great photo opportunity for both of you.”

“Jo Ann, no come on. You’re just still out of it with the medication and all.”

"No, Wesley, I am mad, hurt, wish I had done more to save him."

"It's not your fault, Jo Ann, you can't save everyone." He said, "Jack died saving lives. I can't think of more honorable way to die. We have your shield and sidearm at the station in your desk. You just get some rest, please, and come on back to work when you're ready."

She wiped her eyes and said, "Thanks for the beautiful flowers, Captain."

"You're very welcome, lieutenant." He smiled as he went out the door turning to tell her if she needed anything just call.

She smiled knowing he had ask her out but she felt like it might complicate her job. She felt it was unethical and could affect the decisions she made. But she always thought he was attractive. She always wondered how he might be on a personal level. She sat there, then her mind went to her friend, Jack. She teared up again, then thought to herself, she was going to call Celesta and check on her soon, as difficult as it might be, she owed it to her longtime friend and mentor.

Doctor Mitchell had instructed me to come back to the hospital in a few days to have my wound cleaned and dressing changed. I went in as instructed and had everything checked out, and nurse Atchison let me know everything looked great. I asked her if she knew of Lieutenant Forrester and how she was doing.

"I'm not supposed to discuss patients but then nurse Atchison leaned in and whispered she up on seven, room 428 and she's doing very good."

"Thank you so much, I appreciate it. I've really been worried about her. My wife and I sent her flowers. After I was cleared to go by nurse Atchison, I got on the elevator and went up to see her if I could.

I got off on seven, looked down a hallway behind double doors that were closed. I waited until someone came out then shuffled on through and down the hallway to room 428. I knocked at the door and heard, "come in."

"Hello, Lieutenant Forrester, how are you doing?"

"Avery," she smiled, "How'd you find me?"

I told her I had to come in and get this cleaned and the bandage changed. And just did some recon.

"Oh my, I didn't know you got hit too."

"Oh, it's just a scratch."

She smiled and said, "Tell Michelle thanks for the beautiful flowers." I told her she's very welcome. She said, "I guess you also know about Jack." I could see the sadness in her eyes.

"Yes, I knew that day, and I'm very sorry. He seemed to be a very nice person."

"Yeah," she said, "He had sent his paperwork in for his retirement."

I told her again how sorry I was. But he is in a much better place than us. "Hey," I said, "Lieutenant, can I ask you a question?"

She said, "Yeah sure."

"Did you ever find anything about that person we were talking about in Carlton's file?"

She said, "Ray?"

"No, Art. Remember the post it notes in there call Art."

"No, I couldn't find anything. I did look and nothing in our data base came up on Ray either."

"Why do you ask, Avery."

"Well, maybe it's nothing, but the other day at the church, Elliott Benson was talking to a dark-haired guy, and I swear he said, 'You did good Art.'"

"You're sure that's what he said?"

"I'm like 99% sure that's what he said. Art then gave him an envelope and they were discussing dollar amounts."

"What?"

"Yeah, they shook hands and he said, 'good work, Ray.'"

She looked puzzled narrowing her eyes and at the same time, they both said, “Are we talking about the same person??”

I also heard Elliott say as he put the envelope in his jacket, “this will take care of my girls.”

“What do you think is going on?” I asked her.

She asked me, “Avery have you mentioned this to anyone?”

“No, no, I’ve just been thinking about it. It’s been running through my mind over and over.”

“I will do some work and try to figure this out. Let’s keep this our secret, not to raise any suspicions.”

I said, “Yes, absolutely. I will get a pen and paper and write down everything I remember and text it to you.”

She said, “Put this number in your phone under Jo Ann. This is my private number. She gave me the number and I did just as she said.” I gave her my number to put in her personal phone. After we exchanged numbers, I told her goodbye and told her to keep me posted on anything she found out.

“Thanks, Avery, this will help take my mind off this boredom.”

“You’re welcome Jo Ann, see you soon.”

“Bye Avery..”

Jo Ann Forrester lay there thinking about what she had just heard. Trying to put the pieces together and wondered what it all meant. She fell asleep thinking about Jack, seeing him getting shot. The dark haired man telling her to apply pressure. She struggled to see his face in her dream. Apply pressure, apply pressure. She woke in a cold sweat breathing hard. She looked at the clock in the room it was 9:35 p.m. She called the desk and ask for her things to be brought to her room. She got her phone and noticed she had gotten a message from inspector Mattia.

Attention, Lieutenant Forrester, a detail I forgot to mention to you on the phone the other day. The killer had a tattoo on his neck with an A with a circle around it which we believe stands for anarchy. The tattoo was on his left side behind his ear. Here is a screen shot photo. She rubbed her eyes, focusing on the grainy photo. She inhaled a deep breath, puckered her lips, and exhaled, still focusing on the picture. She had a strange feeling about this guy in the picture. But she thought her mind was playing tricks on her with the pain medication making her woozy. She grabbed her phone and dialed a number.

“Hello, Marty, is it too late?”

“No, not at all.” She had called Officer Marty Zimmerman to find out how the investigation was going. She had assigned Marty as lead man with the Tennessee Power Association.

“Hey, lieutenant, how you feeling?”

“I’m ok, still sore as hell.”

"I bet, hope you're feeling better soon and back to work."

"Thanks," she said. "Hey, have you had any luck on the location of the 2.8 million?"

"It bounced around to several off shore accounts, then disappeared. Vinci said it's impossible to find now. I'm sorry to say, but I have to agree. It is very difficult to follow the cyber trail."

She said, "I understand, Marty. I've got another question for you.."

"Yeah, ask it."

"What's Vinci's legal name?"

"Ah I think it's, it's Andy Ray Turner, I believe."

"Ok, let's keep this question between us."

"10-4, lieutenant."

"Thank you, Marty. I'm sorry to call so late. I've just had more time to think."

"I understand. Just rest. You get well soon, lieutenant. Get some rest!!"

"I will Marty, thanks, bye, bye."

"Bye!!"

She sat there and noticed the initials of Vinci's Name, Andy Ray Turner. The initials ART clearly explains the post it notes that read call ART that Carlton left. And the dark haired man Avery saw Elliott Benson talking to. If that photo that inspector Mattia sent was the same person, then Andy Ray Turner aka Vinci killed Rebecca Ashton. This was a crime of revenge. Then, she thought and wondered, was Elliott Benson involved, or did he know of any of this. I mean it wouldn't be too far-fetched. Revenge is one of the oldest motives in the book. Her mind raced with suspicions.

Karen came in and asked her to take her medication and try and get some rest. She did as she asked, and laid back and tried to relax.

She heard a man's voice. "Apply pressure, apply pressure," the dark haired man said. She could see him, and she could see his neck, but couldn't see the tattoo. She woke up, her breathing was fast, perspiration on her forehead, and cheeks, her hair damp from the sweat. She was certain this man was the same man in the picture Inspector Mattia had sent. She thought, how she would confirm her suspicions. She thought she would pull his file and see his birth marks, tattoos, anything to verify her suspensions. There's always an answer.

Her nurse Karen came In and asked if she could get her anything, and Lieutenant Forrester said, "Yes, please, some coffee."

"Now you can't have coffee."

"Listen I have to be here for a few days but I'm still working on cases. I need some coffee to clear the cob webs out to help me see straight."

"Well, we do have some fresh brewed out there at the nurses station. I guess I could sneak you a cup."

"Or two," Jo Ann pleaded.

"I'll be back soon with you a fresh cup."

"Thank you Karen, I do appreciate it."

After a few minutes Karen returned with a big cup of coffee. After a big sip of coffee Jo Ann said, "Oh my goodness, I think my body has been in caffeine withdrawals. Oh this is so good. Thank you, thank you Karen."

Karen smiled, and said, "You enjoy that, honey. Today Dr. Mitchell has orders for you to be getting out of that bed. Start working that soreness out, moving around."

Jo Ann said, "Awe man, that sounds great."

"You will also be getting that catheter and the IV out today too."

Jo Ann said, "That is more great news, some solid foods. See what happens when coffee is involved?"

Karen said, "Oh yeah," laughing. "I'll be back in a few to get that catheter."

Jo Ann got her note pad out looking at the notes she had scribbled before the meds knocked her out last night. Andy Ray Turner = ART!! She sat there thinking and shaking her head. She called Marty Zimmerman and ask him to pull Vinci's personal file and a background check. Then she asked him to bring her a pair of sweat pants and sweat shirt from her locker. "Bring everything over here to me. Put it in a box so no one can see what it is."

She also told him she wanted to keep this between them. She told him it's something she's working on for Captain Wesley so no one got suspicious. She then hung up and tried to call Celesta Allen. She dialed Jack's private phone. It went to voice mail. She left a brief message for Celesta to call her when or if she got the message. She then called Marty back and asked him to see what Jack's emergency contact number was. Marty was tapping on the keyboard and pulled up Jack Allen's emergency contact number and it was Celesta Allen. He gave the number to lieutenant Forrester then told her he was on his way. She told Marty it was room 428 on seventh floor. "Remember Marty, our secret."

"Yes, lieutenant, I understand."

Karen came back into the room with a walker and sat it beside the bed. She put on her rubber gloves, and removed the IV then she removed the catheter."

"Well, that sure feels better." Jo Ann reached for the walker, and Karen helped her to her feet.

Karen smiled, and said, “Slow and easy now.” A knock at the door startled them both. Dr Mitchell opened the door. Oh good to see you up and about.

“Yes, slow and steady wins the race.”

“Are you feeling any discomfort?”

“I’m just sore,” Jo Ann said.

“Ok try to get some steps in down the hallway and around back by the nurses station. Try for two laps. Ok I’ll do what I can, doctor.”

He turned and left the room. “Oh shit!!”

“What is it honey?”

I thought he was looking at how bad I looked without makeup. There’s a mirror behind me, and my ass is hanging out the back of this hospital gown.”

Karen looked back and they both started laughing. Karen said, “Well, I’m sure he’s seen plenty. I’ll tie you up in the back.”

They opened the door and she went out nto the hallway and slowly completed her two laps then she was ready to get back in bed and relax. She was also ready for some eggs, toast, and jelly.

Wednesday morning I got up when Michelle did to get ready for work. I was moving slowly, but getting it done. Rosie came to the door as I was getting ready to go out and barked. I looked back and laughed, she barked again, and I told her to come on. I opened the door and she jumped up into the jeep. We cranked up and were on our way to the Tennessee Power Association maintenance building. We rolled into the parking lot, Rosie barking with her bob tail wagging enjoying the ride and the sunshine.

We parked and got out and went inside. Chris was in his office going over some paperwork. Rosie ran in and jumped in his lap. Chris laughed and said, “Hey, Rosie.” She sat there looking around. He said, “I knew you’d come check up on me.”

I laughed and said, “You got that right. No, I just dropped by to pick up something.”

“Hey, can you help me buddy?”

Chris said, “Yes, sure I can.”

“Will you get the bolt cutters and cut this lock off?”

“Yeah, no problem.” Chris brought the bolt cutters in and with ease cut the lock off.

I said, “Thanks, buddy, I got it from here.”

“I don’t want you knowing what I’m getting into in case anything is ever mentioned. I think in this case, the less you know, the better off you are.”

He said, “No problem, I understand.”

He turned and went back into the office and Rosie went with him.

I reached into the top of the locker and removed the black cardboard, then the envelope of money, and the closed the locker.

I told Chris I was walking out to the jeep for a second, “Be right back.” I walked out to the jeep and opened my console and put the money inside. I went back in; Rosie was at the door waiting for me. I told Chris thanks for the help and appreciated him taking care of everything.

I told him I would be back soon and hold the fort down. After we left Rosie, and I made our second stop. We arrived at Bates’s markers and monuments. I went inside and sat down with them and explained my idea and told them what I had in mind. They liked the idea and said they would take care of it and notify me when it’s complete. I paid them half now as a deposit. I used the money from the envelope I had taken from my locker at work.

After we left there, Rosie and I had two more stops to make before returning home. We went by Fussell’s Shop For Men and Boys. They had a very big selection of ties. Teddy used his tie on my arm that day at the cemetery to stop the bleeding. I felt like I owed him one for all his help. After picking out a nice one with the help of some folks at Fussell’s, who knows Teddy very well, we headed over to his office. We parked out front and went in where Rosie loved all the attention she got from Mary Catherine and her mom.

Michelle said, “Well, just look at you two out and about.”

Rosie jumped up in her lap. “Yes,” I said, “I brought my buddy, Teddy a present.”

“Oh,” Michelle said, “A present. Well, he will love that. Unfortunately, he’s not here right now he’s at a doctor’s appointment but when he returns I will make sure he gets it first thing.”

I smiled and said, “You lovely ladies have been so helpful, thank you very much.”

I looked at Rosie and said it was time to go as she wagged her bob tail. I gave Michelle a kiss, and Mary Catherine asked, “Where’s mine?”

“There’s only so much to go around, I’m injured.”

“Yeah right,” she laughed. “Bye y’all.”

We went out to the jeep, loaded up and headed home. Officer Marty Zimmerman stepped off the elevator on the seventh floor looking for room 428. Lieutenant Jo Ann Forrester was sitting up in her bed when she heard a knock at the door.

“Yes, come in.”

Marty Zimmerman stuck his head in, smiling from ear to ear. “Good morning, sunshine!!”

Lieutenant Forrester smiled, “Come on in, and sit down.”

Marty said, “I brought you something.”

Jo Ann's face lit up when she saw the large coffee he brought her. "Bless you, Marty, bless you."

"I thought you might want some good coffee. And it's just like you like it!"

She took a sip and swallowed. "Ahh, that's so good!"

He sat the box with the file inside on her tray table she had in front of her. "Good job, Marty." He sat and they talked for a few minutes then he told her he needed to get back.

She thanked him again, and reminded him this was their little secret. He winked as he said bye walking out the door.

Lieutenant Forrester was ready to get into that file. She laid everything on the tray table in front of her.

She opened his department file looking for something specific she then went to his arrest report, and booking report, looking at identification marks along with notable scars or birthmarks. There was no mention of an anarchy symbol or tattoo behind his left ear.

She also knew he was working on the inside and could have had it removed or kept it covered. She could see he had a prior arrest for computer hacking and where it was expunged from his record. The prosecutor was Elliott Benson. She shook her head thinking that could the connection. She scribbled on her note pad again. Vinci, DaVinci, Art, =ART, Andy Ray Turner brother of Carlton Rogers. This picture seemed to be getting clearer. But, this doesn't make Ray a murderer. She still had questions that had to be answered but she had to be extremely careful to accuse another member of the force or a District Attorney. She knew if she accused anyone she better have evidence to back up her claim. Looking through the file she noticed he had his mother's name listed as Hazel Gallimore. No other family was listed. But, she thought once again, someone would only see what he wanted them to see. She had a thought and was curious and called the Hardin County medical examiner's office.

"Yes, hello this is Lieutenant Forrester from Dickson County Police Department. Who am I speaking with?"

This is the chief medical examiner, Dr Jeremy Tagert."

"Oh great, sounds like I got the right person."

"Yes you do, lieutenant."

I was wondering if you have a name of who identified and claimed the body of Carlton Rogers about a month ago?"

"Yes, I would have that here in our files. Yes, here it is, Andy Turner."

"Ok that's what I was looking for, thank you. Bye now."

"Goodbye."

She sat there thinking, when her phone rang and broke the silence, and her train of thought. She picked it up and saw Jack's number, and she knew it was Celesta.

"Hello, this is Jo Ann speaking."

"Hello Jo Ann, this is Celesta."

"Yes, ma'am I called and left a message yesterday."

"Yes, I saw that, I've been so busy taking care of Jack's arrangements. Sorry it's taken so long to get back with you."

"No, I understand completely with all you are dealing with."

"They had a story on the news last night about the shooting, did you see it?"

"No, no ma'am, I didn't."

"My, my, we had planned on moving to Florida where our two girls and grandchildren live. I just never thought I'd be making those plans alone." Celesta said, "It's crazy how things just happen."

Jo Ann said, "I'm so sorry it happened this way." Then there was a moment of silence both women were thinking of Jack.

Celesta then said, "I'm having Jack cremated and we will bury him down there close to his brother, Edward. We will still see those Florida sunsets together. I promised him we would."

"I'm so sorry, Celesta, I wish I could have done something more to save him."

"Honey, Jack thought the world of you. It's not your fault. Jack knew the dangers of this job. I've prayed for years for God to bring him home safe to me, and he did. I thank him for those years. But this time Jack went home and he is now waiting on me."

"That's a beautiful way of thinking of his passing, but it's still tough.

"God will guide us through the pain and give us comfort."

Jo Ann wiped her tears and admired her strength and faith. "I will keep in touch, Celesta. And I told Jack I would come see you both."

"Honey, you do that, and Jo Ann, get well soon. I'll be praying for you."

"Thank you, Celesta. I'll get off here now and thanks for calling bye now."

"Bye honey, please stay in touch."

"I will Celesta bye." She sat there in tears thinking and missing her friend Jack. After she cried a while, she pulled the story up on her phone and pushed play.

"Hello, I'm Ken Katel reporting to you on location where a deadly shooting took place a few days ago. We reported a few days ago of a shooting out of Dickson County TN. The shootout took place at St Patrick's Catholic Church cemetery which left two people injured and two people dead. The shooter, Tommy Mason, an ex-employee of the Tennessee Power Association showed up here at the St Patrick's Catholic Church cemetery with a gun, stating he wasn't going to no prison. Mason had been charged with arson and was out on bond awaiting trial. The arson charge involved a former co-worker who is still employed at the Tennessee Power Association. Which that employee, Avery Jackson, was one of the victims in this shooting, along with Lieutenant Jo Ann Forrester, and the deceased, Veteran Officer Detective Jack Allen. Timmy Mason also died by his own hand. All this occurred as I said, here at the St Patrick's Catholic Church cemetery where a former Tennessee Power Association employee was being laid to rest after dying under suspicious circumstances. We reached out to the Tennessee Power Association for comment and a Spokesperson did responded saying, Timmy Mason was a former employee terminated for breaking company policies. They were very sorry to hear of the loss of lives or injuries that occurred involving this distraught ex-employee. We also asked the Tennessee Power Association about the missing 2.8 million dollars for which was still unaccounted. Their response was, "There is still an ongoing investigation." There you have it. I'm Ken Katel coming to you live from St Patrick's Catholic Church in Dickson Co, TN. News Channel 3 WTVR-TV.

After watching the video, she was still in disbelief remembering the incident like it just happened moments ago. It was all still so clear. She turned the volume down on her phone and sat there in the dark looking out the window for a while. A few hours had passed so she got up out of bed and went to the closet to get her jogging pants and sweat shirt on, then got her walker and opened her door. She went out into the hallway and decided to take a little walk to clear her mind and do some light stretching. She knew she wouldn't be there but a few more days. She also knew Elliott Benson would be the first person she would talk to about her suspicions of Andy Ray Turner killing Rebecca Ashton. She just needed to feel him out and get his thoughts on Ray being a killer.

She made six laps around the nurses desk before she realized it, lost in her thoughts. When she went passed the stairwell, she opened the door going inside putting her leg up on the third step and stretching then changing legs, careful not to pull her stitches open. She thought to herself I will sleep good tonight and be a day closer to going home.

Thanksgiving was a few days away she planned on being in her apartment watching the Macy's Thanksgiving Day parade stretched out on the couch enjoying Chinese food from Ching Court Buffet And Grill. Just thinking of their egg rolls or spring rolls made her mouth water. Her little Thanksgiving day ritual, just something she had been doing the past four years.

She got back to her room, got undressed and took a shower. The hot water helped relieve some of the soreness. She got out and towel dried her hair, put on a fresh clean soft cotton gown, and got into bed. She looked at her phone saw the time was 9:35, pushed the button on the side, making sure the phone volume was turned completely down for some good uninterrupted sleep.

The next morning, Dr Travis Mitchell came in as Jo Ann was finishing her breakfast. "Good morning, Jo Ann, how are you feeling?"

"Fine doctor."

"Let me get a look at those stitches. All looks good. How's your appetite?"

"Good I've eaten everything they have brought."

"Bowel movements?"

Jo Ann said, "Everything seems to be working fine."

"That's great news. I see no reason you can't be discharged today."

"Oh," Jo Ann said, "That's great news, doctor, the news I was hoping to hear. Thank you for all you and your staff have done for me."

"You are very welcome, Lieutenant Forrester, and thank you as well, for all you do to protect and serve, keeping us all safe."

The next morning Michelle got up and was getting ready for work while I fixed her a waffle, a glass of milk, and coffee to go. While she ate, we went over the grocery list for the Thanksgiving dinner. She had invited Teddy, Mary Catherine, and her boys over for dinner. I was ready to throw down on some deviled eggs, chicken and dressing, turkey, and rolls. Oh and green bean casserole. Yes, just thinking of all that good food was making me hungry. After a trip to the grocery store, I was back home using my mother's recipe, cocking cornbread for the dressing. I've always said Michelle makes the best chicken and dressing I've ever had. Thanksgiving day, Michelle was up early cooking and getting everything ready before our guests arrived. I was the official taste tester and took that job seriously. Michelle would stick a spoon in my mouth and say, here test. As usual, everything was scrumptious. We would laugh, and she would say, you know it's good.

I asked what she thought about us taking Lieutenant Forrester a plate to the hospital. She agreed it was a great idea for us to do this afternoon. I got my phone to call her and let her know we would stop by this afternoon. I dialed her number and no one answered. I called the hospital and asked them to connect me to Jo Ann Forrester's room 428. They let me know she had been discharged yesterday. I dialed her number again.

"Hello."

"Hello, Jo Ann, how are you feeling today?"

"Pretty good now that I'm home."

"Yes, I heard that."

"You did, from who?"

I called the hospital and they told me you were discharged yesterday."

"Yes, I was so glad to get home and just relax in my own bed and lounge around on the couch watching TV."

You have any Thanksgiving day plans I asked her?"

She said, "No, I'm just doing my thing."

"Well, Michelle and I wanted to invite you over for dinner today."

"Oh, thank you both, that's so nice, but I'm so sore, and I'm just not feeling much like getting out," she said. Besides, I have a little ritual and I've ordered my Chinese food, and it should arrive anytime now."

I laughed and said, "Ching Court."

"Yep!"

"They do have the best spring rolls."

"Thanks again, Avery, and tell Michelle thanks and Happy Thanksgiving to you all."

"You too, Jo Ann, I'll talk to you soon. Bye."

"Bye Avery."

I gave Michelle the message Jo Ann sent and how much she appropriated the invitation.

Teddy and Mary Catherine arrived and the boys weren't far behind. Mary Catherine had sweet potatoes and pumpkin pie and Teddy brought two pies, pecan, and a chess. Teddy thanked me for his new tie I had gotten him more than once. Trevor and Troy were watching Fox pregame show getting ready for the game between the Lions and the Cowboys. Everything looked awesome on the new 65" TV we had gotten with the newly remodeled living room suite. Michelle had apple cinnamon candles burning throughout the house and I just thought everything felt great today. We gathered around the table and Teddy said grace. After what happened at the cemetery, it put so much into perspective. He emphasized on the fact that tomorrow wasn't promised. We should never take our days for granted. We all had so much to be thankful for. I couldn't help but think about the Benson's and how they are coping without Steven. We all enjoyed the good food and fellowship.

Then we munched and watched football the rest of the afternoon. The boys were telling Teddy and me about the recruiting letters they had gotten from some big name schools and many being in the SEC. Neither had made any final decisions just yet on which school they wanted to attend. Both weighing their options. The day was a great day. Rosie really enjoyed the attention, and especially the table scraps. Michelle and I called our parents later that afternoon wishing them a Happy Thanksgiving. This was the first year we hadn't traveled for the Thanksgiving holiday.

Jo Ann Forrester reported back to work December 1st bright and early, thinking everyone would be pretty busy and her return wouldn't be too noticeable. Little did she know, Captain Wesley had let everyone know of her returning that morning. As soon as she walked into the squad room, everyone started cheering. Congratulating her of her full recovery and return to work. They lead her into the conference room and immediately she could smell bacon and maple syrup as she walked through the door. And then a picture of Jack on the memorial board on the wall which made her tear up.

Captain Wesley had it catered, coffee and donuts, pastries, breakfast foods, fruit and a cake which read, welcome back Jo Ann, now get back to work. She was so surprised and overwhelmed by all the love, kindness, and support from her co-workers.

Jo Ann said, "I just want to thank you all so much. The flowers were beautiful. I can't help but think of our co-worker, my mentor, and my friend, Detective Jack Allen. They had a moment of silence in his honor. They all toasted his picture yelling his name. She held up her glass of orange juice. "Jack!!"

She then thanked everyone again, and after a while, made her way to her office. Not long after she got seated at her desk, her phone rang. It was Marty Zimmerman.

"Hello, stranger."

"Hello, Marty."

"I heard you were in the building."

"Yes, It's back to the grindstone."

He laughed said, "Takes news a while to get down here to the dungeon, I mean basement."

She said, "Well, when you get ready for a break go by the conference room and get your sugar rush on."

Marty laughed and said, "ok, I will, and be by to see you soon."

"Ok Marty, see you in a few."

Marty knocked on the door and lieutenant Forrester waved him on in, she could see through the window in the door he had his hands full with two plates of food stacked on top of each other, with a cup in his mouth to free up a hand to open the door. He came on in, she couldn't help but laugh as he used his foot to close the door and set the plates on her desk, sat down, and put his cup down too.

Laughing, she said, "You didn't have to bring me anything."

He laughed, and said, "This is better than Shoney's breakfast bar. He said, "Hell, next time I may shoot you myself."

Both laughing. He said, "Maybe graze you."

She asked him if he found anything out about the 2.8 million.

I have found out something that's interesting. I found that the account was frozen, then unfrozen, then closed by Rebecca Ashton. But, the dates just don't match up to be right because she was already deceased."

"So, could we say whoever killed her knew about the money, then had to know how to transfer or bounce the money, then close it out, or make it disappear."

He sat there then, taking another bite of his donut, and said, "Yes, but that takes major skills."

Lieutenant Forrester said, "You could do it, couldn't you?"

"Well, yeah probably."

She asked, "Could Vinci do it?"

He said, “I knew where you were going with this. But, yes he could do it for sure.”

“But, he couldn’t kill anyone. I’ve been around him and he’s just not capable of something like that.”

“Revenge will bring out the worst in people. Revenge, don’t you mean greed?”

“What are you thinking?” Marty asked her.

“I believe Carlton had a brother.”

Marty looked very surprised. “And you think that brother is Vinci? Andy?” Marty asked, “Where did you come up with this theory?”

I went by to see Carlton’s mother or stepmother to tell her about Carlton’s passing and they said her son, Ray, was the contact number. And in Carlton’s file it was listed that Ms. Hazel Gallimore was his mother.”

“Oh, ok, I see now how this picture is coming together.”

And Lieutenant Forrester added, “Ray signed for Carlton’s body to be released. So here’s what I need you to do, we need to verify that they are brothers through the state. And we need to keep this between ourselves for now. Is he here today?”

“No, he comes in tonight or sometimes he works from home.”

"Alright, let's do some digging."

"Ok."

"Lieutenant, so glad you're back."

"Thanks, Marty, glad to be back. See you later."

"Ok, keep me posted," she whispered as he went out the door. She sat there and knew she needed to speak with Elliott Benson soon to see what, or if, he knows anything. And she also knew she wanted to go by sometime soon and see Ms. Hazel Gallimore again.

She picked up the phone and dialed Elliott Benson's office.

"Good morning, District Attorney Elliott Benson's office, Brandy speaking, how may I help you?"

"This is lieutenant Forrester; I'm calling to speak with Mr. Benson if that's possible."

"I'm sorry, that's not possible at this time, he's in court this morning and won't be in until this afternoon, or in the morning."

"Will you give him a message to call me at his convenience."

"Yes, lieutenant Forrester, I sure will."

"Thank you so much, bye now."

Lieutenant Forrester thought about how she really wanted to see him in person to see his body language in response to her questions. It was about one that afternoon when Lieutenant Forrester got a call from the office of District Attorney Elliott Benson.

She answered, and it was the District Attorney himself. “Hello, Lieutenant Forrester. How are you feeling today he asked?”

“Fine sir and thank you so much for the flowers you sent.”

“You’re very welcome.”

“The reason I called was I have a few questions about Rebecca Ashton’s death, and I was hoping you could help me.”

“Well, I’d be happy to help anyway I can lieutenant.”

“How about 4:30 this afternoon. I have a few things to take care of at the Courthouse.”

“That would be great, thanks.”

“You’re welcome, see you then.” She was very pleased to get this meeting with him to maybe find out some answers.

At four twenty she was in the front office of District Attorney Elliott Benson’s. The young secretary smiled and asked her if she had an appointment.

Lieutenant Forrester answered, “Yes, I’m here a little early, my appointment is 4:30.”

The secretary looked at her appointment book and said, "Lieutenant Jo Ann Forrester, I presume."

"Yes. I'll let him know you are here."

"Thank you."

The secretary picked up the phone and said, "Lieutenant Forrester is here sir."

"Ok, I'll let her know." The young lady hung up and said, "he will be just a few minutes."

Lieutenant Forrester thanked her and sat patiently waiting. It wasn't ten minutes and his office door opened and Elliott Benson came out and greeted her giving Lieutenant Forrester a hug. And told her to come on in and grab a seat. He asked if she would like something to drink or coffee.

Jo Ann said, "a bottled water."

Elliott looked at his secretary, "Brandy, honey, bring us a couple of bottles of water, please."

"Yes, sir, Mr. Benson."

They sat down and Elliott told her how sorry he was about Jack being killed. He said, "You know you two saved several people that day."

She shook her head and modestly said, "We were just doing our jobs."

Brandy came in and sat the bottled water down and asked if they needed anything else.

"No, I think we're good thank you."

"So, how can I help you today, lieutenant?"
"I was wondering how well you know Andy Turner?"

"Andy Turner, I can't say I do know him."

"Andy Ray Turner, you prosecuted him in nineteen ninety two for computer hacking. Then a few years later signed off on getting his record expunged."

"Ray Turner, yes, yes, I do remember him, is he in some kind of trouble? I thought he straightened up."

She could tell he was being deceptive, acting as if he didn't know him. Jo Ann said, "Well, he is Carlton Rogers brother."

"No, I didn't know that," Elliott said quickly looking down at some paperwork on his desk not making eye contact. Elliott Benson had been a prosecutor for more than thirty years and also knew the signs of deception.

She said, "Yes, you know I've been thinking, Rebecca Ashton's death could have been motivated by revenge."

Elliott said, "Andy just didn't strike me as a killer. He was a quiet guy, nerdy type, best I can remember. And she was killed in Sicily! How are you coming up with this theory? I just have a feeling this wasn't random."

Jo Ann wasn't going to give up too much information and sure wasn't going to tip her hand this early in the game they were playing. "I don't know just yet," she said, "It's just a thought I can't get out of my head. I read the description of the suspect; he matches that description. Well, so does another few million people on this planet," Elliott answered quickly.

"The description was of a dark haired man with dark beard stubble and glasses. The strange thing is when I got shot it was a dark haired man telling me to apply pressure there at the cemetery. That description matches Andy Ray Turner to a tee."

He looked at her, shook his head, and said, "Lieutenant, you are letting you imagination run away from you. Could be the medication you're still on."

"How well do you know Andy Ray Turner, Elliott?"

"What are you implying, Lieutenant?"

"Oh, I'm just asking questions."

He laughed and said, "What happened over there is over there. We have no jurisdiction over there."

She smiled, "Oh, I know that. But, justice knows no boundaries, like revenge, you could say."

He looked at his watch and asked if there was anything else he could help her with. He said he needed to get home, "the girls have a piano recital tonight."

"No, sir I just wanted your thoughts on my thoughts."

"Well, if you have anything, else just let me know."

"Yes, sir I will. Thank you for seeing me and listening to me ramble."

"Oh, that's fine, lieutenant. Good seeing you and glad to see you back on the job. Bye now."

Jo Ann said goodbye and left. Elliott sat down thinking and picked up his office phone then hung it up and reached into his bottom drawer of his desk and got a phone out, turned it on and dialed a number. "Hey, we need to talk soon. Call me when you get this."

Jo Ann sat out in her car for more than ten minutes waiting to see when he left. He wasn't in as big of a hurry as he acted. She figured as soon as she left he called Ray to let him know she was asking questions. He did come out and leave very casually. She was on her way back to the office. She got back to the office and called Marty.

"Hello lieutenant, what have you found out?"

"Hey, Marty I thought about something, pull up Andy's time sheet for the week Rebecca Ashton was killed. Let's see here, 10-02-14 and here it is. Shows he was here all week.

She said, "I wish we could verify that."

Marty said, "Oh, there is."

Jo Ann said, “How?”

“We can pull up the security or video from that day.”

“Wow,” she said, “We can go back that far?”

“Yes, our security records are downloaded and saved.”

Lieutenant Forrester could hear Marty typing on his keyboard. “Yes, here is the day and Andy came in at 7:00 a.m. until 7:00 p.m. and here he is in the flesh.”

Jo Ann said, “Save that week, in case I need that for reference.” She felt confused, but in a way she felt relieved.

She exhaled and Marty asked, “Are you ok, lieutenant?”

“Yes, Marty, I am. Don’t worry about saving that information. I think I have been wrong about all this.”

Marty said, “Well, you have been through a lot here lately.”

“Sometimes, it is what it is.” She closed the file in front of her and placed it in the bottom drawer with the other files on this case.

“You may be right, Marty. I’m going to call TPA and let them know we have no new findings.”

She called the Tennessee Power Association and reported that the money trail had dried up in cyberspace. It would remain open, and she would have officers from the Tech department try to trace its whereabouts."

. . .

I had been back to work for two weeks now, getting stronger every day. Chris did a great job while I was absent the week I was shot. We were up to a full crew now and I was very pleased with the new hires. Chris and I had implemented a more diverse group of employees in the TPA facilities department. Something the other group would never have had. I know I wasn't the only one to notice, but no one said anything. That was then, and this is now, and I won't allow it. I was in my office when my cell phone rang and It was Bates Markers and Monuments, letting me know the monument I had made was almost complete. They would take it to the cemetery and place it after Christmas. They would call or text me when it's placed. I thanked them for the update. Michelle and I had plans to go visit her parents and family in Lexington, Kentucky, and then my parents and family in Gatlinburg. We have had this planned since the day after Thanksgiving.

The week of Christmas was for volunteers for those who wanted to come in. Michelle, Rosie, and I were all packed and loaded in the car, and ready to hit the road. After a check and a recheck, we were on our way to Kentucky.

Lieutenant Forrester was in her office when she heard a knock at the door. She looked up seeing the figure of a man standing there looking around, and then recognizing the face and hair. She yelled, "Come in."

He entered the room and said, “Hello Lieutenant Forrester, and welcome back.”

She smiled and said, “Thank you. And I also want to thank you for saving me at the cemetery.”

He said, “You’re very welcome, just trying to help as many as I could.”

She asked him, “What should I call you, Vinci, or Ray, or Andy?”

“Ah yes, I understand you have been asking questions. Just call me Ray.”

She said, “I’m very sorry about your brother, Carlton.”

“Yes, me too. He was a very big hearted guy. He wasn’t a mastermind in their theft. They used him, then killed him. You believe they killed him? Or did he just have an accident as it appears. Everything’s not always as it appears, lieutenant. I loved my brother and there’s nothing wrong with that. But I didn’t kill anyone for revenge.”

She stared at him, he stared at her. He asked her if she had any other questions. She also knew she couldn’t give up any information because she had no proof.

“No,” she answered, “I’ve just been looking at all the angles, trying not to leave any stones unturned.”

He said, "I completely understand, lieutenant. But, your looking in the wrong direction. I believe the guilty got exactly what they deserved."

She said, "An eye for an eye."

He smiled and said, "Or even a life for a life."

She felt as if she were being toyed with in a way. She looked as he got up looking for a tattoo or any kind of marks or scars. Something that could be used to identify Ray as the killer in that grainy photo, but she couldn't see anything, nothing at all. "Lieutenant Forrester, I'm glad you are feeling better and back to work. If there is anything I can do to help with any questions, please feel free to ask."

"Thank you, Ray," she said.

He smiled and said, "Have a good day, Lieutenant Forrester," and walked out.

Jo Ann just sat there shaking her head thinking she must have gotten it all wrong.

...

Our Christmas with her parents and family was a lot of fun. It was great seeing her aunts, uncles, and cousins. Michelle really enjoyed the country traditions with her family in Kentucky. She was so happy to see her parents and remembering all their childhood and family memories, and waking up on Christmas morning. Lots of great food and football. After three days we were on the road again heading toward Gat inburg to have

Christmas with my parents. And as usual, mom and dad were asking about grandkids. Michelle was blushing and pushing the blame on me saying I was working too much or getting shot. We hit the strip in Gatlinburg all the Christmas decorations were beautiful as always. Rosie enjoyed all the attention of the strip. Decked out with her little sweater and booties on. We had a wonderful time with them, and it was so much fun. The following day we were packed up and ready to hit the road back home goodbyes are bitter sweet.

We were on the road again, in about seven hours we would be home, home sweet home, if the traffic cooperated, and it did. We were on the road when I received a text from Bates Markers and Monuments letting me know they had set the monument at Steven's graveside. They had sent a picture and it looked awesome.

Black with engraved white writing and a Blackbird on a tree branch with the full moon behind it. I couldn't wait for Michelle and I to go see it tomorrow. The next day was unusually warm, a beautiful day for December. I actually had on a t-shirt, shorts, and sandals. Michelle had on a t-shirt and sweat pants. A beautiful day for our trip to the cemetery. We arrived at St Patrick's Catholic Church cemetery and I noticed the birds were singing and chirping beautiful melodies. The sun was beautiful, the day couldn't be any more perfect. The monument had a black base, black pedestal, and a black smooth top surface with white letter engraving that read:

"Blackbird, Blackbird"

Many times I have seen you,
on my windowsill. Doesn't matter day or night

with your eyes dark as coal, I can feel you staring into
the depths of my soul. I see you
In the moon light a shadow of uncertainty.

Blackbird, blackbird why don't you sing,
Blackbird, blackbird tell me what you
have seen. Can you see the darkness
that dances in my dreams, I can hear the voices on the
wind beneath your wings.

I've heard it said don't look into your
eyes for you'll see the darkness and hear
my silent cries
I can't help but wonder what it is you
bring do you have the answers to the
questions unforeseen.

Blackbird, blackbird why don't you sing,
Blackbird, Blackbird tell me what you
have seen. Can you see the darkness
that dances in my dreams, I can hear the
voices on the wind beneath your wings.

Blackbird, blackbird can you set me
free, can you show me love and prosperity.
Do you bring the white bird to
help me travel on, am I strong enough
to make this journey on my own.

Blackbird, blackbird please don't fly away
stay here and protect me so I can
see another day, stay here, and protect me

so I can see another day....

Michelle was amazed at how awesome this monument turned out. She said it was beautiful as she wiped tears from her eyes. Steven would be so proud of this gesture.

I too was very impressed with this beautiful monument. We left the cemetery and I couldn't help but have a feeling of tranquility. The radio said the high was 79° but Michelle's car said it was 83° and sunny. We took some backroads going home, and stopped off at a little gas station to get gas. I pulled in and Michelle got out and was going inside to pay.

She asked, "Twenty be good?"

"Yeah."

"Hey, do you want a beef jerky or some chips?"

"Yes, sounds good, and a Dr. Pepper, please." I heard the pump set and kick on. I couldn't help but notice a beautiful yellow convertible 57 Chevy Bel Air next to us getting gas. The guy finished pumping and got in on the passenger side. He had on a hat, sunglasses, and leather jacket. I thought to myself, It is a beautiful day for a cruise.

"Let's go, Arty!" the man yelled!

"Hold your horse's, Ray, this damn machine took my money," he kicked the machine. I looked at the guy at the machine and then back at the guy in the car, they looked as if they may be brothers. The guy at the machine kicked it again and a drink fell out. He walked towards me talking to the guy in the car. He said, "You see, Ray, you just got to be patient."

My thoughts raced trying to place the names. Call Ray, call Art. Could this be Carlton's brothers! Was one of these guys at the church and cemetery that day? The driver also had on sunglasses, a hat and hoodie.

I noticed as he sat down in the driver's seat he had a tattoo behind his ear down on his neck of an "A."

"Let's roll, brother," the driver said as they cranked up and casually drove off slow and easy in the beautiful classic car.

The license plate had a personal tag that read, Ms. Hazel. They pulled out heading west on highway 70. Michelle came out and saw the confused look on my face. Smiled and said, "Yeah, cool car."

I said, "I think one of those guys was Carlton Rogers' brother."

"Oh, the one you saw at church?"

"Yeah, I think so. But, I couldn't tell for sure. I'll give Lieutenant Forrester a call tomorrow and ask a few questions."

We took our time and drove the backroads home. There we lounged around enjoying the rest of the beautiful Sunday afternoon. We discussed getting tickets to see 24 Seven at The Mic Stand in Huntingdon, TN. Where they are playing this year for New Year's Eve.

Lieutenant Forrester went by to see Ms. Hazel Gallimore at Whispering Oaks Assisted living. She went down to the room she was in, but the name on the door was not Ms. Hazel Gallimore. She ask someone coming down the hallway. Her name tag said Certified Nursing Assistant, Tina Brooks.

Jo Ann said, “Excuse me, I’m Lieutenant Forrester, and I was looking for Ms. Hazel Gallimore.”

“Oh, dear,” she said, “Ms. Hazel died the week before Christmas.”

“Oh, ok, I was just going to stop by and see her.”

Jo Ann said, “Thank you,” and turned around walking back down the hallway and saw Phillis Johnson at the nurses desk, and Jo Ann said, “Hello.”

Phillis said, “Hello Lieutenant, how are you?” I was just going to come by to see Ms. Hazel. I was just told she passed a few weeks ago.”

“Yes, she was ready to go home.” Phillis turned and pointed to a box and said, they still haven’t gotten all her things yet. Jo Ann looked at the box, seeing a few pictures and picked them up looking at the pictures. She looked and put on her glasses, and focused very intently at one picture in particular.

Her phone rang, she reached into her pocket looking at her phone seeing Marty Z on the screen.

“Hello, Marty.”

"Yes, Lieutenant, I know you said you thought you were wrong about your gut feeling, but you're not gonna believe this but, I just got all the records back from the state and it's very interesting, very interesting. Seems Ms. Hazel Gallimore was married twice. She had a daughter and two boys."

Jo Ann said, "Twin boys."

Marty said, "How'd you know?"

"I'm here at Whispering Oaks, and I just saw a picture, and it just clicked, Arty Raymond Turner and Andy Ray Turner."

Marty continued, "And their sister is Carlton Rogers's biological mother, Melinda Suzanne Turner."

"So, Arty and Ray were Carlton's uncles?"

"Yes," Marty said.

"Damn! I can't believe I missed this," Lieutenant Forrester exhaled blowing out frustration.

"Great work, Marty! I want to get Arty in here to answer some questions. I have a strong feeling he's nowhere to be found."

Marty asked, "Should I put out a BOLO?"

"I have a feeling DA Benson will not issue a warrant. It didn't happen here, and a suspicion doesn't get you a warrant." She was pacing up and down the hallway. She waved at Phillis on her way out to her car. "Let me get back to you, Marty."

Lieutenant Forrester was already feeling she had been played. She got into her car, slammed the door, cranked up, and floored it. She pulled up at District Attorney Elliott Benson's office, seeing his car, got out, and on her way inside to speak with him.

Lieutenant Forrester came into the office, her frustration very visible and Brandy, Elliott's secretary, could plainly see it on the lieutenant's face. "Can I help you, Lieutenant Forrester?"

"Yes, I'm here to see Mr. Benson."

"Do you have an appointment?"

"No, I do not. Is he in?" Brandy didn't answer. I asked, is he in?" Brandy still didn't answer. Lieutenant Forrester walked to his office door, and grabbed the doorknob.

"Excuse me, but you can't go in there." Brandy grabbed the door.

Lieutenant Forrester pushed the door open and District Attorney Elliott Benson yelled, "Jo Ann, what's going on here?"

"Brandy, it's ok, Brandy!"

"What's the meaning of this, Jo Ann?"

"You knew the whole time, Elliott, you knew!"

"Knew what Jo Ann?"

"He had a twin!"

"What?"

"You knew what happened to Rebecca Ashton! You were in on it!"

"I told you; you're letting your imagination run away with you."

"Don't patronize me, Elliott!"

"Listen, Jo Ann, I have been doing this a long time, and you can't just make wild accusations if you can't prove it. And I don't like being accused of murder," slamming his fist on his desk and pointing at her. "So, I'm going to pretend you didn't just bust into my office accusing me of a crime So, unless you have anything that would justify your behavior, good day Lieutenant Forrester."

She stared at him, turned, and walked out. She got to her car, got in, and slammed her fist on the dash. "Dammit!!" She knew she had no proof of anything illegal.

She sat there and her phone rang she ignored it. It continued to ring, she looked and saw it was Avery.

"Avery, hello, what can I do for you?"

"I meant to call you earlier about something that I saw yesterday that I thought might be interesting Michelle and I were at a gas station on highway seventy and two guys were there getting gas. One of the men's name was Arty and the other man's was..

Lieutenant Forrester spoke up and said, "Ray."

"Yes, that's right, Lieutenant, Arty, and Ray Turner. They got their gas then drove off heading west in a yellow convertible 57 Chevy. It had a personalized tag that said, Ms. Hazel."

"Marty Zimmerman got the records from the state today verifying Arty and Ray are twins."

Avery was silent, thinking. "So, do you think one of them killed Rebecca Ashton?"

"Yes, Avery I do. If I had to bet, it was Arty Turner who was responsible for Rebecca's death. But, I don't know if I can prove it. I also believe District Attorney Elliott Benson was in on it or knew of his actions. As I've been told revenge is one of the oldest motives in the book. I don't believe the DA will issue a warrant because the murder didn't happen here in the United States."

Avery felt it was Rebecca Ashton who was responsible for Steven's death. He thought maybe she got what was coming to her. "Well, Lieutenant, please keep me posted if you hear anything or if I can help answer any questions."

"I will, Avery, and you keep in touch."

"You too, lieutenant." She could hear the despair in his voice. "I will keep looking, Avery, to untangle this web of corruption."

The Tennessee Power Association settled with Tommy and Darlene Ashton. Tommy Ashton bought his grandfather's farm. Darlene negotiated the deal on behalf of Tommy since he was still a minor. I heard the amount was 750,000 dollars, but like I said, that's just hearsay. TPA claimed the investigation was still ongoing to recover the 2.8 million, but, I believe they know they won't ever see that money again. Lieutenant Jo Ann Forrester continued working with the Dickson County Police Department for another three years. She relayed her suspicions to Inspector Mattia and how she believed Arty Turner was involved, and possibly in Rebecca Ashton's murder. She later married her Captain Daniel Wesley. They now have two children together. She told me she misses the excitement but after her friend, Jack Allen, was killed, it put things into perspective for her. I still work with the Tennessee Power Association and have now for six years. Michelle still works for Teddy, alongside Mary Catherine. Michelle moves a little slower these days though being an expecting mother. Yes, Michelle and I are expecting our first child. Our parents are beyond excited about finally becoming grandparents. We don't know what gender our child is yet, but I've thought if it's a boy, I would name him Steven. I go to his graveside often and visit. I see his girls around town from time to time and think how much they resemble their father. He was an innocent victim who accidentally got caught up in the greed of others. They say time eases the pain. Time keeps on going, and the world keeps on turning and memories fade. But, I think back and remember, seeing it all so clearly. That yellow 57 Chevy convertible casually pull onto the highway as if the two men inside didn't have a care in the world as they slowly drove off. They say justice is bittersweet. Rebecca Ashton's murder is still an unsolved homicide. Was it karma? Or an eye for an eye? Or in this case a life for a life? Steven's death was ruled accidental overdose, which was far from the truth. There was no justice, no justice for Steven. Fly High Blackbird!!

About the Author

My name is Shane Bates, I'm 52 years old and live in Tennessee. I'm married to my beautiful wife, Michelle, and am a stepfather of two and a grandfather to seven grandchildren.

I enjoy writing!! This is my first book, and I am planning on drafting another book soon. I also enjoy writing songs.

I wrote the song lyrics to Blackbird, Blackbird that's in the book. I chose the title Blackbird, Blackbird because I felt the song related perfectly to the dynamics of this book. The song Blackbird, Blackbird is available on Spotify and iTunes. My friend and co-writer, Anna Watkins Anawalt performs Blackbird, Blackbird, and other songs I've written. Everyone should check out her page Fiddlin Momma.

This book is sold on Amazon
and is available in e-book and paperback

ISBN: 9798325523823

Published through
Galah Bookstore
www.galahbookstore.net

Made in the USA
Columbia, SC
15 December 2024

49411291R00167